THE MISSOURI RUN

THE MISSOURI RUN

THE ROUTE 66 STEAL
BOOK TWO

LIZ HARTLEY

RAINY VALLEY PRESS

Salem, Oregon

*For all those who travel Route 66 searching out the hidden heart
of America.
For all those who live along the Route who keep that heart
beating, make us welcome, and share their lives, knowledge and
love of place with us, however briefly.
With gratitude to the artists who create all the wall murals.
What joy you give us!*

*And in memory of my dear friend Gretchen Hohn Olson.
The world is poorer for your absence.*

"...there is hope on the road... A sense of opportunity as wide as the country itself. A bone-deep conviction that something better will come. It's just ahead, in the next town, the next gig, the next chance encounter with a stranger."

Nomadland
Jessica Bruder

CONTENTS

CHAPTER 1
A FRESH START

"I still can't believe you threw $40,000 in gold into the Mississippi," said Tish O'Donnell.

She shoved her fingers up to her hairline, dislodging a mass of gray hair. "Holy Mary, I'm glad to have that wig off," she added, dropping the lifeless thing onto the Buick's leather bench seat. "I thought my brain was going to melt." She grabbed the long tail of her gray-streaked red hair and pulled it up through the scrunchy making it into a messy knot above her neck.

Kat Merevec, sitting behind the wheel, had tossed her gray wig into the back seat, but damp spikes of her burgundy-tinted dark hair still clung damply around her face. Her brain felt a bit squishy, too.

She didn't really want to talk about the gold. Neither she nor Tish had said much on the drive over the broad Mississippi River from Illinois. The snarkiness that had defined their relationship during their first week on the road had evaporated in the events that had shaken them earlier that day. They were delicately navigating this new truce, and Kat was afraid that bringing up the gold would shatter it.

"I explained all that back at the bridge," she said, then winced inwardly at the defensive note in her voice.

"Oh, I'm not complaining about it," said Tish, putting her hand out toward Kat. "I understand why you did it. Those ingots would have pegged us as the ones who'd cleaned out the store safe. But still..." She sighed. "$40,000. In gold."

"Yeah, I know," Kat agreed, thinking briefly about what she could have done with her share of that money. But there hadn't been any choice, really.

From the moment they'd surprised each other in Fitz O'Donnell's jewelry store office in the middle of the night, both intent on taking from that lousy, lying snake's safe what was rightfully theirs—Kat her severance pay and bonus, and Tish the gemstones that would give her a fresh start—Kat had known they could sell the diamonds and gemstones. They were anonymous, as were the bundles of hundred-dollar bills stuffed in the duffel bag they'd found there.

But the gold...

They'd had to take it, of course, because what kind of burglars would leave behind a pile of gold? But stamped with the Superior Jewelers' logo, it would announce to anyone they tried to sell it to that they were behind the burglary. And they were both too old to go to prison.

So, Kat had done the only reasonable thing: tossed the incriminating ingots into the Mississippi off the old, crooked, Chain of Rocks Bridge.

She'd used the opportunity to get rid of her set of keys to Superior Jewelers, too. She'd meant to leave them in her car after the heist, but she'd stupidly left them in her jeans' pocket.

Tish took another bite of frozen custard, closed her eyes and moaned. "I could get used to having this for breakfast every day. This is sooo good," she said.

"No argument from me." Kat dipped up another bite. Her body temperature fell another fraction, and her jangled nerves settled just a little more. "It looks like everyone driving Route 66 stops here. And half the population of St. Louis."

She nodded toward the iconic building housing Ted Drewes' Frozen Custard stand across the parking lot. Long lines of customers trailed from almost every window.

"I wish we could get rid of Clapham's diamonds, as easily," said Tish.

Kat really didn't want to talk about the diamonds—at least *those* diamonds—either.

When Tish had opened the safe, they'd been shocked to discover two boxes of diamonds that didn't belong to Superior Jewelers. It appeared that Fitz—Tish's philandering, lying husband of thirty-five years—was money laundering in partnership with Alfred Clapham, the notorious Chicago-area fence, known—or at least strongly suspected —to use bodies as landfill.

"We can always go back to the river and throw them in," said Kat. But at Tish's pensive look, she added. "I'm joking, Tish. There's no reason to. Any pawn shop will take them. They're middling-quality stones. Easy for them to resell."

"Yeah. I know, but..."

"The whole point of raiding the safe was to give us both a new start in California. What we can get for those diamonds will be a nice addition to the 'Fitz Fund.' How much did you say they were worth?"

Tish sighed again. "Way more than $40,000. And you're right. In for a penny… But I feel like they're a big eye, watching us. Like he can see us."

Kat barely refrained from eye-rolling. "That's just the guilt of the newly larcenous."

Tish glared at her.

Kat gave her a wide-eyed look and raised her hand.

"I'm including myself. You think I don't feel it, too?" she said. Tish's glare faded.

"He has no idea we have them," said Kat. "No one does. You know that. As far as Clapham knows, Fitz has those diamonds."

Tish wrinkled her nose. "You're right. I know you're right. I'll still be glad when they're gone."

"That's why we're trying to sell them first."

Kat didn't admit to her own wiggling worm of fear. If the police, for any reason, came to suspect them of the midnight assault on the black safe at Superior, they wouldn't be sympathetic to the women's reasons for unloading the safe, but at least Kat and Tish would survive the encounter. However, if Clapham discovered they were the ones with his diamonds and—until this morning—a pile of his gold ingots, the encounter would be fatal.

Kat noticed that neither of them were mentioning the roughly one million in cash they'd also found in the safe, money that most likely had been meant to be exchanged for the diamonds. Whoever the cash had belonged to—and they knew it wasn't Fitz—might be even scarier than Clapham.

"Do you think those guys…" Tish hesitated, her pause pregnant with the weight of the terror that had driven them off the Chain of Rocks Bridge at a dead run. "Well, that they would have...maybe... killed us, if they'd caught us?" She waved the spoon vaguely over her shoulder toward the Mississippi River which formed the Illinois-Missouri state line a few miles behind them.

Mention of the five gang members who'd surprised them as she'd lofted the duffel bag over the bridge railing and into the "Big Muddy" was enough to curdle the custard in Kat's mouth.

So much for soothing her jangled nerves.

She swallowed.

"I don't know," she said. "But I wasn't about to stay to find out. Quit waving that spoon. I don't want you to get custard on the seats."

Tish looked at her. "It's *my* car," she said.

"Legally, yes," Kat agreed. "But spiritually," she ran a hand, in its black driving glove, lovingly over the steering wheel of the two-tone, yellow and white, '57 Buick rag top, "spiritually, this car is mine."

Tish snorted and almost spit frozen custard. "Spiritually?"

"Yep." Kat grinned, happy to change the subject. She pushed her black-framed glasses back up her face with the back of her hand and sliced off another bite of custard. "Some people have spirit animals or animal familiars. Beauty, here, is my familiar."

"Beauty?" asked Tish. "You named my car?"

"I didn't have to name her," said Kat, looking out over the hood possessively. "It was obvious."

Tish shook her head.

"Tell you what. If it means so much to you, when we get to California, you can use your share of the money to buy it from me."

Kat froze, spoon halfway to her mouth, and stared into the distance through the windshield. Ice formed around her heart.

She hadn't thought past the End of the Trail sign in Santa Monica. Couldn't think past that. Couldn't breathe.

End of the road.

Moving was everything. Stopping gave her nightmares. What would happen at the end?

"Kat?"

She managed a shallow inhale. "Sure," she said weakly. "I could do that."

From the corner of her eye, she saw Tish's puzzled look. Kat finished taking her bite of custard, but her appetite for it was gone.

"We should put the top down," she said, changing the subject again. She stuck her spoon into the remains of her custard and ran a hand through her short hair, making it spikier than normal. "It's going to be a scorcher."

After the bridge incident, they'd decided they were too rattled to hit any pawn shops and attempt to sell "inventory"—which is what they were calling the stolen gems and cash in the trunk—that day. Instead, they'd amble along, taking in the sights of Route 66, starting with their frozen custard. The Buick's windows were all open, the breeze coming through them thick with the buzzing of cicadas. But this close to the Mississippi, the Missouri humidity was especially oppressive.

"Too bad your dad didn't have AC installed in this car when he had it restored," said Kat. "We could have kept the windows up and the heat out."

"Well, hey there, Cutie!"

Tish screeched and almost dropped her custard, as a

grinning face, scruffy with two-day stubble, popped into the passenger-side window.

"It would have kept out the irritating bugs, too," murmured Kat, frowning.

A chubby, sun-leathered face under curly, dyed blonde hair popped in next to Stubble. The top of her generous cleavage was visible at the edge of the door frame. "Hey, girls," she said.

"I told Erm, soon's I saw the car, that just has to be Katie and Mary," said Stubble. He slapped the Buick's door. Tish jumped again, and Kat's eyes narrowed. "No ma'am. Not many like this around anymore."

Uly and Erma Armentrout. Kat and Tish had picked them up in Pontiac, Illinois, like the smell of dog doo you can't get off your shoes.

"I'm surprised to see you're still driving her," said Erma. "When we saw you in Springfield, you said you had a buyer for her."

The lie had been an attempt to get rid of them, Kat remembered. Who would have believed they'd run into the too-friendly couple again?

Kat had convinced Tish that Route 66 would make an excellent escape path after their heist, assuming that no one would think to find them wandering America's "Mother Road," meaning not Fitz, not the police, and certainly not Alf Clapham. She hadn't figured on anyone like the Armentrouts popping up. Although their appearances seemed accidental, they made Kat nervous, considering what was in the Buick's trunk.

"The deal fell through," said Kat. Tish was as mesmerized by the Armentrouts' faces in the window as a small mammal facing a couple cobras.

"Guess they didn't know a cherry Buick when they saw one," said Uly.

"Lucky for us, though," said Erma. "I wasn't foolin' when I said we'd buy her from you."

"Too late," said Kat. "I decided to buy it."

Kat thought she saw a flicker of avarice in Erma's eyes, but it was gone so fast...

"Offer still stands," said Erma, her friendly face back in place. "Bet we can give you enough, you could get something even better."

"Not for sale. At any price," said Kat.

Greed flicked in Erma's eyes again, and her smile tightened.

Anger? wondered Kat. *Strange.*

"Well, it's lucky for us you still have her," said Uly, "otherwise we might have missed you."

"Yeah. Lucky," murmured Kat.

"You two heading to Meramec, too?" he asked.

If we had been, we wouldn't be now. "No," lied Kat. "We're spending some time here in St. Louis."

"Oh, say, why don't you come and join us?" said Uly, leering at Tish, who had slipped across the bench seat until she was only a few inches away from Kat. "It's a classic Route 66 sightseeing spot, you know. You can't drive the Route and not stop at Meramec. If you call now, you maybe could get the same reservation time as us. Or we could switch ours around so's we could go through the caverns together. What do you say? You can always come back to St. Louie. It's not very far. They say Jesse and Frank James holed up there, you know. At the caves."

"They have a wonderful patriotic show, too." Erma shivered. "Just gives me chills, I tell you. We've been five times."

Erma's face was aglow with innocent kitsch-loving pleasure. But Kat's mistrust meter began pinging more loudly.

"The guy who started promoting Meramec invented bumper stickers to advertise it. Did you know that?" said Uly.

"Should we?" asked Kat.

"Used to hire kids to put 'em on cars while people were in the caverns. Smart marketing," said Uly, and winked.

"I may not like this car, but no one's putting a bumper sticker on it," said Tish, finding her voice.

"Too bad," said Uly. "It's got bumpers just crying out for a sticker or two. Come on with us anyway." Uly gave a tug to the worn baseball cap that featured the faded logo of some boat chartering place. "It'll be fun!"

"Thanks," said Kat. "But we have reservations for a riverboat cruise this afternoon."

"Well, okay then," said Uly. "We'll see you on the road somewheres else, I'm sure." He slapped the car again, earning another death-stare from Kat. "Bye there, Cutie." Uly winked a leer at Tish.

The faces disappeared from the window. Kat and Tish watched Uly's butt and Erma's bust bounce and swing in time as they crossed the parking lot to their tiny blue Nissan Cube.

"How do they find us?" asked Tish. "It's creepy."

Kat slid a wicked glance toward her friend.

"I still say it's your pheromones," she said.

"Don't start," said Tish, turning her own death-glare on Kat as she slid back toward the passenger door.

"No, seriously. I'm telling you, he has the hots for you."

"Kat..."

Kat laughed. "Look on the bright side," she told Tish.

"You wanted to spend a few days in St. Louis sightseeing. A couple days here, and maybe your stalkers will have moved on down the road far enough that we won't run into them again." *And St. Louis would be a great place to hit a few pawn shops*, too, thought Kat, though her heart quailed at the thought right now.

Tish brightened. "Then we really can do that cruise?"

"Sure."

Tish watched the Armentrout's Nissan Cube pull out of the parking lot and onto Route 66. Uly beeped the horn, and Erma waved at them.

"Ugh," said Tish. "Kat?" she added, after a moment.

"Umm?"

"You don't think I look like Erma, do you?"

Kat looked across at Tish, tendrils of red hair curling around her clear peaches-and-cream cheeks slightly flushed with the warmth of the day. There was a sweetness and honesty in her deep brown eyes that even thirty-five years with Fitzpatrick O'Donnell hadn't dimmed.

The extra weight Tish carried clearly bothered her, but Tish was a beautiful woman who had no idea just how lovely she was.

"You look nothing like Erma," said Kat firmly. "Which is probably why Uly keeps following us..."

"Stop it," said Tish warningly.

"...but now that you mention it, Hilary will probably look like her in twenty years," said Kat, mentioning Fitz's much younger girlfriend. Fitz announcing that he was going to marry Hilary was the reason Tish had decided to clean out the safe in their Evanston, Illinois, jewelry store and leave him first.

Kat had had her own reasons for making the same decision.

But Fate, with her peculiar sense of humor, had determined they would decide to burgle the store on the same night. At the same time.

Slowly, Tish grinned back. "It'll serve him right," she said.

Kat smiled, leaned forward, and turned the key. The big car purred in response. Kat turned out of the parking lot and onto Chippewa.

"Get your phone out," she told Tish, as she pointed the Buick back toward downtown St. Louis, "and find us a cruise. With luck, it'll be cooler on the water."

CHAPTER 2
THE GOLD FLOATS

From his thickly carpeted and densely paneled office, high above Michigan Avenue in downtown Chicago, Alfred Clapham had a breathtaking view of Lake Michigan, from the Navy Pier to the planetarium, not that he ever looked at it. It was enough that he was able to pay for it.

Hungry little Alf Clapham, one-time runner for mobsters. Little "Elf" Clapham, who'd had to put up with jokes about his height for years after he got out of juvie. Alf Clapham who'd had to make it on his own when his father and brother went to prison, after that little weasel snitched on them.

Now the mobsters came to him, along with the attorneys, financial planners, stockbrokers, and other sharks like Alf Clapham, who skimmed, scammed, and flat-out stole jewelry, paintings, and rare coins from their clients. They all depended on him to turn their gleanings into honest, untraceable cash. No one laughed at Alf Clapham now.

Certainly not the man standing in front of him.

Everyone but Alf stood. There was no second chair in the room.

"So, where'd they get it?" Clapham asked him, leaning back in his chair. With his desk and chair on a raised platform, Clapham was eye-to-eye with his lieutenant.

"They say two old women walked up on the bridge with it and tossed the bag over the railing. It caught on a catwalk. One of these losers was drunk and stupid enough to crawl over the railing and get it."

"What about the women?"

"They didn't give us much. Old. Gray hair. One tallish and fat. One small and thin. The thin one tossed the bag. When they saw our guys, they ran."

"Car?"

"Again, not much. Big. Old. White. Caddie, they thought. They didn't see the tags."

"They didn't go after them?" asked Clapham.

The man shrugged. "Didn't see the need. They opened the bag, saw the gold, and that was it."

"They didn't know the women?"

"They say not."

"You sure?"

"Oh, yeah. We're sure. They were begging to make up names for us before we finished."

"But they're sure it was old ladies, not guys in drag?"

Another shrug. "They didn't pants 'em, Boss. But the big guy, Ty? Almost wet himself laughing when he told us how they ran away. I'm guessing they were what these guys say they were."

"That's all we got?"

The standing man nodded at the shiny pile on the desk. "All but the gold."

"And these." With his middle finger, Clapham leaned

forward and flicked a set of keys lying on his desk. They slid across the slick surface and hit the stack of gold ingots with a dull *clink*. The keys had been in the bag with the gold ingots. "*These* tell me those morons did the job themselves. This crap about 'old women' is bullshit."

"You're sure those are the keys to the store?"

"You said your clowns had their own car keys on them," said Clapham.

"True. They did," said his lieutenant.

"If they have the keys, they did the job. If they did the job, they have my diamonds."

"They say the gold was the only thing in the bag."

"It's a bullshit story," said Clapham, again. "No one throws forty grand in gold into the river, least of all two old ladies who probably eat cat food on their Social Security checks."

The standing man stayed silent. When Clapham's tiny dark eyes looked up from the gold and drilled him, he shifted but stared back.

"Boss, normally I'd agree with you," he finally said. "But these guys… They all stuck to the story, even the young kid. Crying and puking, he kept saying they didn't do it. That he climbed the rail to get the bag." He shook his head. "I gotta say, I believe them. Stupid as it sounds."

"And there were no diamonds."

"Nope. No diamonds. We stripped the car, stripped them. If there'd been diamonds, they'd have given them up."

Clapham picked up one of the ingots, turned it in his hands, and thought.

"We have no way to find these old ladies?"

"Not without a better description or plates on the car. They could be anywhere."

"Where's this bridge again?"

"Down in St. Louis."

"That's where these clowns are from?"

"Yes sir. Most likely the women, too, but who knows?" said Clapham's associate, lifting his hands and one eyebrow "Could have come up from Memphis."

"No. Not Memphis. The gold's from Evanston," said Clapham. "That's where the store is. That's where my diamonds were. If these 'old women' are real, they came from right here." He slapped the ingot on the desk. "Chicago."

Clapham took up the ingot again, tapped it against its reflection on the desk. Flipped it. Tapped it. Flipped it. Tapped it.

His associate wisely stayed silent.

Finally, Clapham gave a short, sharp nod. "Well, if that's all we've got, that's all we've got." He looked up at his lieutenant. "But if those bitches ran south, maybe they'll keep running south. You tell all our connections in St. Louis, I want those stones back. It won't be healthy for anyone trying to turn them behind my back."

"I'll put out the word."

"*And I want those old hags.*" Clapham drove his fist into the desk and stood up, so he loomed over his associate.

"I'll let them know."

"You do that. About the other thing... I don't want any comebacks when those guys float."

"There won't be. The bodies won't come up until they reach the Gulf. If then."

Clapham nodded again.

"Okay then. I'll take it from here."

As his associate left, Clapham sat again and began spinning the ingot on the desk.

Finally, he came to a decision, picked up his phone, and dialed.

"Yeah?" said a voice on the second ring.

"Got a job for you. Down in St. Louis. Usual rate. You free?"

"Yeah."

"Not much to go on, but you've had worse."

"What's the job?"

"Couple old bitches have some diamonds that belong to me. I want my diamonds back, and I want the two hags to disappear. But first, I want to know who sent them against me."

"No problem."

CHAPTER 3

NOT ACCORDING TO PLAN

The hackles on Kat's neck were standing at full alert. The pawnbroker was trying too hard. His colleague had made a phone call not long after they walked in. Kat hadn't thought anything of it—until this guy started stalling.

Tish, beside her, was tense. She felt it too.

"Ladies." He smiled his crocodile grin again. "Like I said, my boss is the only one who can pay out on this kind of a purchase. He should be in shortly. Just a bit late today. If you'll take some time, look around..."

The sooner we get out of here, the better, thought Kat.

She made a point of looking at her watch.

"Well," she said, giving the pawnbroker an apologetic look. "We really can't wait right now. My cousin here, she needs her insulin in a bit, and probably a bite to eat. Give us say, half an hour? Forty-five minutes? Your boss should be in then, and we'll come back and talk to him."

"I think that's best," said Tish. "I *am* feeling a bit light-headed."

Kat took Tish's arm. "Come on, hon. Don't want you to have a seizure."

As they turned toward the door, Kat looked back over her shoulder. "We'll be right back, as soon as my cousin's feeling more settled."

They were out of the pawn shop, around the corner, into the car, and down a block almost before the door had swung shut behind them.

Kat made several random turns. Tish kept her eyes glued on the right-side mirror, another addition her father had made when he'd restored the big old '57 Buick.

"Anyone behind us?" asked Kat.

Tish shook her head. "No. I don't think so."

Kat searched the rearview mirror again. "I don't think so, either." She glanced at Tish. "Can you get us to Forest Park?"

"Sure, but why?" asked Tish.

"We need time to think."

"Right at the next corner."

Kat turned obediently.

Tish's younger son, Luke, called his mother's faultless sense of direction her superpower. Born with no sense of direction at all, Kat had found her partner's ability unsettling at first, but Tish's built-in cranial compass was less supernatural to her as the days went on. In fact, she was coming to depend on it.

Twenty minutes later they sat, cold bottles of water in hand, under trees at Forest Park, which they'd delightedly discovered two days before. Kat kicked off her high-heeled sandals and managed to fold to the ground—less than gracefully, thanks to her black, pencil skirt. She pulled off what she'd taken to calling the red-haired Dolly wig. She ran her hands through her short—and damp—burgundy-tinted hair. In moments, the familiar spiky look was back.

Tish didn't try for graceful. She plopped to the grass, arranged her navy-blue skirt under her, and yanked off the mousy brown wig she'd chosen that morning, scattering hair pins in all directions.

"I can't believe it," she said, digging through her massive handbag to come up with a hair clip. "It's not even mid-morning. It must be almost 90 already." She twisted her long red hair and massed it into a messy knot on her head, corralling it with the clip.

"Better?" asked Kat.

"It would be better if the air would move." Tish pulled the front of her flower-printed cotton blouse away at the neck, settled her icy bottle of water against her soft bosom, and sighed.

Kat shoved at the heavy black glasses sliding down her sweat-slicked nose.

"I'm glad your costuming instincts did not dictate stockings today," she said.

"Ugh," was Tish's only comment. She toed off her low-heeled pumps. "I wish I'd worn sandals, too."

They sat quietly for a few minutes, drinking their water and lowering their body temperatures as well as their heart rates.

"Something's wrong," said Kat finally. "You felt it, too, didn't you? In both those places?"

"Maybe we're having an off day?" said Tish, after a moment. "We were bound to have one sooner or later."

"You didn't feel like the pawnbrokers were looking for us?"

"Maybe it's part of the Missouri character? It *is* the

'Show Me' state. Maybe people here are just normally suspicious."

When Kat remained silent, Tish shot her a sidelong look.

"You don't think so," she said. A statement, not a question.

"Neither do you," said Kat. "Remember what you said after we walked out of that first pawn shop? You said the broker made you feel naked."

Tish shivered. "You're right. I did. He did."

"I just can't figure out why they each tried to keep us waiting for someone. I don't believe for a minute they couldn't make a buy. All I know is that it scared the hell out of me."

"But Kat, why would anyone be looking for *us*? Do you think we're wrong? That maybe Fitz *did* call the police? Told them *we* robbed the safe? Do you think the pawnbrokers were waiting for the St. Louis police?"

Kat saw splinters of fear in Tish's wide brown eyes.

She reached out and squeezed Tish's arm, as much to calm herself as to soothe her partner.

"No," she said, with more assurance than she felt. "Fitz will believe your note threatening to sue him in court. He won't suspect you. Or me."

In fact, I'm sure he's forgotten I exist, she thought, with a flair of white-hot anger.

She took a long pull on her water bottle. "Besides. I think you're right. Once he found the office safe was empty, and all the best stones were gone, not to mention all Clapham's stuff, he'd have to clean everything out of the big vault. He'd need all the money he could get from the jewelry and gemstones in it to maintain Hilary. She's probably not low maintenance."

She saw the stricken look on Tish's face and realized what she'd said. "I'm sorry, Tish. I didn't mean to pour salt in that wound."

Tish scrunched her face up in a way that was meant to show Kat it wasn't a big deal, but it looked more like she was trying not to cry.

"You're right, though," said Tish, once she'd regained control of her face. "And he'd need the insurance money to pay Clapham for the missing diamonds."

Not to mention repay the other shady character that had to be involved, thought Kat. *That money came from somewhere.*

She thought a minute more.

"Though..."

"What?" asked Tish when Kat hesitated.

"Well, when the police called you, back in Illinois, you told them to talk to your attorney. Do you have one?"

Tish gave her a panicked look. "What? No, of course, I don't have one! I've never needed one! Besides, don't they have to tell the police if they have knowledge of a crime?"

"You don't need to tell her about the safe," said Kat. "Just tell her you've left Fitz, but because there was a burglary about the same time, the police are adding two and two and coming up with seven. You need someone to run interference."

Kat pulled her tank top out and blew down her front. "I think I'm going to get another one of these," she held up the almost-empty water bottle, "and pour it over my head.

"Besides," she said, continuing her previous thought, "if you *are* planning to get a divorce, you'll need an attorney anyway. Two birds? One stone?"

Tish pulled a brochure from the river cruise out of her purse and fanned herself with it. "Sometimes this just gets too real, you know?"

"Yes. I know."

A slight hint of breeze blew past them. "Oh, please!" said Kat, turning her face into the faintly moving air. "More of that. Please!"

When the baby breeze died down, Tish turned to Kat. "If they can't be looking for *us*, why all the suspicion at the pawn shops, do you think?" She tipped up her warming bottle of water and drank down half.

Kat watched traffic on the road through the park. A jogger passed on the path behind them. *Courting heat stroke,* she thought.

"Maybe they *are* looking for someone," she said pensively. "Not necessarily us, but maybe we fit a description."

"I guess that could be true," Tish agreed. "But if that's the case, what do we do?"

"Stay away from pawn shops, at least for now, I think," said Kat. "But an out-of-the-mainstream jeweler might be a safe place to try. After all, pawnbrokers and jewelers attract different types of people selling jewelry, right?"

Tish produced what Kat was coming to think of as her "annoyed mother" look. "You ask me that like I'm an expert at this."

"Well, I'm not an expert, either, but it makes sense."

Tish sighed.

"The abusive husband story, rather than the dead mother story?" she asked.

Kat nodded.

"Okay," said Tish, and finished her water. "I think my nerves can take one more try. But if we get the same vibes, we leave St. Louis. At laser speed, as Luke would say."

"I think you mean warp speed."

Tish waved a hand. "Whatever. Just really fast!"

CHAPTER 4
FITZ GETS A FRIGHT

"**B**ut Fitzy, when are we going to get married? I want to get married," pouted Hilary.

When he'd first seen Hilary Schoenmeyer pout, there behind the counter of The Koffee Kup where she was a barista, all Fitz O'Donnell had wanted to do was kiss that mouth until it stopped pouting. He hadn't considered that she was younger than his son Luke.

Lately, though, with so much on his mind, he was finding it harder to concentrate on erasing that pout than on what was causing it.

"So do I, sweetness," Fitz lied. "But I have to get divorced first, and my attorney can't find Tish to get her signature."

"You said you loved me." Hilary's lower lip stretched out further.

"I do, sweetness. You know that." He put his arms around her and petted her hair.

God damn it, he thought. *I've got to find Tish. The store's gone, and so's all the money and the gold and the diamonds. I can't lose Hilary, too.*

He didn't plan to *marry* Hilary. But if he could get Tish back to Evanston, it would at least *look* like he wanted a divorce. He and Hilary could escape with whatever money his son Carlisle, a hedge fund manager, could scrounge up for him.

Tish could deal with the rest of the mess. The police. The angry customers. The suppliers. The employees.

And Clapham.

Fitz shuddered.

She was the one who'd always wanted the damned store anyway, he thought. *Let her have it.*

Of course, Hilary thought the store was going to be *hers*. Breaking it to her that they weren't coming back might be tricky. But once they were settled in the Bahamas, he was sure he could make her forget about the store. And marriage.

He sighed inwardly.

It should have been so easy. He'd arranged a trade-off of diamonds and cash between Alf Clapham and the mystery man Carlisle called the Shady Sheik. Then, while all of it, diamonds and cash, was in the store over the long Memorial Day weekend, he and Hilary would clean out the safe and head to warmer climates before anyone knew they were gone.

He'd about died when they'd found the safe empty. When the insurance company told him the old black safe wasn't insurable, Fitz had told them the big vault had been broken into as well.

Unfortunately, the vault was on a time lock and couldn't be opened until two days after Fitz claimed the break-in had taken place.

So, when Carlisle had suggested they empty the big, walk-in vault—which held the rest of the store's gemstones and all its jewelry—before the store opened on Tuesday, after the holiday, it had seemed like a godsend.

But the damned police hadn't liked the timing of the "burglary" any more than the insurance agent had. At one point, they'd even suggested he might have killed Tish! Thank God, they'd found her alive.

No, he thought. *I can't lose Hilary. I've done all of this for her.*

"Look," he said, with sudden inspiration. "Until we can find Tish, why don't you move in here with me? We can sell the condo." *And I can stop paying for an extra piece of property,* he thought."

"Here?" Fitz felt her recoil.

"Why not?" he said. "I have a Jacuzzi in the bathroom upstairs, a massage bed..."

"But Fitzy. It's all so...ugly." Hilary's lip curled as she looked around the O'Donnell living room. Suddenly she brightened. "I know! I can redecorate!"

Fitz froze. How could he tell her there was no money for that?

I've got Alf Clapham on one side of me, wanting his money. The Shady Sheik's on the other side, wanting his fucking diamonds. Carlisle, Mr. Oh-So-Smart Money Guy, said we had to take the customers' jewelry, too, so now they're screaming. I've got employees hollering about severance and paychecks, and the goddamned suppliers are kvetching about money for their jewelry and gemstones, which are who-the-hell-knows-wherever Carlisle has stashed them. I've got to sell this fucking house, a chunk of commercial property that won't be easy to move. Then there's Hilary's condo. And she wants to redecorate!

If Carlisle would just bring back some that jewelry, like Fitz had asked him to, he could give Hilary something to make her happy. But, damn him, Carlisle had refused! If he did that, his son said, the police would know Fitz really *had* burgled his own store, and so would the insurance company. Then Fitz would go to jail for fraud.

Fraud!

He'd finally blackmailed Carlisle into liquidating some of his stocks, or whatever hedge fund managers dealt in, and advance him the money. *After all, it's his fucking fault I'm in this mess,* thought Fitz.

There's no way Fitz was going to waste any of *that* money on a house he never planned to come back to. A house he already had on the market.

Hilary nuzzled his neck. Any fledgling doubts he might have had about any of his recent decisions, died quickly.

Fitz's phone vibrated in his pocket. His fingers twitched. He was desperate for a call from Carlisle saying he'd sold whatever he needed to sell to give Fitz the cash he wanted. But his instinct told him that Hilary, beginning to soften in his arms, would slip away from him if he made the wrong move—and reaching for his phone was definitely a wrong move.

He let it go to voice mail.

"I'll tell you what, sweetness," he said, sliding his hand under her pink, cropped T-shirt. Geez. Her skin was so soft he almost forgot what he was saying.

What was he saying?

Oh, yes.

"Why don't you start selling what you hate the most." *I can use the money to start paying off Clapham*, he thought. "Once things are cleared out a bit, you'll have a better idea of how you want to redecorate."

"Oh, Fitzy!" Hilary danced backward and clapped her hands. "I'm going to start with that ugly couch," she said.

"And that ugly painting..." She went into the dining room and picked up her phone.

His phone buzzed again. Fitz slipped it out of his pocket as he stepped into the foyer and glanced at the caller ID.

His blood drained to his feet. He was sure his heart would stop.

Clapham. Calling for the second time.

Hands sweating, he let it go to voice mail again. He didn't want to take the fence's call in front of Hilary. She didn't know...

Fitz got his breathing under control and went into the dining room. Hilary was snapping pictures of everything.

"Sweetness, while you're busy here, why don't I go out and...and pick us up some lunch?"

"No Italian," she said, continuing to create her catalog of things to sell. "It's too fattening."

"Fine," he said. "I'll be back like lightning." He turned toward the kitchen.

"Fitzy!"

He turned back, pasting a smile on his face.

She was pouting. "Hillie wants a kiss."

"Always, my sweetness," he said.

For the first time since he'd met her, her lips tasted like sawdust.

CHAPTER 5
THE GREEDY JEWELER

Tish searched her phone, and they made a short list of jewelers near the park. Back in the car, with Tish navigating, they drove by three of them. The fourth was in a mixed area of strip malls and stand-alone businesses. It looked like the area had served the local community for years but was slowly upscaling. The street was busy, but it wasn't a main thoroughfare. The jewelry store, holding down the end of an older strip mall, was settled next to a secondhand store parading as an antique shop, a family-owned Italian restaurant, a small clothing shop, and a tattoo parlor. All but the tattoo parlor looked like they'd been there a long time.

Kat parked.

Tish took a deep breath. Another.

"Ready?" Kat asked.

"As I'll ever be," said Tish. She looked Kat over. "But you'll have to wear the jacket."

Kat groaned. "Tish. It's 92 degrees."

That morning, hoping to distract pawnbrokers from paying close attention to them, Tish had decided Kat needed to "sex it up." Kat had strapped herself into a black lace push-up bra that exaggerated her already generous attributes and topped it with a slinky red tank top about a size too small. It had gotten attention, all right. Just not enough.

Now, they needed to tone down their performance, so Kat had to cover up.

She reached into the back seat and dragged forward the black jacket that went with the pencil skirt. "Sometimes I hate you," she said to Tish.

"What are you complaining about?" asked Tish. "I'm the one wearing a sweater."

Tish opened the Buick's enormous glove box and handed Kat a sedate, shoulder length brown wig. "You'll have to lose the purple."

"Burgundy," said Kat, taking the wig with a sigh.

Tish pulled out a short, gray wig for herself, along with a high-quality gold-filled bangle, a strand of imitation pearls, and matching clip-on earrings they'd found at a thrift store. Tish hadn't lied, thought Kat, when she'd said she was an ace at thrift-store buying.

She handed the bangle to Kat, hooked the pearls around her own neck, and clipped on the earrings.

They adjusted wigs and reapplied makeup. Tish leaned over and yanked off Kat's long eyelashes.

"Ow!" said Kat. "I hate when you do that."

"Shoes," said Tish, draping a lanyard around her neck and settling her reading glasses onto her generous bosom.

"Now I know I hate you," said Kat. She opened the Buick door and forced her damp feet into black pumps. Tish was doing the same.

Now, with a black suit covering Kat's red tank top and lacy bra, and wearing her brown wig and black glasses, and

Tish in her navy skirt, flowered blouse, cotton cardigan, pearls, and sensible heels, they looked like two severe daughters of the Confederacy.

"Okay, Sarah Bernhardt, we're on," said Kat.

"Very funny," said Tish, but Kat could see she was pleased by the nickname.

They'd decided to sell some of Superior's high-quality diamonds, with a variation of the story that they'd told at the Markers' store in Joliet, Illinois—that Tish was trying to leave an abusive marriage and wanted to sell the diamonds that she'd had removed from her wedding and engagement rings. If asked, she could truthfully say the stones in her rings were now cubic zirconias.

Tish gave the store owner, Mr. Jessup, her story, but from the beginning, Kat had seen the look of avarice in his eyes. While the Markers—at least Mrs. Marker—had had a great deal of sympathy for Tish's story, Jessup was no Monica Marker. He was older, crustier, and much more tight-fisted. Not to mention, greedy.

"That's my best offer," he said to them after he offered Tish less than a third of the market value. "Take it or leave it."

"These are worth much more than that," Tish said. "I don't expect to get what was paid for them…"

"And you won't," Jessup said bluntly.

Sensing that Tish was about to step out of the sweet, soft-spoken character she was playing, and tell this cheapskate jeweler that she knew exactly what the market value was for secondhand diamonds, Kat quickly intervened.

"Terry, honey," she said, using the name on the fake driver's license she'd made for Tish a few days before, "let's go have coffee and talk about this. I'm sure Mr. Jessup is offering all he can." She tugged gently on Tish's arm. "Come on, hon."

Tish held onto her composure and allowed herself to be pulled out of the store.

"That cheap...son of a...a...so and so," Tish snarled when they were half a block away.

For the last few days, Tish had recommitted herself to not swearing. If she ever dared to go to confession again, she'd told Kat, she didn't want to break the priest who would be forced to give her a thousand Hail Marys.

"We can't expect every jewelry store to be like the Markers'."

"I know that. But that was ridiculous."

They went around the corner, and Kat pulled Tish to a stop.

"What?"

"I have an idea," Kat told her. "You still have Clapham's stones in your purse? The ones we were going to sell at the pawn shops?"

"Of course, I do. Where else would I have put them?" Tish said irritably.

Kat pointed to the coffee shop across the street, part of a national chain. "Let's go get that coffee and use the ladies' room."

Tish's eyes narrowed as she looked at her partner. "What are you thinking?

"Come with me, and I'll tell you."

They got two iced coffees and sat down in a corner of the dining area. The place was noisy with loudly playing world music, the roar of steam heating milk for cappuccinos, and voices raucous from the caffeine hits. The bedlam covered their conversation as Kat outlined her idea.

Tish was quiet. She turned the cup holding her iced coffee. Turned it again. And again.

"What?" asked Kat.

"This feels dishonest," said Tish.

"So, we don't do it?"

"We'll be cheating him."

"Are we?"

"Well, we aren't giving him what he thinks he's getting."

"Is the price he offered a fair price for the diamonds we'll be giving him?"

"You said Cl... the Collection is all VS to high SI grade, and J or better in color, right?"

Kat, who'd been Superior Jewelers' gemologist as well as store manager, had inspected all the stones in their "inventory" carefully during their prolonged stay in St. Louis.

"Yes," said Kat. "Except for the twenty or so stones that were I clarity grade."

"Wholesale value for those stones is at least twenty-five percent higher than what he offered us for the VVS diamonds we showed him," said Tish without hesitation.

"Then are we cheating him?" asked Kat again.

Tish glared at her partner in crime. "You're beginning to sound like a Jesuit," she said.

Kat tried not to smile, but her eyebrows danced.

Tish gave a light shake of her head, then turned her attention back to her iced coffee. A moment later, she turned the cup pensively. And again.

"Tish. Unlike Mrs. Marker, who was sympathetic to your plight as an abused wife, I think Mr. Jessup sees an opportunity to take advantage of the situation. All I'm proposing is that we reduce his advantage."

"You're rationalizing again."

"I am," admitted Kat.

"What if he checks the stones?" asked Tish, looking up.

Kat shrugged. "It's a possibility. But I think he has a low opinion of us. Of women in general, probably. He's already checked them once, and very carefully. I don't think he'll look again."

"It would serve him right, too," Tish said in mock anger. "Trying to take advantage of a woman in my situation."

Kat sat silently, as Tish continued to meditate on her coffee.

Kat had lived in shadows much of her younger life, and her line between right and wrong had been...more fluid... than Tish's. For the last thirty years or so, however, that line had become less permeable, and Kat had stayed on the "white" side of the line between black and white. Mostly. The only shadows she'd lived in were the ones she carried with her.

The night she decided to raid the safe, though, she knew she was stepping decisively into the gray.

No, she thought. *I knew I'd be over the line into the black.*

It wasn't the same for Tish. Tish had lived her life in the light.

Correction, thought Kat, smiling to herself. Tish had a hidden safe in her closet where she kept the jewelry she'd had their goldsmith make every time Fitz cheated on her. Fitz didn't know anything about it.

Tish had also dived, head first, into putting together their disguises and coming up with "scripts" for their sales encounters. Tish had adapted to the gray zone more quickly than Kat had expected.

Maybe so. But in the last ten days, Kat had gained a tremendous amount of respect for Tish. She was damned if she was going to drag Tish any farther into the shadows than they already were.

"We didn't do this at the Markers," said Tish, interrupting Kat's thoughts.

"No, we didn't. They agreed to give you a fair price for your diamonds."

More cup turning and pensive looks.

"Are you're comfortable with doing this?" asked Tish.

"Yes, I am," said Kat immediately. "But I meant what I said, Tish. If you're not good with it, then we don't do it. We're in this together. We decide together. I won't push you into something you won't be able to live with."

Something, thought Kat, that would shatter this delicate budding friendship.

This, she was surprised to realize, was becoming more valuable to her than anything in the trunk.

"You don't want to break that priest," Kat added.

Tish's eyes smiled at her briefly, before she turned to watch the traffic passing on the street. Kat gave her space.

"You know, it's odd," said Tish finally, "but I *am* okay with it." She turned back to Kat, with a one-sided smile. "Though I'm not sure what that says about either of us."

She nodded. "Yes," she said firmly. "But that's our baseline, Kat. Whatever diamonds we give someone, the price has to be fair for what they get. And we don't switch unless provoked."

"Agreed," said Kat, relieved, yet amused by the word "provoked." "Tonight, we'll come up with some kind of code, so that you can pull the plug any time we don't reach the baseline, or if for any reason, you're not comfortable with the situation."

"Me?" said Tish, startled. "Why me?"

"You know the prices, Tish. You can figure weights and

prices faster in your head than with that fancy calculator on your desk. Besides," Kat straightened, finished off her iced coffee, and grinned, "you're our moral compass."

"Moral compass?" asked Tish ruefully. "Not sure I have one anymore. Not since..." She trailed off.

Kat's smile vanished. She leaned forward, utterly serious.

"Tish," she said, "we were both furious that night, and we landed ourselves in a situation neither of us is cut out for. Especially you. And yes, we've rationalized and justified that decision and every decision since. But I don't think either of us wants to go down the road to perdition any farther than we have to. Redemption lies only in the choices we make from here on out. But not all of them will be 'right.'"

"Redemption?" said Tish, raising an eyebrow.

Kat's smile came back. "Once a Catholic, you never lose the guilt."

Tish laughed out loud.

CHAPTER 6

FITZ BLABS

Fitz pulled into a parking spot near the lake. He tried to take a deep breath, but an iron band was around his chest. He was going to have a heart attack. He just knew it. In fact, he wasn't sure he wouldn't welcome it. He doubted Clapham would let him get away with anything that easily, though.

He tried again, managed a shallow, shaky breath. With a sweaty hand, he dialed Clapham's office. A secretary put him through.

"O'Donnell? What the hell...?"

Fitz's words were a blur in the ear.

"Mr-Clapham-I'm-really-sorry-I-couldn't-take-your-call-earlier-and-I'm-really-sorry-I-didn't-call-you-sooner-about-the-loss-of-your-diamonds-and-money-in-the-robbery-but-it's-been-total-chaos-and-with-the-police..."

"You moron!" shouted Clapham. "Use the app!"

Suddenly Fitz was talking to air.

App?

Fitz flushed and cursed himself.

When they'd set up their deal, Clapham had told him

never to call on the office line. He was only to use a phone app that encrypted their calls. It had taken Fitz three days to figure out how to use it, and he'd only used it once.

The freaking app.

For a moment, he considered driving straight to O'Hare and getting on the first plane going anywhere. Hilary or no Hilary.

He would have, too, except without cash and with his credit cards probably maxed out...

Fitz fumbled with his phone, trying to remember how to use the encryption app. The phone's buzz startled him. He dropped it, and it slithered toward the floor. He grabbed for it, thumping his head on the steering wheel.

The phone buzzed.

Fitz threw open the Corvette door, caught his foot on the threshold, and crashed to the pavement. He crawled back on hands and knees and scrabbled for the phone. It slipped from his sweating hand and slid, buzzing like a swarm of yellow jackets, under the carpet protector.

He shoved at the stiff plastic, swearing. He almost sobbed when his fingers locked onto the phone.

Clapham was screaming as Fitz, still kneeling next to the car, opened the connection.

"You're a total fuck up, O'Donnell! A complete and total fuck up. I told you never to call me on the office line."

"Yes, Mr. Clapham, you did and I'm sorry, it's just so much..."

"Where's my money?"

"I'm sorry, Mr. Clapham, but you see the store was robbed..."

"I *know* that, O'Donnell. I hear the news."

"It's just that they took all the diamonds and the gold and the cash, and now the police..."

"The police?" Clapham shouted. "You called the fucking *police*?"

"I had to!" whined Fitz. "I needed their report for my insurance company."

"O'Donnell, if you mentioned my name to the police..."

"No! No, Mr. Clapham. Of course not. But they think I'm involved..."

"Are you?" snapped Clapham.

"Am I? Am I what?" asked Fitz.

"Are you fucking involved, O'Donnell! Did you steal my money?"

Fitz's jaw froze. *Shitshitshitshit*, echoed in his head.

"Did you?" screamed Clapham into the silence.

"No! Of course not." Even to his own ears, Fitz didn't sound innocent.

"O'Donnell, you'd better not be double crossing me."

"No, Mr. Clapham! I swear! I'd never do that! I'm an honest businessman."

Clapham snorted.

"Then tell me, O'Donnell, tell me how a bunch of two-time losers down in St. Louis turned up with a bag full of *my* gold stamped with *your* store logo?"

What? thought Fitz.

"I...I...I don't kno..."

"You don't know."

"No! Mr. Clapham, I swear. The police think it was a domestic dispute..."

There was an ominous silence on Clapham's end of the phone.

"Are you trying to tell me your *wife* took my money and my gold?"

Fitz's strangled laugh was the sound made by a man

who'd just stepped through a trap door with a noose around his neck.

"Tish would never have the nerve to do that," he said.

"Good. Because I'd hate to think you're bullshitting me."

"No, Mr. Clapham. Definitely not. I would never..."

"You have five days, O'Donnell."

"Five days?"

"Five days to get my diamonds back or give me the money you owe me."

"Five da...?"

"Since you're more than a week late with the payment," Clapham went on, "I'll expect interest, too. Ten percent per day."

"Ten perc...?"

"Five days."

Fitz mobilized his brain and coordinated it with his tongue.

"Mr. Clapham, I can't do it in five days. I have to sell the store. I have to sell the house. I'm still waiting for the insurance company to pay my claim." No need to mention that that was not going to happen. "I need..." Fitz swallowed hard. "I need at least three weeks."

"Fine," said Clapham.

Fitz almost fainted with relief, until Clapham added, "The interest is still ten percent per day. In cash."

"Yes, Mr. Clapham. I'll get the money for you."

"Don't let me down again, O'Donnell. You won't like what happens if you let me down."

"No, I won't, sir," said Fitz. But the connection went dead.

The gravel in the parking lot was cutting into Fitz's

skinned knees. He had a sudden, urgent need for a bathroom.

IN DOWNTOWN CHICAGO, in a non-descript office in a non-descript building, two FBI agents stared at each other.

"Did we just catch a break?" asked Special Agent Julia Weyburn, peeling off her headphones.

"Play it again," said Special Agent Jason Watson.

Weyburn reversed the recording and hit PLAY.

"O'Donnell? What the hell...?"

"Mr-Clapham-I'm-really-sorry-I-couldn't-take-your-call-earlier-and-I'm-really-sorry-I-didn't-call-you-sooner-about-the-loss-of-your-diamonds-and-money-in-the-robbery-but-it's-been-total-chaos-and-with-the-police..."

"You moron! Use the app!"

The recording stopped.

Watson looked at his partner as a slow smile began to spread across his face.

"I just love stupid criminals, don't you?" he said.

They both started to laugh.

CHAPTER 7
THE SWITCH

Kat got the bathroom key from the barista while Tish walked casually toward the ladies' room. They slipped in together and locked the door, then sorted through the diamonds in Tish's purse, the ones from the boxes they believed had belonged to Alfred Clapham. They chose stones that were the same size as the high-quality stones from Superior's stock that Tish had first offered Jessup. They bagged them up, just as the other stones had been packaged, in a small, ziplock plastic bag. Then one at time, they slipped back out of the ladies' room, and Kat returned the key to the counter.

Dropping their empty cups into the trash as they left, they walked back to the jewelry store, slowing their steps as they approached, as if reluctant.

As they went in the door, Tish said, "Kitty, I still think we should try somewhere else."

'Honey, we've tried somewhere else. And something is better than nothing."

"I'm just not sure about this…"

Kat patted Tish reassuringly on the arm as they

approached the counter and asked the sales assistant for Mr. Jessup. As if she couldn't see him through the open office door. As if she hadn't seen the momentary predatory look on his face.

As he came out to the counter, Kat and Tish were having an intense, whispered conversation.

"Kitty, these were my mama's diamonds before they were mine. I feel like I'm letting her down by selling them so cheap."

"Terry, you have got to have money to leave Harry. This is the best offer we've had. I think you have to take it."

"Ladies," said Jessup swimming up to them like a shark moving toward a school of guppies. "Did you have a change of heart?"

"My cousin is still convinced the diamonds are worth more than you're offering, Mr. Jessup," Kat said. "I can't say I disagree with her. But we've talked it over, and I've convinced her to take your offer. I'll help her figure out some way to cover the rest." Kat held out the small ziplock, acting reluctant to turn it over.

Next to her, Tish made a small protesting whimper which Kat pretended not to hear.

The stage lost a great actress when that high school teacher thought Tish was too heavy to play leads, Kat thought.

The glint of victory snapped in Jessup's eyes as he took the ziplock baggie. "I'll get you that cash," he said.

Kat simply nodded.

No matter what she'd told Tish, if he checked the stones again...

She needn't have worried. She'd read him right. Jessup was back in a few minutes with the promised money. He didn't ask for ID or for an address or anything else. Kat was reasonably sure he wouldn't even remember the names they'd given him.

"Thank you, sir. Here, honey," she said, handing the cash to Tish. "Put this in your purse. Now let's get on the road to Memphis."

Tish nodded, clicked her purse shut, and the two left the store. They walked calmly until they reached the end of the strip mall, where they turned the corner and quickened their pace. Down a block and across the street, they hurried to the Buick, stripping off jacket and sweater, and tossing them into the backseat. As she turned the ignition key with one hand, Kat dragged off the brown wig with the other and tossed it on the bench seat between them, before driving away quickly.

She thought she'd handled everything very calmly. They'd gone a mile or so before Tish pointed out that they weren't heading west but were heading east back toward Illinois.

CHAPTER 8

DETECTIVE LYONS GETS THE CASE

Evanston police detective Adam Chung glanced up when his senior partner, Sam Lyons, stopped by his desk.

A tall, dark-skinned woman in her early forties, her slightly graying Afro cut longer on top, Lyons was dressed for court in a charcoal-gray linen suit and a cream blouse, open at the throat. She was wearing small gold hoop earrings, something she only did on court appearances. The lines carved in her dark face from twenty-plus years of police work seemed deeper than usual this morning. Her mouth was tightened in a grim line.

"Oh oh," said Chung. "That's *not* a happy face."

"They jumped bail," said Lyons, holding up her phone. "I just got the call."

Chung didn't have to ask who she meant. Lyons was scheduled to testify later that morning in the electronics store flash mob robbery case from the previous January. Two of the perpetrators involved in the robbery had been out on bail pending their testimony against the store manager, who, Lyons and Chung were sure, had master-minded the robbery.

"Crap."

"You could say that."

"We don't have a case without them, do we?"

"No," said Lyons, slumping into a chair. "I need caffeine before this day gets worse."

"Where do we go from here?"

"I'm not sure. I'll have to call the DA's office." Lyons rubbed her face and muttered what sounded like a string of profanity.

"Well, maybe I can give you some better news," said Chung. "At least, better for us."

Lyons looked up. "I'm listening."

"I got a call, just a few minutes ago, from a Mrs. Fielding. She said she knows you?"

"Elspeth Fielding?" Lyons sat up. Her voice rose in surprise.

Chung nodded.

"Really?"

Chung nodded again.

"My, my." Lyons shook her head and sat back again.

"Who is she?" asked Chung.

"She was the vice president for student affairs at Northwestern University almost forever," said Lyons. "Her husband, Mercer, was the university's General Counsel until he died a few years ago. My, my," said Lyons again.

"So, she's someone I should know?"

"Oh, yes. Mrs. Fielding is very much someone you should know. She's connected to pretty much any Northwestern student of any consequence who's graduated in the last thirty years, or more. And I mean *any* grad. She's on a first name basis with celebrities, politicians, athletes..."

"How do you know her?" asked Chung. "Did you go to Northwestern?"

Lyons gave him a crooked smile. "No. There were some hate crimes on campus about fifteen years ago. I was one of the few black detectives in the department—and the only female at the time—so the chief decided I'd be the best choice to deal with it."

"You find out who was responsible?"

Lyons nodded. "Yeah. Some disgruntled students with lousy GPAs who decided they were being discriminated against because the scholarships they thought their white skins and mediocre grades deserved were given to students of color who happened to be top of their class."

"What happened to them?"

"Mrs. Fielding happened to them," said Lyons.

"She had them expelled?"

"You'd think that, wouldn't you?"

Chung nodded.

"Not Mrs. Fielding. Oh, we charged them. But she spoke up for them. Got the judge to give them a *lot* of community service hours, but she also insisted that, as part of the deal, they had to attend tutorials—which she personally oversaw—and get their grades up to at least 3.5. If they didn't, the judge could revisit the sentencing and give them jail time or fines or both."

Chung looked skeptical. "Did it work?"

"It did. With Mrs. Fielding watching, and the threat of jail time hanging over them..." Lyons smiled, shaking her head in admiration. "After a year, the community service had improved their attitudes, and their grades were up. Mrs. Fielding helped them get scholarships. Later, she wrote recommendations for them."

"Wow," said Chung. "She must be something."

"She is."

"So, if her diamond wedding ring was at Superior Jewelers for repair, and was stolen in the burglary, then we should pay attention?"

There was a long silence.

"You're telling me O'Donnell had jewelry in that vault that belonged to other people?"

"That's the way it looks."

"He didn't mention that."

"He did not."

"So, if he engineered this thing..."

"Oh, he's behind this all right. Missing jewelry. Missing diamonds. Missing cash..."

"Cash?" asked Lyons, brow furrowed.

"Hmm." Chung scrolled through his notes. "Remember when we questioned him at the house?"

"Yeeess..."

"The daughter. Remember she was desperate for the money she thought her father had in that safe? The one that supposedly had nothing in it?"

"Oh, yes! Twenty thou, wasn't it?" said Lyons. "I'd forgotten that."

"All of that missing and a young girlfriend, too. No, he's definitely behind this."

"Aren't you too young still to be so jaded?"

"Picked it up from my partner," said Chung.

"Now there's jewelry missing that belonged to people other than the O'Donnells, so it isn't only a domestic dispute. It's theft," mused Lyons.

Chung grinned.

"That grin tells me you've already checked and found out Mrs. Fielding isn't the only one to complain about missing jewelry."

"No, ma'am, she is not." He nodded toward his monitor. "I'm putting together a list right now. And not only that…"

"There's more?"

"Yep. I'm not the only one convinced O'Donnell was behind the burglary," said Chung. "I checked with the insurers. They were cagey about it, but they indicated that they'd declined his claim and canceled his insurance."

"So…?"

"That means the 'loss' of the customers' jewelry isn't covered by his insurance."

"In other words, he settles with them out of his pocket or faces lawsuits. Or, should the customers hear he may be behind this, he faces criminal complaints against him."

"That's about it."

"Well, well, well," said Lyons. She looked at Chung, her face serious. "Any word on the wife? Or the store manager?"

"No sign of the store manager. Her phone is off. Her car hasn't been sighted. We're tracking the wife's phone. She's down in southern Missouri right now, but…" Chung made a face.

"What?"

"I don't think she's involved, Sam."

"Why?" asked Lyons.

Chung huffed. "She's not acting right."

"How do you mean?"

Chung lifted his hands from his desk, then dropped them again. "Well, for one, she's driving an old Buick, according to O'Donnell. I mean, those gas guzzlers had big trunks, but not big enough for all the jewelry taken from that store. I talked to one of the long-time employees. We're talking a *lot* of jewelry.

"Second, other than St. Louis, she hasn't stopped in any large cities where she might be able to get rid of a bunch of jewelry, assuming she *could* fit it all into the car. She's been staying in smaller cities and, frankly, little towns. I mean, Pontiac? I hadn't even heard of it until I got the records."

"Pontiac, Michigan?"

"No, Pontiac, Illinois," said Chung.

"Then, she's still using her phone," he continued. "I mean, anyone in this day and age knows you have to get rid of a phone because you can be tracked. She's even been contacting her younger son. I talked to him. He's out in Oregon. He claims she hasn't told him where she is. Doesn't want the husband to know. Just told him she's spending time with a friend.

"And that's what she's acting like, Sam. Like she's on vacation. She's just ambling along."

"Where's she getting the money?"

"Don't know. Maybe they kept money in the house. She did have that safe in her bedroom closet. That had been emptied. Or maybe it's a male friend she's traveling with. Maybe the husband isn't the only one with someone on the side."

"Could be a female friend."

Chung nodded. "Agreed. Could be."

Lyons drummed her fingers, with their closely trimmed nails, on the edge of Chung's desk.

"When you talked to her, she *did* say she suspected her husband of emptying the vault for the insurance money," said Lyons, thoughtfully. "She'd certainly be in a position to know."

"She could be saying that to throw us off."

"Also possible," said Lyons. She frowned in concentration. "No. I agree with you. At least for now, she isn't our first suspect. That doesn't mean we set her aside altogether, though." Lyons rolled her shoulders. "Let's start with this new angle first, the theft of customers' jewelry."

"Mrs. Fielding said she has a photo and an appraisal," said Chung. "She's going to send them over."

"Oh, no. I think we should go get them personally," said Lyons, smiling as she stood. "I'd like to see her again, and you should meet her. Besides, she might have some insights into Fitzpatrick O'Donnell or the wife—what's her name?"

Chung turned to the computer, pulled up his report. "Mary Patrice," he said. "Her husband says she goes by Tish."

Lyons nodded. "Like I said, Mrs. Fielding knows everyone. If Mrs. O'Donnell has done any charity work in the community or been involved at the university in any way, Mrs. Fielding will probably know her. If she does, maybe she can give us a better idea of whether either of the O'Donnells would engineer a jewelry store heist." She started toward the door. "Besides. I'd be interested in knowing which option she's favoring: lawsuit or criminal complaint."

"What about your coffee?" asked Chung, as he logged off his computer and snatched up his jacket and phone.

Sam Lyons turned around and threw her arms out wide as she walked backwards. "Caffeine? Who needs caffeine, Adam? We have a case!"

CHAPTER 9

BACK ON THE ROAD

Tish stuck both arms straight up into the Buick's slipstream as they rolled down Route 66. "Wheee!"

Kat laughed. "I thought you didn't like the top down."

Tish, strands of auburn hair whipping wildly around her face, pulled her hands down and grinned.

"I'm probably going to regret it," she said, touching her nose, generously coated in 50 SPF sunblock. "But it's so deliciously cool this morning after that storm last night. I feel like I just want to eat the air!"

She punched the slipstream again. "Wheee!" she squealed, then laughed.

A man in a white "mom van" shook his head and smiled as they passed him. But there was a look of envious longing on his face as his eyes slid over the classic 1957 Buick.

"Eat your heart out, people!" Tish shouted into the wind.

"I think you're beginning to like Beauty," laughed Kat.

"Let's just say I'm appreciating her better qualities today."

"You're just glad to be out of St. Louis."

Tish dropped her arms. "I really am." She gave a theatrical shudder. "I was beginning to think we were being stalked by a jinx there. Didn't you?"

"I'd have to say I felt unwelcomed if not exactly jinxed," said Kat, then grinned again. "Except for the day we spent at Forest Park. I will never forget you hunched over the handlebar of that Segway, going full tilt."

Tish laughed. "That *was* fun," she said, then looked directly at Kat. "I think we need more of that, don't you? Vacation time?"

"We have work to do, Tish. I'm sorry."

"I haven't forgotten. But remember when we started this? Back in Chicago? You said it could be fun, too. Like a vacation. Because Fitz never took me on vacations."

"I did?"

"You know you did. You told me about all the kitsch on Route 66. You threatened to stop at as many of those big plastic people as you could find."

A wistful look came to Kat's face.

"Fiberglass. And you're right. I did."

"Once in a lifetime, I think was the phrase you used," said Tish, pushing through the crack opening in Kat's defenses.

Kat threw her a glance, that Tish couldn't quite interpret.

"Once in a lifetime," murmured Kat, her eyes back on the road.

"Don't you think your dad would want you to enjoy the trip that you planned together for so long?" said Tish.

Kat didn't respond, and Tish decided not to push it further.

But as the suburbs of St. Louis rolled by, she watched Kat, one gloved hand on the wheel while the other squeezed a pink tennis ball. Though Tish felt they'd left the threatening atmosphere in St. Louis behind them, Kat was still tense. Still spooked.

Tish didn't understand why, but she'd decided not to pursue it. Somewhere in the last ten days—had it only been ten? twelve?—anyway, between the night they'd surprised each other at her husband's jewelry store, and the long, long run across the Chain of Rocks bridge pursued by a bunch of terrifying thugs, things between the them had changed. They'd become, well, maybe not friends, not yet, but at least not enemies. Today, Tish, who a week ago would have pushed at Kat's nervousness, was less willing to poke at her new partner's apparent fears.

She was embarrassed to remember she'd once thought Kat had been having an affair with Fitz, just because, at 45, Kat had the body of an exuberant 30-year-old and hair the color of a teenager, while Tish, at 55, had the body of a woman whose round figure had only added weight with the birth of each of her three children.

Kat also had brains and a kind of cunning that had kept the two women safe for their first days on the run. She'd kept them ahead of the police who, at first, had suspected that Tish might be involved in the store robbery. (Well, she was involved in the *safe* robbery, just not the *vault* robbery. It was complicated.) Kat had kept them ahead of Fitz— well, a ham sandwich could stay ahead of Fitz, and what did that say about Tish, and what she'd put up with for thirty-five years? And she'd even kept them ahead of the Armentrouts, who kept popping up like gophers in a new lawn.

Yes, Tish would never have made it this far without Kat.

She *did* have a number of questions about the source of Kat's cunning, however, her ability to forge—no, no, *fake*, Kat insisted on the difference between the two skills—pieces of identification, and how she knew so much about how to sell hot diamonds, but Tish was now a partner in the hot diamond business. There were certain questions you didn't ask about your partner.

Honor among thieves, as Kat had said that night.

If Tish ever had the courage to go to confession again, she had no idea where she would even start.

Kat suddenly changed lanes and cut in front of oncoming traffic to turn left.

"Whoa!" Tish braced herself against the passenger side door, as her seat belt snapped tight. She stared at Kat. "What was that about?"

Kat's eyes were fixed on the rearview mirror.

"Kat?"

"What? Oh, nothing. Sorry. Thought I'd missed a turn."

Tish frowned and studied the right-hand sideview mirror. It was empty. Not a car in sight. They were already half a mile down the side road.

"Well, if you keep going this way, you'll end up at Six Flags," said Tish.

Kat waved her hand dismissively.

"Anybody can make a wrong turn."

Tish shook her head. "I can't believe that anyone who loves cars as much as you do can have such an astonishingly bad sense of direction," she said.

Kat made a non-committal noise but didn't turn back.

Tish's smile faded, as Kat checked the rearview mirror again.

"It was an SUV again, wasn't it?" said Tish, when Kat continued south, away from Route 66.

No answer.

Maybe Kat hadn't heard her, over the roar of the wind pouring over the top of the windshield, but it was more likely that she was simply *pretending* not to hear.

Tish gave her another half mile.

"Why do you freak out whenever you see a black car?" she asked, making sure she was loud enough Kat could not ignore her. "It's like a black cat crossing your path."

Kat lifted fingers off the steering wheel, like she was shooing away an insect, as if to say, I really don't want to talk about this.

"Kat. What are you not saying?" Tish persisted.

"Nothing!" said Kat. "I'm not not saying anything. I don't know what you're going on about."

"Yes, you do. In St. Louis, you started making all kinds of turns after you saw that big black car downtown. You said it reminded you of those gangsters on the bridge. But we didn't run into them until Chain of Rocks, yet you started hyperventilating back in Springfield when you saw that convoy of black SUVs."

Kat slowed and pulled into a driveway to turn around, apparently deciding that they *weren't* being followed.

"I did not 'freak out,'" said Kat, her voice adding the air quotes. "I just said they looked suspicious."

"Suspiciously like what?" Tish prodded.

Kat lifted a shoulder. Started to speak. Stopped.

"Like what, Kat?"

Kat sent an annoyed look her way.

"It's just that... Don't you think anyone who drives a car with the windows blacked out is some kind of trouble? Either it's some kind of government department or some kind of criminal—like drug lords or even corporate crimi-nals. And why are the cars always black?"

Tish wasn't sure what to make of that statement.

"Seems a little overboard," she said after a few moments. "You're equating drug lords with the convoy in Springfield that probably belonged to the governor of Illinois?"

Kat took a hand off the wheel and waved it as if to say, you know what I mean.

But Tish didn't know what she meant.

"You keep saying we don't have to worry about anything. You're sure Clapham can't be looking for us."

"I *am* sure."

"Then what else can you be suspicious of?"

"Nothing!" Kat waited for a car to pass, then backed out of the driveway.

"There's something you're not telling me," said Tish. "It's beginning to make me nervous."

"You're making something out of nothing," said Kat. "Anyway. I thought we were going to get breakfast on the road. I'm starving."

Kat was never hungry.

She was acting like she didn't have a care in the world, and Kat was a good actress. But Tish was learning to read her better. She wasn't finished asking questions, but she would let it pass.

For now.

"Good idea," said Tish. "It'll give me a chance to change your costume, too."

Kat briefly dropped her head back as if she were beseeching a higher power.

"Oh, Tish," she said on a long, drawn-out moan, as she brought her eyes back to the road. "Do we have to? It took almost an hour this morning for you to figure out what you wanted me to wear."

"Well, it's hard to dress you to be ready for everything from a high-end jewelry store to a down-and-dirty pawn shop. And you're beautiful. After our experience in St. Louis, I want to make the most of that to distract whoever we're working with from asking too many questions."

"I'm not beautiful. I just have big tits."

Tish stared at Kat open-mouthed.

Kat glanced over at her. "What? You think I didn't know why men always come on to me? Why women want nothing to do with me?"

"I'm...I'm sure most women wish they had your figure..." Tish felt herself coloring.

"No, they don't. They may say that, but what they're really saying is 'I don't like the way my husband, or my boyfriend, looks at you.'"

Guilt stabbed at Tish. She'd been one of those women for years.

"But..."

"But nothing. No one looks beyond the tits." Kat waved a hand toward the front of her tank top. "I've come to terms with it."

No, you haven't, thought Tish, hearing the false brightness in Kat's tone of voice.

"I've even learned to use it," Kat went on. "I'm using it now. You're helping by the clothes you choose for me to wear." Kat reached between her breasts and snapped the low neckline of the tight black Spandex camisole she was wearing. The sheer, lace-edged bra peeped over the neckline. "You chose this for a reason. The right reasons."

Tish's face went from warm to burning.

Kat glanced at her again. "Don't be ashamed of it. I do it

myself whenever I need to. Right now, we need to. Because you're right. We want men looking elsewhere.

"But Tish. It's not because I'm 'beautiful.' It's the tits, baby. The tits are all I got," she said bitterly. She snapped the tank top again. "Without them, I'd be just another face-less, plain Jane. A nobody."

Tish remembered Kat, standing in front of a mirror, appearing to admire her "tits" and her figure. Had it been remorse rather than admiration?

"But your friends, surely…"

"I don't have friends, Tish."

Kat kept her eyes on the road as a strip of light indus-trial buildings rolled by.

"I've never had friends. Girls hated me in school. Boys just wanted to cop a feel. Nothing's changed now that I'm older."

"You said you made fake IDs for friends at school," protested Tish.

"That was a business," said Kat. "They weren't friends. They didn't seek me out until they wanted an ID. It was just something I could do for them." She grinned and flashed her eyebrows. "If I'm honest, charging them fifty bucks per ID was a way for me to get even for them using me."

She hesitated.

"In fact, Tish, you're probably the closest thing to a friend I've ever had," Kat added, almost shyly.

Tish didn't know what to say that wouldn't sound phony or patronizing.

"Breakfast?" Kat asked her again.

Tish fumbled in her purse and pulled out her phone.

"You do know we have to turn left up here, don't you?" she asked, as they neared the intersection with Route 66 where Kat had gone astray.

"Yes. I know."

"Oooh. Testy."

Kat looked over long enough to glare.

Tish gave her a lopsided grin.

Kat rolled her eyes, shook her head, and slowed for the turn.

CHAPTER 10

WHAT MRS. FIELDING HAD TO SAY

The door was opened by a tall, slender woman on the far side of 70 wearing jeans and a long-sleeved white shirt, sleeves shoved up above her elbows. Her straight gray hair, going white, was cut to chin length in front, and angled to a shorter length in back. Bangs fell to touch the brilliant blue glasses framing equally brilliant blue eyes. She wore a watch on her left wrist.

The upright bearing, the direct stare. Elspeth Fielding would have terrified Lyons if she'd been a student at Northwestern.

Then she smiled, and the sun shone more brightly.

"Detective Lyons. You didn't have to make the trip over here," she said, "but it's delightful to see you again."

"Mrs. Fielding. My partner, Adam Chung."

Lyons noticed Chung straighten up. She knew he was rethinking the royal blue T-shirt he was wearing with his khakis, even though he had a lightweight navy blazer over it.

Elspeth Fielding had that effect on people.

"Ma'am," said Chung.

60

"Detective Chung." Mrs. Fielding offered her hand. "A pleasure. We spoke on the phone?"

"Yes, ma'am."

"Please come through," she said, ushering them in. "Let's sit in the garden."

She led them to a shady, bricked patio where a pleasant fountain splashed amid well-tended beds. On a table, sheltered by a pristine white umbrella, a pitcher of iced tea sweated gently, and three glasses waited with ice.

An envelope rested next to the glasses.

"I won't waste your time with small talk," said Mrs. Fielding as they sat down. She pushed the envelope toward them, diplomatically not directing it to either detective. She smiled. "I had my fill of that during university gatherings."

As she withdrew her hand, Lyons noted the wide white line on her empty left ring finger.

Mrs. Fielding lifted the pitcher and poured, while Lyons removed an appraisal and photograph from the envelope.

"You had the appraisal done last year?"

"Yes," said Mrs. Fielding. "Mercer and I updated our appraisals every five years. I have a few other pieces of jewelry worth appraising, and there's also some antique silver we collected."

"This is your wedding ring?"

"Yes. Well," she paused and smiled. "It's a copy of my actual wedding ring, which was a carnival midway prize made of pot metal and rhinestones."

"You're serious?" asked Lyons.

"I am."

"There's a story there, I think," said Lyons.

Mrs. Fielding laughed. "Thank you for asking, Detective. It's a story I never tire of telling."

She picked up her tea. "Please," she said, waving a hand at the glasses in front of the detectives.

As they obeyed, she said, "Mercer and I were as broke as two sticks when we met as students. Here at Northwestern, as it happens. Mercer couldn't afford a ring, when we got engaged. I told him it wasn't important, but he was a romantic." Her eyes softened as she remembered.

"Then at the county fair, he spotted one of those machines, you know the kind? Where you manipulate a claw to pick something out of a pile of prizes? There were all these little vials with, oh, all kinds of things in them. Like those tiny troll dolls with the wild hair or a set of jacks. One of them had a ring in it. Mercer was determined to get it. And he did." Her smile was, at once, sad and happy and very much that of a woman still in love. "He proposed with it, then and there."

She shook her head.

"It took him 25 years," she went on, "and the plating was almost worn off of that original, but he finally replaced it with a replica in gold and diamonds for our anniversary. It's the most precious thing I own."

"I can understand that," said Lyons.

"I hadn't taken it off for more than 20 years, Detective. Not until a prong broke. Fortunately, I heard the diamond hit the counter in our kitchen when it fell out. You can imagine how devastating it was, with Mercer's death so recent."

"I can."

"I want my ring back, Detective Lyons." The icy eyes and diamond-hard voice that had terrified Northwestern students into good behavior and better grades were back. Lyons only just prevented herself from squirming. Chung, she saw from the corner of her eye, wasn't as successful.

"At the very least, I want it replaced," Mrs. Fielding continued. "But Fitz O'Donnell won't return my calls. Now I'm beginning to hear rumors that the safe wasn't insured or, worse, that it might have been Fitz himself who engineered the theft. I want you to know, I'm fully prepared to press charges if you think that's what's happened."

Lyons wasn't surprised to hear that Mrs. Fielding knew almost as much about the burglary as she did. As she'd told Chung, Mrs. Fielding knew *everyone*.

"To tell you the truth, Mrs. Fielding," Lyons was holding the older woman's gaze only with great effort, "until your call, we thought it was a domestic dispute—husband or wife cleaning out the store before filing for divorce. We didn't realize that there was jewelry in that vault that belonged to anyone other than the O'Donnells. With this," Lyons lifted the appraisal, "we can open an investigation."

"You think one of the O'Donnells did this?"

"We don't know for sure. You've been doing business with them for years. Do you think they're capable of it? What can you tell me about them?"

Chung quietly pulled his tablet and stylus out of his bag, as Mrs. Fielding sat back, sipped her tea, and thought.

"Andy Ryan, Fitz O'Donnell's father-in-law, owned Superior previously. Mercer knew him from here at Northwestern. I never cared for Ryan. He was a condescending, narrow-minded misogynist, which is why, I suppose, he left the store to his son-in-law, rather than his daughter. But Ryan knew his business, and he employed skilled craftsmen. The work was always excellent. So, we never hesitated to take our work there."

A cardinal called loudly in the trees directly overhead. There was a flash of red, and it disappeared.

"I don't think Fitz has the knowledge, or, frankly, the

interest in the business that Ryan had," said Mrs. Fielding. "The only times I've seen him, he seemed to be flirting with customers or admiring himself in mirrors."

Ouch, thought Lyons, though she'd noticed O'Donnell's fixation on mirrors, too.

"What about his wife, Mary Patrice?"

"Tish is a nice woman in a marriage that I don't think was of her making. She's way too smart for Fitz, and I think she knows it."

"Oh? Was she a student at Northwestern?"

"No. Her father didn't believe in educating women who were supposed to be having babies, not running businesses, though he didn't mind her working in the store for low wages. That's not catty gossip, Detective. Tish told me that herself once. We were at a fundraiser for the community theater, and I asked her where she'd gone to university. She'd had a couple glasses of wine, otherwise I don't think she would have said anything."

Mrs. Fielding paused, frowned. "I'm trying to remember why I think the marriage wasn't her choice. There was a scandal... Well, I doubt it would be a scandal now, and probably shouldn't even have been one then." She paused again, then, her gaze turning inward, she added, mostly to herself, "It had to do with a Northwestern student...a clandestine engagement...an elopement?"

She shook her head. "I can't remember. I don't usually pay attention to teenagers' scandals. There are so many of them." She frowned again. "But whatever it was, whenever I run into Tish, especially if she's with Fitz, there's always a...a lingering feeling of sadness surrounding her. Maybe that's why I always have the sense that Fitz wasn't her choice."

"If that's the case, do you think she might have engineered the store burglary in order to get back at her husband?" asked Lyons.

Mrs. Fielding shook her head emphatically. "No. Tish loves the jewelry business. That's the one thing that lights her up—talking about the store. Well, not the store, actually. But talking about styles of art especially as they apply to jewelry design and manufacturing. She loves designing jewelry. In fact, at fundraising dinners, the times I've been at the same table, I've noticed she rarely listens to the speakers. She's always drawing jewelry in a notebook she keeps in her purse."

Lyons tapped the appraisal on the table. "I notice this is signed by Kat Merevec."

"Yes. Kat does all their appraisals.

"Now there's a smart woman, Detective," Mrs. Fielding went on. "Fitz brought her in six, seven years ago, I think. Before that, with Ryan and Fitz trying to run the store together, the staff turnover was outrageous. The same salespeople were never there twice in a row. The jewelers were in and out of there almost weekly. But once Ryan retired, and Fitz brought Kat in to manage, the staff started to stay."

Mrs. Fielding shot Lyons a glance.

"You don't think Kat Merevec is involved with this?"

Lyons hesitated. "In confidence, Mrs. Fielding, we don't know. She's missing. Right now, I just hope she's safe."

"Oh my God," Mrs. Fielding whispered. "I like Kat. I'd find it hard to believe she's involved, and I really hope she's not been hurt."

"Since you know the O'Donnells, Mrs. Fielding, do you know their children as well?"

"Only the older boy, Matthew. Their daughter—Maggie?—I don't believe went on to college." She frowned.

"Or did she drop out? Tish mentioned once, but... No. It's gone. I can prod my memory if it's important, Detective Lyons."

Lyons shook her head. "Not really. What about the younger son?"

Mrs. Fielding smiled. "Luke. The only topic Tish is more enthusiastic about than jewelry design. He went to the School of the Art Institute of Chicago. He's quite a good painter. I've been to his openings. Tish is always there, though I've never seen Fitz. I understand Luke's quite a talented teacher as well."

Lyons nodded. "Thank you, Mrs. Fielding. We'll talk to Mr. O'Donnell, and we'll do our best to get your ring back for you."

"I appreciate that."

Lyons stood. "May I take your appraisal with me? I'll make a copy and bring it back to you."

"No need, Detective," said Mrs. Fielding as she, too, rose. "Those are copies for you to keep."

As they reached the front door, Lyons hesitated.

"Mrs. Fielding, you talked about the two younger O'Donnell children, Maggie and Luke. But you didn't say anything about Carlisle."

"Carlisle?" asked Mrs. Fielding. "Oh. Matthew. Yes, I heard he'd changed his name. Matthew O'Donnell." She shook her head.

"He was a student at Northwestern?"

"He was," said Mrs. Fielding. "He even graduated. But he was never as smart as he thought he was, though he was too smart for his own good."

"What do you mean?"

She looked at Lyons for a long moment, then nodded almost imperceptibly.

"I'm talking out of school, here Detective, because we were never able to prove anything. And I know you're discreet."

Now Lyons nodded.

"A couple of our professors believed Matthew—or Carlisle—had bought the answers to exam questions as well as paid other students to write his papers. His work in class, and grades on quizzes, were at odds with his final scores. Mercer and I were also pretty sure he was selling alcohol and marijuana on campus, bankrolled, we strongly suspected, by his grandfather, Andy Ryan. When Mercer confronted Ryan about it, he brushed it off as if it were a joke."

Lyons tipped her head slightly, as if listening to a voice in the distance.

"Lots of students get up to things on the illegal edge in college," she said thoughtfully. "But they straighten out as they get older."

"Many do," agreed Elspeth Fielding. "Others don't."

Lyons heard what she wasn't saying.

"So, someone like Carlisle O'Donnell, if his grandfather encouraged him to take those kinds of risks when he was younger, do you think he might be willing to try something a little more...illegal, now? Thinking there might be no consequences?"

"Or that someone else might suffer the consequences in his place? Yes." Mrs. Fielding regarded Lyons shrewdly. "Though I hesitate—only briefly—to say it, Detective, it wouldn't surprise me in the least, if the rumors of Fitz O'Donnell robbing his own store turn out to be true, that you find Matthew O'Donnell is involved."

CHAPTER 11

GOING ON VACATION

Tish was busy with her phone, glancing up at the countryside passing by, catching street names, and going back to her phone.

"What are you looking for?" asked Kat.

"Hmmm?"

"What are you looking for?"

"Are we in Sullivan?"

"Yes. We just passed the water tower. The name was on it."

"Okay, then..."

Tish started looking at street names again.

"Tish, what are you looking for?" asked Kat again, and Tish laughed.

"Do you know they decorate the fire hydrants in Sullivan?" she said.

"They what?"

"Slow down a bit," said Tish, scanning both sides of Route 66.

Slowing wasn't a problem. There was rarely anyone behind them. Even when there was, Kat could simply pull over to let them pass. It was one of the great joys of driving Route 66.

"Look, look!" exclaimed Tish, pointing. "Turn there!"

Kat braked, swung into the side street, then started to laugh.

"Can you park in there?" asked Tish.

"Absolutely!" said Kat, smiling. She turned into a parking lot in front of a group of service businesses, pulled to the end, and parked.

In a strip of grass between Route 66 and the parking lot sat a fire hydrant. It had been painted to commemorate two of the most iconic Route 66 sites in Illinois, both of which Kat and Tish had visited: the Gemini Giant and the Polka Dot Drive-In.

Tish jumped out of the car and circled the fire hydrant taking pictures with her phone.

Kat stood nearby, watching.

"I told you all the kitschy sites are why people come from all over the world to drive Route 66," said Kat.

"I'm beginning to believe you," said Tish.

Kat pointed across the street. "Do you see the one over there?"

"No! Where? Oh! I have to get that one, too." Tish ran across the quiet two-lane road, took some photos, patted the hydrant on its rounded head, and darted back.

Kat was grinning at her. "You are too funny," she said.

"Why?" asked Tish. "You were the one who said this trip should be fun. And these are cute."

"They *are* cute," Kat agreed.

"Let's look for some more." Tish headed back to the car.

For the next hour, Tish looked up hydrant locations on her phone, pointed, Kat parked, and Tish took pictures. Tish was thoroughly enjoying herself and had completely forgotten what was in their trunk. Kat seemed to have forgotten whatever had spooked her a short while before.

But Tish was very aware of the new tender spot in her heart where Kat's words had stuck.

You're the closest thing to a friend I've ever had.

"Turn here," Tish told Kat at one point, pointing left.

"Another fire hydrant?"

"Just turn."

"Okay. Okay."

"It should be around here, I think... Keep going... Yes, there."

Tish was pointing to a small café/bakery in an area that looked like it might once have been the heart of this small town. It was close to railroad tracks bracketed by brick buildings that had once served heavy rail traffic. Many of the buildings had been removed, leaving bare lots. Yet the remaining businesses looked like they were thriving.

Kat pulled to the curb. "Looks like we're done with fire hydrants?"

"You said you were hungry. So am I."

"Cute place, but to say it's off the beaten track would be an understatement."

"Look at the bright side," said Tish. "The Armentrouts will never find us here."

"Hallelujah," said Kat. "So how do you do that?"

"Do what?"

"Find these out-of-the-way places."

"Superpower," said Tish with a straight face.

"No, seriously."

Tish held up her phone. "Tripadvisor."

Kat gave her a look. "Must be good," she said, pointing at a line of motorcycles in the parking lot next to the café.

She pulled forward, turned into the lot, and parked behind the array of bikes.

"I'm going to put up the top," said Kat, getting out of the Buick. "If I don't, by time we finish eating, the seat will be like a griddle."

"Oh, look!" said Tish, as they locked the car.

"What?"

"Over there. Butterfly wings on the wall across the road. I want to take your picture."

"Oh, no," said Kat.

"Oh, yes," said Tish, pulling her by the arm.

"Only if you do it."

"Deal. But you first." Tish towed Kat across the street.

She took several pictures of Kat, then handed her the phone. As they walked back across the road to the café, Tish scrolled through the images.

"You look good with wings," she told Kat, holding out the phone. "They go with your purple hair."

"Burgundy," said Kat.

Tish smiled.

As it was late morning, the small café was only partly full. It was quiet except for the table full of booted motorcyclists on the patio, leather and denim jackets hanging on the backs of chairs.

"You fit in," said Tish, nodding toward the group.

"What do you mean?"

Tish plucked at the sleeve of the black denim jacket Kat had put on to cover the tightly fitting camisole.

"Ah," said Kat, then shook her head. "Nope," she said, but the corners of her eyes were crinkling. "Motorcycles are not me. Not enough wheels."

Tish snorted. She was enjoying this new, more relaxed side of Kat.

They examined the menu posted behind the counter as they waited their turn. A lone woman got into line behind them.

Laughter and some lightly accented comments rose from the table on the patio. Tish cocked an ear to the conversation.

"Are you eavesdropping?" asked Kat.

"Irish," said Tish, happily.

"Are you sure?"

"Absolutely. My grandmother was Irish."

"Ah! That's why Mary Patrice Geraghty," said Kat, referring to one of the not-quite-aliases Tish was using.

"Of course."

"She was Irish from Ireland, then. Not American Irish?"

Tish nodded. "I heard her accent every day for most of my life."

"She lived with you?"

Tish made a face. "No. She and my mom didn't have a great relationship. But Mom didn't mind Gran taking care of me after school."

"Your mom worked at the store?"

Tish nodded again. "Gran was a free babysitter." She sighed. "I didn't want to go home in the evenings. I got along better with Gran than with Mom."

"Ladies, what can I get for you?" asked the young woman behind the counter.

They ordered, then found a place out on the covered patio where they could keep an eye on the car.

"This is a sweet place," said Kat. She put their claim number on the table as Tish sat down. "I'll be back in a minute," she said. "Restroom." She headed toward the front of the café, passing the woman who'd been behind them in the counter line.

Tish looked around the café, easily identifying the few regulars who, elbows hooked over the backs of their chairs, were trading gossip about the local high school baseball team.

The Irish motorcyclists had pushed a couple of tables together and were teasing each other good-naturedly. From what Tish could hear of their conversation, they appeared to be a family. The woman who had waited behind Tish and Kat in the counter line was heading to their table.

Tish stopped eavesdropping and bent over her phone. She wanted to text Luke before Kat got back. She didn't know Tish was in contact with her younger son, and Tish wanted to keep it that way.

Look at these, she wrote, after she'd uploaded pictures of the fire hydrants. *Town in MO called Sullivan. Community project for Portland? Love you.*

She followed the text with a string of heart emojis.

She was smiling to herself when a woman's voice said, "Mary Patrice Geraghty?"

CHAPTER 12

FITZ FEELS THE PRESSURE

"They're accusing *me* of theft?" said Fitz. "*Me?*"

His legs went rubbery. He left the detectives standing in the doorway, wobbled across to the dining room, and sank onto a chair.

As Detective Chung closed the front door, Detective Lyons followed Fitz across the living room. Fitz saw her eyeball the indentations in the carpet left by the furniture. She raised an enquiring eyebrow at her young partner as he approached her.

"Don't they realize I'm the *victim* here!" said Fitz.

"So are they, sir," said Chung, and Fitz heard the veil of condescension over his voice. "They left their jewelry with you to be repaired, expecting it to be safe, but they trusted that, should anything happen to it, you would cover the loss. You haven't responded to their calls. You can see how they might begin to get suspicious."

"Those news vultures looking for a story aren't helping, either," said Fitz.

"That's to be expected, Mr. O'Donnell," said Lyons.

"Some of your customers have quite a lot of standing in Evanston and the surrounding area."

"Don't I know that," said Fitz. "They make very sure to tell me every time they come in."

Just before they ask for a discount because of the "exposure" they can give my business, he thought. *Talk about vultures.*

"Right now," said Chung, "these are just complaints. No one is pressing charges. Yet."

"As you're probably aware, it's not so much the monetary value of the missing jewelry that has people angry," said Lyons. "It's the emotional loss of that jewelry."

"Oh, sure," said Fitz. "But I'm sure a large monetary settlement will soothe their 'emotional loss.'" Fitz rubbed his temples. "This is a fucking nightmare."

"I'm sure it must seem like that," said Lyons. "But if you don't start talking to these people, sooner or later one of them—or several of them—are going to come in and press charges. If that happens, we'll be forced to arrest you."

Fitz muttered profanity under his breath.

"Do you understand, Mr. O'Donnell?" asked Lyons.

"Yes!" shouted Fitz. "I fucking well understand!"

"Good," said Lyons, irritatingly calmly. "Then I hope we don't have to come back."

"You're not the only one," muttered Fitz, as Lyons moved toward the front door.

When she turned back suddenly, he froze, thinking she'd heard him.

"I can't help noticing, Mr. O'Donnell, that a lot of your furniture is missing since we were here last," she said.

"I didn't realize there was a law against redecorating," said Fitz.

"There isn't," said Lyons. "But I wouldn't want you to leave Evanston. Or the state, until we've sorted out the...

incident at your store." She nodded and followed Chung out the door.

"Shit!" cried Fitz, slamming a fist on the dining table. "Damn Carlisle."

He snatched up his phone and dialed.

"Yeah, Pop?" said Carlise, warily.

"The police were here. Again. People are telling them I stole their jewelry. I told you we should have left it! But oh, no. You said we had to take it, or it would look suspicious."

"It would have. Can you imagine..."

"What I can imagine, is that if Clapham doesn't kill me, I'm going to prison!" yelled Fitz. "This is your fault."

"I'm not the one who called to report a burglary *before* the burglary took place!"

"I didn't! I reported the theft from the safe."

"Which wasn't insured, but which you thought was the best place to keep all the most valuable gemstones, not to mention all the stuff you were holding for your shady friends."

"It wasn't *my* idea to rob the vault afterward," said Fitz. "And *I'm* not the one holding the jewelry—including the stuff that belongs to customers."

The threat hung in the air.

Too late, Fitz realized that if he turned his son into the police, Carlisle would implicate him—and Hilary—in the robbery. And he'd still go to prison.

Breathing hard, Fitz adjusted his tone. "Carlisle, you're my son. I need help here. I need you to give me..."

"Pop. We've talked about this. I can't give you the jewelry back. There's no way you'd be able to explain that. Not without convincing the police you took it in the first place..."

"Not the jewelry, Carlisle," said Fitz, his voice rising

again. "I need the goddamned loan I asked for so I can make some of this go away!"

"I can't give you any money, Pop! I'm a breath away from jail myself!"

Fitz inhaled to yell back, then Carlisle's words sank in.

"What?" he said. "What?"

"Shit, Pop," said Carlisle. "You think you're the only one with troubles? I told you. Marcy wants a divorce. She's got her accountants and lawyers crawling all over me looking for money. I'm surprised they're not here tearing the cushions off the sofa. I think she turned me in to the IRS, too, because suddenly *they* want an audit. If that's not enough, the fucking SEC has started sniffing around my company. Now, Pop, is *not* the time for me to show up with a bag of cash to give my old man!"

"Jesus, Carlisle. I thought you were smart."

"Oh, fuck you, Pop."

Fitz backpedaled. "Sorry. Sorry. That came out wrong."

He paused. They both thought.

"What the hell are we going to do?"

"I keep telling you. Pin it on Mom," said Carlisle. "The store is robbed. She disappears. She's the obvious choice."

"And I told *you*. No one would believe Tish could pull off something like this."

"The police don't know that," said Carlisle. "Neither do your customers."

Fitz was about to argue, then stopped.

"You're right," he said, scratching his chin. "They *don't* know that."

He sat up straight and smoothed his moustache. He could see it... Fitz O'Donnell. Wronged victim of a cruel divorce plot.

"I could hold a press conference. Tell everyone that she did it..." he started to say.

"Sure. Then Mom hears about it on the evening news and disappears for good. Your three-week deadline passes, and Clapham kills you like he promised, either before or after the police arrest you. Hilary mourns for maybe four minutes before she finds another guy to keep her."

"Hilary loves me."

"Sure, Pop."

Silence smoked between them for a full minute.

Fitz was the first to speak.

"So, what do you suggest, genius? As far as I know, the police aren't even looking for her. How can I pin this on her if I don't know where she is?"

"Help them. Hire a private detective. When he finds her, have him tell her you want an amicable divorce. You'll give her half of everything—the insurance settlement, the house, the store. When she comes back, you turn her into the police, and the heat will be off you."

"The insurance company won't pay me anything. They think it's fraud."

"Pop. You're missing the point. If the police arrest Mom, the insurers will change their tune."

Fitz perked up. "You're right! They only refused to pay because they think I took the jewelry. But if I didn't, then it can't be fraud. They'd have to pay up!"

"You're getting it, Pop."

"I can't turn her in before she signs the divorce papers, though," said Fitz. "Hilary is set on getting married."

Even though he didn't mean to go through with the marriage, he had to at least look willing. At least until they got to the Bahamas...

"Whatever," said Carlisle.

"Once the police have Tish locked up, and the insurance money is paid, I can get the jewelry back."

Then Hilary and I can leave town, he added to himself, *and go anywhere warm that isn't* here.

"Pop, that's not how it works. You can't have it both…" Carlisle was saying, but Fitz was deaf to him.

"I don't know any private detectives," he said. "Do you?"

There was hesitation at the other end of the line.

"I do," said Carlisle finally. "And he works cheap."

Special Agent Jason Watson flicked off the recording, pulled off his headphones, and looked at his partner, Julia Weyburn. She was smiling.

"That's it," he said.

"Clapham threatened to kill him," she said.

"Sounds like it."

"We can use this," said Weyburn.

Now Watson smiled. "Yeah," he said. "I think we can. Suppose we should turn the son in to the SEC or alert Evanston PD that he has the jewelry?"

"Probably," said Weyburn. "When we're done with him. For now, I think he'll keep."

CHAPTER 13

THE IRISH CONNECTION

"Mary Patrice Geraghty?"

Startled, Tish looked up.

"Yes?" she said, before she thought, then kicked herself mentally.

It was the woman from the order counter.

She smiled at Tish. "I hope you don't mind me pushing myself in like this, but I heard your friend mention your name," she said. There was no mistaking the familiar music of Irish in her voice. "I'm a Geraghty, too. At least by marriage." She pointed over her shoulder to the table behind her and raised her voice a bit. "I'm wed to that handsome lad there, who won't admit to the bald spot," she said, glancing back. "So, we all agree to pretend it isn't there."

"I'm not deaf, you know," her husband called to her.

She grinned and turned back to Tish. "The whole lot of us came over here looking for dead relatives," she said. "I never expected to stumble on a live one. You're not a ghost now, are you?"

Tish couldn't help but smile. "Not yet," she said. "I hate

to disappoint you, but even though Gran came from Ireland, I doubt that makes us relatives."

"Ah, you never know. Or rather, nowadays you can know. That gossiping DNA, it tells everyone's secrets." She held out her hand. "I'm Maureen."

Kat's going to kill me, thought Tish, as she took Maureen's hand. But what could she do? The sound of Irish made her homesick for Gran Geraghty.

"Where was your granny from, then?" asked Maureen.

"I don't know, really," said Tish. "Wherever Geraghtys are from, I guess."

"Well, then, maybe we are family. Seeing as you're a native here, maybe you can recommend some local cemeteries where we might find our connections?"

"Oh, we're not from here. We're from...we're from Illinois," said Tish and winced.

"Are you following Route 66, too, then?" If possible, Maureen lit up even more.

The hell with it, thought Tish. Let Kat kill her. It was a pleasure just to have a normal, unguarded conversation.

"We are," she said. "My...cousin's dream."

"For us, too," said Maureen. "We've planned it for more than two years, now. We'll be at it for a couple months or more."

"That long?"

"Sure. Once in a lifetime, you know."

"Is it your first time in the US?" asked Tish.

"No, goodness. Tim and I have been here any number of times on business. But look, why don't you join us? We enjoy talking to captive Yanks. It's the accent we love." Maureen's grin was wicked.

Tish laughed. The Irish woman had heard her comments to Kat at the counter.

"Thanks," said Tish, regretfully. "But we wouldn't want to intrude."

"Don't be daft," said Maureen. "You're practically family. We'd love to hear your stories about Route 66."

"I'm sure yours are more interesting," said Tish, "from a non-American point of view."

"Then you'll join us?"

"I will," said Tish, making up her mind and pushing back her chair.

Just for a few minutes, she thought.

Kat wouldn't be happy with her, but at least she wouldn't kill her in front of witnesses.

KAT SKIDDED to a stop when she saw Tish laughing with the Irish motorcyclists, like they were old friends.

An icy breeze blew over her heart, chilling her bones.

Once again, she was outside looking in.

Always the odd one out, the one with secrets. Unable to bring friends home, and her mother fearful of letting her go to sleepovers, Kat had earned the reputation of being stuck up. The other girls began to ignore her, and the sleepover invitations stopped.

Her father had been unusually unsympathetic. "Friendship is an illusion," he'd said, when she was snubbed again at school. "You can never really trust anyone."

"Nick is your friend. You trust him," eight-year-old Kat had retorted.

"That's different," was all her father would say.

After her mother had died, and they'd left Fargo so abruptly to settle in Madison, Kat had hoped for a fresh start. Hoped things would change when her father had gotten the garage and even found friends.

But high school had been a nightmare of cliques, and the people her father had taught her to trust had eventually turned on her.

Trust only yourself, her father had told her.

And you, she'd said.

He'd smiled. *And me.*

But now he was gone, teaching her the hardest lesson: What you love, leaves you.

During these days with Tish, the lonely space in her heart, the one she tried to hide even from herself, had grown smaller. But Tish, it now appeared, was leaving her, too. The hole gaped painfully wide again.

Tish looked up and saw her. A sheepish but defiant and wholly delighted grin lit her face. She waved, *Come on,* and pointed to the open seat next to her.

For a split second, Kat thought about running. Just...going.

The moment passed, because the reality was, there was no place to run. Not now. There was only Route 66 and the choices she'd made—they'd made—that night in front of the safe.

There was no choice but to do what she'd always done: brazen it out.

Kat bent her mouth into a smile and dragged reluctant feet across the floor to join Tish and her new friends.

"This is my cousin, Katherine Miller," Tish told the table. "Like Maureen told you, Tim, it's always been Katherine's dream to drive Route 66."

Kat felt naked as she heard her private longing tossed out to strangers. Her lips felt like cardboard as she clung to the smile.

My fault, she thought. *I told her to stick—mostly—to the truth.*

Still. She had to get them out of here as soon as possible. Tish looked far too comfortable.

A man of middle height—trim and fit in his forties with a complexion that would have been peaches and cream when he was young—stood up to reach across the table. "Tim Geraghty," he said. "Mary Patrice said you're the one wheeling that beautiful motor along the road."

Kat shook his hand. "A pleasure," she said, not meaning it. She tried to concentrate on names as Tim went around the table introducing what turned out to be a big family.

"This beauty I'm lucky to be married to is Maureen," he said, setting his hand on the shoulder of the slender smiling woman next to him whose short strawberry blonde hair was starting to go gray. "She's the one thought we should spend this trip looking for dead family, though what she plans to do with them, I'm sure I don't know."

Tim nodded to the two young men sitting across from Maureen. "She's also responsible for those two troublemakers. The dark one whose hair needs a good cutting and who is attached to his phone by his thumbs is our younger son, Jamie..."

The phone, thought Kat anxiously, watching Jamie, his eyes focused on the phone in his hand, his thumbs moving at light speed across its surface. *What if he takes pictures of this happy group and posts them online?*

"Or so they tell us, anyway," said the young man sitting next to Jamie. "But it's my belief he was left on the doorstep at birth."

Jamie's left hand shot out—just as Tim was telling Kat and Tish, "...and that one is his brother, Connall"—and clipped his brother lightly on the shoulder. Connall laughed.

The two boys were unlike each other, though in a

genetic sleight of hand, both resembled their father. Jamie's dark blue tank top put his gangly late-adolescent—Kat guessed 18 or 19?—body on full display. Connall, probably in his mid-20s, had filled out into full manhood.

"This beauty," Connall was saying, as he laid adoring eyes on the face, and a gentle hand on the wrist, of the young woman sitting opposite Tim and between him and Tish, "is the love of my heart, Deirdre."

In Deirdre, Celtic and Scandinavian genes had long ago blended into a head-turning mix. Large tortoiseshell-rimmed glasses did nothing to hide her deep brown, long-lashed eyes set on either side of a straight classic nose. Her unblemished skin was blushing now, and her rich autumn-auburn hair was pulled back in a clip.

She looked, thought Kat, a bit like Tish.

Deirdre turned to Tish and Kat. "Deirdre Byrne," she said. "Ignore Connall's rubbish."

"Oh, sure," said Jamie, rolling eyes as startlingly blue as Kat's. "Anyone with eyes to see can tell the beauty part's rubbish." He shook his head and smiled at her fondly. "You can't deny the obvious, Dee."

If anything, Deirdre blushed harder.

"What's true, is that all three are troublemakers," said Tim. "Jamie's probably live-streaming our conversation, even now."

Oh, shit, thought Kat.

"Just the interesting bits," said Jamie, grinning.

"You're not too old to drown," said Maureen calmly.

"Always with the threats," said Jamie, his soft accent almost erasing the "h," changing the word to "t'rets." "You can see," he said, turning those blue eyes to Kat, "I'm hard done by."

Although determined not to feel friendly, Kat couldn't help falling, just a bit, for the mischief in those eyes.

"Lastly, this is Siobhan O'Hanlon, to whom I'm grateful every day for giving me Maureen."

Siobhan was a smallish woman with short, gray softly curling hair. The resemblance between her and her daughter, Maureen, was strong.

"She writes for the *Irish Times*," added Tim. "She's using our trip and our search for ancestors as fodder for her column, so watch what you say."

The brothers hooted.

"That's not all she writes," said Jamie, grinning fit to split his face.

"Oh, yes. "Tell them, Gran," said Connall. His eyes flashed with mischief, too, making the resemblance to his brother clear.

"You're both swine," said Siobhan, without heat. "You really are."

On Siobhan's right, Tim's face was spasming as he tried to keep it straight.

Siobhan sliced her eyes sideways at her son-in-law. "You, too, boy," she said. She looked at her daughter. "Am I not getting any support here?"

"Oh, I think you can take care of yourself," said Maureen.

When Siobhan turned to Kat and Tish, her eyes were dancing. "I write a bit of romance," she said, sending Jamie and Connall into convulsions.

Kat looked to Tish for clarification, but Tish looked just as mystified.

"She writes *sexy* romance," Deirdre finally told them.

"Hot," said Jamie. "Absolutely carnal."

"You're not old enough to read them," Maureen told him.

"It's all right, Ma. I explain the smutty bits to him," said Connall.

As the laughter died away, Maureen turned to Kat and Tish.

"You're probably wondering why anyone would bring a lot like this on a road trip with you, if you had another choice," said Maureen. "You should have run like you were demented when I suggested you could be family."

"I promise you," said Tish, wiping tears from her eyes, "my family was never this much fun."

Truer words, thought Kat, thinking of Fitz O'Donnell and Tish's two heartless older children. It was clear why Tish had warmed to this family.

But as their server arrived to put Kat and Tish's iced teas, muffins, and quiche on the table in front of them, Kat wished they'd gotten the food to go.

"Did you rent the bikes in Chicago?" Tish asked Tim, forking off a piece of muffin.

"We brought them over with us," said Tim.

Kat felt her eyebrows go up.

Tim saw it and grinned. "You're shocked, thinking we'd be better to burn the money for warmth."

"No, really..."

"Sure, you are. But it's not anywhere like as dear as it would be to rent them all summer. We've a good shipping agent, too."

"Besides, if anything goes wrong with them, we know how to fix them," said Connall.

"And when we curse them, they know we mean it," added Jamie.

Kat laughed in spite of herself. It was so like something her father might have said.

Too many heartache landmines here, she thought. *Time to move back to our own table.*

"It's been great meeting you," she said, beginning to slide her chair back. "But we've probably intruded enough."

"Don't be daft," said Maureen. "It's grand being with people other than ourselves. No need to hurry away."

"We're on vacation, remember, Kat..herine?" said Tish, pleading in her eyes.

No, we are not on vacation, thought Kat angrily. But she couldn't argue with Tish in front of an audience.

"I guess you're right," she said settling a bit resentfully back into her chair. Disaster loomed. She was sure of it.

Tish's eyes lit up. She turned a bright smile back to the Geraghtys.

"Maureen said you're going to be on the road for several months," she said to Tim. "What kind of work gives you that kind of vacation time?"

"Vacation!" Maureen snorted.

"I'm the only one on holiday," said Deirdre. "I work for theater and film production companies in make-up and hair design. Right now, I've nothing on."

Tish was clearly puzzled. "But the rest of you...?

"Tim and I design security systems for companies," said Maureen, nodding toward her husband. "We can work from anywhere. Those two," she gestured the across the table to Jamie and Connall, "have their own electronic and internet security business."

"We keep the world safe for celebrities and others with too much money," said Jamie.

"So, except for Deirdre, you're all working while you're on the road, then?" asked Tish. There were nods all around.

"We have extended stays planned in several places, just for that reason," said Maureen.

"You've heard all our secrets, now, Aunt Mary Pat," said Connall. Tish startled at his casual inclusion of her in the Geraghty family, and Kat felt another pang of jealousy. "You said Cousin Katherine, here, always wanted to drive along Route 66, but tell us, was that your dream, too?"

Tish caught Kat's eye, and though her hesitation couldn't have lasted two seconds, the momentary silence seemed to stretch on forever. Before Kat could decide if Tish was silently asking her to jump in, though, Tish turned back to the table.

"I left my husband," she said.

CHAPTER 14

ALMOST THE TRUTH

The look on Connall's face said he wanted desperately to take back the light-hearted question that had elicited this answer.

Kat was afraid her face looked the same way.

"Oh, Mary Pat," said Maureen. "We didn't mean to pry…"

"You're not," said Tish, and shrugged. "It's the same old story. He found a younger woman. So, I took my jewelry and what cash I could get my hands on, and I left him to it. I'm going to California to start over." She nodded toward Kat. "Kat…Katherine was at loose ends, too, so I asked her to come with me. She suggested we take Route 66. And here we are."

Well, thought Kat. *It wasn't* not *the truth.*

As such, it was easier to remember. But also so much easier to sail into the much more dangerous sea of the *complete* truth.

Once again, though, she had to admire Tish's ability for improvisation and for saying exactly the right thing at the right time. Kat might have spun a story they'd have trouble remembering and sticking to. But Tish, by telling almost the truth, had shut down all other questions.

Even so, Kat uncrossed her legs, freeing a foot to kick Tish if she got a little *too* honest.

Siobhan leaned forward and reached across the table toward Tish. "I know how you feel, love. I had one of those myself. They were a lot harder to get rid of in Ireland. I had to wait until 1997."

Tish took the offered hand. Kat heard her shaky inhale. "1997?" she said to Siobhan.

"The year divorce became legal."

"*1997?*" said Kat, with disbelief.

Siobhan nodded.

"Good heavens," said Tish.

"I'm not sure heaven had anything to do with it," said Siobhan, tartly. She squeezed Tish's hand and sat back.

"Yes. The living are always more difficult than the dead," said Maureen.

Jamie thumped his head down onto the table, narrowly missing his coffee, and crossed both arms over his head. "Cemeteries. I knew we'd end up talking about cemeteries."

Siobhan laughed, buried her fingers in her grandson's dark hair, and shook his head lightly. "So much carry on over a bit of old bones," she said. "And here we have fellow travelers who we can, perhaps, enlist to your mammy's cause."

"Run," said Connall to Tish and Kat. "Run now, before it's too late."

"Oh, it's not that bad, you." Deirdre laughed and slapped Connall playfully on the arm.

Tish grinned and looked past Kat to Maureen. "Tell me about your genealogy search," she said. "Who are you looking for?"

"Someone give me something stronger than coffee, please," muttered Jamie from deep beneath his arms.

Siobhan shook his head again gently. "You're not old enough to drink in this country," she said.

"Why did we come here, then?" asked Jamie, sitting up.

"Dead folks," said Deirdre and Maureen at the same time.

Everyone laughed.

As Tish became more rapt with the Geraghtys' story about their search for brothers Eamonn and Hugh, who had left Ireland during the Great Famine, Kat felt herself disappearing, like she had so often. Almost unconsciously, she inched her chair backward, out of the circle around the table.

"Their last letter indicated they were moving west from the mines in Illinois, but they didn't say where they were going," said Maureen. "Their families were left to survive as best they could. We've exhausted our online resources, so now we're looking in cemeteries and local history archives trying to find them."

"It seems like a pretty random way to search," said Tish.

"As we've said continually," said Connall.

"Don't listen to him," said Deirdre. "He and Jamie are literally along for the ride. They love these roads. So often we have the whole thing to ourselves. In big cities, like Chicago, a motorcycle rider can feel like a target. But out here...well, it's a joy. It's a bit like Ireland, if I'm honest. It's a treat to discover this part of your country."

"Mary Pat said driving along Route 66 has been your dream, Katherine," Tim startled her by asking. "What should we be seeing along the way?"

"Besides cemeteries," said Jamie.

"Yes, please," said Siobhan, reaching into the jacket

hanging on the back of her chair and pulling out a well-marked map. "I can only write so much about cemeteries."

"Have you seen the fire hydrants here in Sullivan?" asked Tish before Kat could respond.

"The what?"

"A lot of them are painted. Some look like the different landmarks all along the Route," she explained. She pulled out her phone and opened the photos she'd taken not long before. She handed it to Maureen. Tim leaned in over her shoulder.

"Oh now, those are quite clever," said Tim. He passed the phone to his left. "Siobhan, you should write about these," he told her.

"There are more, I think," said Tish. "There's a website with a bunch of pictures. It's kind of a community project."

Siobhan was making notes in a notebook. "Where are these?" she asked. "I'd quite like to see them."

Tish started to explain, but Jamie jumped in.

"I've got them," he said, and was already marking them on a Google map of Sullivan.

That damned phone, thought Kat. She'd forgotten about Jamie and his phone. Had he taken a photo of them all? She couldn't remember. She didn't think so.

"Will they make a story, do you think?" Maureen asked her mother.

"Certainly part of one," said Siobhan. She turned to Kat and Tish. "Have you seen the murals here in town?"

"Or the Muffler Men," said Kat quickly. "Did you s…"

She wasn't fast enough.

"Oh, yes! We saw the murals," said Tish. "Have you been to Pontiac, Illinois?" As everyone nodded, she went on. "There's a mural there with a big yellow car in it. Well, Kat parked right in front of it."

Yep, Kat thought. *She's going with all the truth.*

Tish hadn't thought the incident was very funny when it happened, but now that it was in the past, she seemed to think it was hilarious. She'd brought it up several times in the past week.

That was fine, when it was just the two of them, but now...

Kat had to stop her before she mentioned what was in the trunk.

Under the table, she tapped Tish's foot with hers. Engrossed in her story, Tish moved her foot away.

"As you can imagine that big yellow Buick, parked in front of a big old, yellow car painted on the wall, drew a lot more attention than we wanted."

Kat kicked her again. Hard.

Tish spun toward Kat.

Kat, keeping what she hoped was a friendly smile on her face, stared into Tish's brown eyes, trying to burn a warning into her friend's mind with mental telepathy.

It worked. Tish's face froze as she recognized what she'd been about to reveal.

Kat turned to the Geraghtys.

Mostly the truth, she thought.

"We came back from a short walk around town," she said, picking up Tish's story, "to find the car surrounded by tourists taking pictures. Two were actually on the car." The thought of those two guys standing on Beauty's bumper made her angry all over again. "But the worst part was the Armentrouts."

Kat hoped only she heard it, but Tish sucked in a big breath of relief as Kat got the story back into a—relatively —safe lane.

"Who are they?" asked Maureen."

"Vintage car groupies," said Kat. "Who want to be our best friends."

"They keep popping up everywhere," added Tish.

"We've noticed that, too," said Tim. "More than once, we've seen people along the road that we've seen elsewhere."

"We're all looking for the same things," said Connall.

"Except for the graveyards," said Jamie.

"Remember what I said about the drowning," said Maureen.

"How long have you had that big Buick, then?" asked Tim.

"It's actually Ti...Mary Patrice's," said Kat, kicking herself mentally. They were both getting too comfortable with this group. They needed to get away from them. Soon.

"It was my father's," said Tish. "But I've never liked it. Katherine claims it's her spirit vehicle."

As Tish started to tell the story of the car restoration, Kat relaxed enough to finish off her muffin. She lifted her coffee mug, glancing over Jamie's shoulder at movement in the parking lot.

She set her mug down with a thump.

"Oh, shit no," she said. "Oh, no, no, no."

CHAPTER 15

FITZ HIRES A GUMSHOE

"So… This is a sideline for you?" asked Fitz, pulling in his stomach as he glanced at himself in the mirrored closet doors that formed one wall of his office. He smoothed his moustache with one hand.

Henry Fox recognized the vanity in the gesture and inwardly rolled his eyes. He'd heard about Fitz O'Donnell.

He knew that O'Donnell, at roughly six feet tall, was comparing himself favorably to Henry's more modest 5'9". No doubt Fitz was also disdainful of Henry's salt and pepper beard and mustache, and the thin spot on the top of his head. But while Henry's hair was still naturally dark, he was pretty sure Fitz's hair color was courtesy of a bottle, and careful styling was covering O'Donnell's own thinning spot.

"Yes, it is," said Henry.

"It seems a bit…strange for someone who runs a bookstore to be a 'private eye,'" Fitz made air quotes, "on the side. I mean, isn't it…dangerous? Guns, and all that? Sit, sit." Fitz waved to the seats in front of his desk while he sat in his own expensive, ergonomically designed, leather chair.

The big desk. The big chair. All the mirrors. Henry had wondered why Fitz would want to meet at the empty store rather than at his home, but now it was obvious. This was where Fitz felt powerful. In control.

Which he obviously wasn't if he was hiring a private investigator.

"I get that a lot," said Henry. "But I've always loved mysteries and the old 'gumshoe' novels."

"Gumshoe novels?"

"You know, Philp Marlowe and Sam Spade. The noir detective novels of the 1930s and 40s."

A blank look from Fitz.

"Then there are the modern detective stories, like the Elvis Cole series. There's also the explosion of female detectives, like Sue Grafton's Kinsey Millhone or Dana Stabenow's Kate Shugak. I even enjoy the PIs in the urban fantasies, like Devon Monk's Allie Beckstrom."

"*That's* your background?" said Fitz, his eyes opening wide. "Reading detective stories? I mean, my son said..."

"No," Henry chuckled. "Of course not. That's only what triggered my interest. So about ten, twelve years ago, I took a course in private investigation."

"You can do that?"

"Sure. Then I spent a couple years working with a licensed private investigator who liked all the confrontational stuff—like process serving—but who hated the paperwork end of it. That was okay with me. I prefer doing background checks and so on. So, to answer your other question about the guns—no. No guns."

"That's what you've done for Carlisle, then?"

"Skip tracing, yes. Not for his company. He got my name from other people I've worked for."

"But you still have a bookstore." Fitz seemed unable to get beyond that, but then, a lot of people had a hard time with it.

"Yes."

"Why? I would think you'd make more money doing private investigating."

Fox laughed. "Well, the money helps," he said. "But if you love books, you love books."

"Oh," said Fitz, clearly puzzled. "My wife has a bunch of books, too."

Henry made a noncommittal sound.

"Your son said it's your wife you're looking for?" he said.

"Yes," said Fitz. "We've separated. I've met someone else you see. I understand she's angry, but she's disappeared and she's not taking my calls. I need to find her so she can sign divorce papers."

Henry could see that Fitz was edgy. Rocking and swiveling in his chair. Toying with his moustache. Casting nervous glances at himself in the mirrors. He'd been really intent on hiring Henry that day, too.

Fitz could have left the search for Tish to the divorce attorney, assuming he had one. *So why hire me?* wondered Henry. *What's the real story here?*

"You've suffered a grave financial loss, too," said Henry, taking a shrewd stab in the dark.

"What do you mean?" Fitz sat up fast, the chair almost catapulting him across the desk.

Henry shrugged. "It's an odd time to worry about getting divorced and remarried." He waved a hand toward the front of the store. "I understood that you lost everything in the robbery. At least, that's what the newspapers said. I would think you'd want that resolved first."

"Well, actually…"

Henry waited, watching Fitz fidget.

Fitz leaned forward across the desk.

Henry obligingly leaned in as well.

Here it comes, he thought.

"Well, I wouldn't want this to get out," said Fitz, lowering his voice, although it was just the two of them in the immense building. "You see, I do want to get the divorce papers signed, of course. Hilary means the world to me."

Henry returned the sappy lovelorn look on O'Donnell's face with a bland, but slightly curious, one of his own.

"But… But you see… Between the two of us… I think Tish is behind the robbery. Anything to hurt me, you know."

Henry kept his eyes pinned on Fitz's, though Fitz was looking everywhere but at Henry.

"Oh, I know," said Fitz. "People will say she doesn't have the brains to pull off something like this. They're right, of course. She must have had help."

Henry stayed silent, breathing evenly. He forced himself to relax his tightly clenched left fist.

"Have you told the police this?" he asked Fitz.

"Of course. But the police think…" He stopped as suddenly as if he'd swallowed his tongue.

But the police think you did it, thought Henry.

A few phone calls had told Henry the insurance company had doubts about what had actually happened in the store. He'd also heard that customers' jewelry was missing, and that the police had opened an investigation.

"The police aren't even looking for her," continued Fitz. "That's why I need you. I need you to find her so I can get my property back. Once she's here, I can prove she took everything, and the police can arrest her."

O'Donnell sat back triumphantly.

Henry sat back, too.

Ordinarily, he would think twice about taking on someone like Fitz as a client. But Henry had reasons for taking this one.

"I'll do my best, Mr. O'Donnell," said Henry. "But your wife may not want to be found. I can give you no guarantees."

"And even if I find her," Henry continued, "she may choose not to return to Evanston. I certainly can't force her."

O'Donnell looked surprised.

What does he think a private investigator can do? wondered Henry. *Tie her up in the trunk of his car?*

Then Fitz produced a look that Henry was sure the man thought was sly. Or cunning. Or clever. But definitely not... well, stupid.

"I'm sure you'll find a way to convince her," said Fitz. "You won't find me ungrateful."

He didn't really say that, thought Henry, trying not to laugh. *Does he think he's some kind of mafia don?*

Henry leaned down to cover the twitching of his lips and reached into his messenger bag to pull out an electronic tablet and stylus.

"Okay," he said, sitting back up and in control of his face again. "First, I'll need some information about her."

"Like what?" asked Fitz, clearly puzzled.

Henry mentally rolled his eyes again, as he thumbed on the tablet.

"Name, birthdate, Social Security number, phone,

friends and relatives she might have sought out. I did email you a list of what I needed."

"Oh," said Fitz. "All that?"

"I have to start somewhere, Mr. O'Donnell."

"Well, her name is Tish."

"Is that her given name?"

Fitz stared at the stylus, poised over the tablet, like it was a snake.

"It's what I always called her."

A spark of anger flared in Henry. *No wonder she disappeared,* he thought. *You can't even tell me her given name or her birthdate.*

He sighed with deliberate exasperation and clipped the stylus to the side of the tablet. Reaching back into his bag, he pulled out a sheet of paper.

"Here's a printed copy of the information I need in order to start," said Henry. "I'll leave this with you. When you've got it all together, give me a call and I'll come back."

"Well, I'd like to get this done today," said Fitz irritably. "I can look around here, if you can just hold on."

"I charge by the hour, Mr. O'Donnell."

That got Fitz's attention.

"You're right. You're right," said Fitz, shooting to his feet. "I'll get back to you when I have it all together."

"In the meantime," said Henry, putting his tablet in the messenger bag and getting up, "perhaps you have a recent photo of your wife?"

"Photo?"

"Yes. Perhaps something taken during the holidays? Or at an event?"

"Oh, yes. An event." Fitz brightened and went across the office to a credenza and brought back a framed photo. "This was taken last year at a very important jewelry industry dinner in Chicago. I was getting an award." He handed it to Henry, pointing at the trophy he was holding in the photo. "See?"

Fitz, grinning at the camera, was shaking hands with the person who had handed him the award.

"Is that Eddie Redmayne?" asked Henry.

"Who?" asked Fitz.

Henry pointed. "Eddie Redmayne? The actor?"

"I guess. He signed the picture, see? I could never read his handwriting."

Henry came close to shaking his head in disbelief, then turned back to the photo.

He wasn't looking at Fitz's image, though, or the Oscar-winning actor's. He only had eyes for the lovely redhead standing just behind her husband's right shoulder. She was paying no attention to the award-granting ceremony at all. Instead, she was laughing at something or someone off to her right.

"May I take this?"

"Oh. You need to take it?"

"Unless you have something else."

"Oh. I guess you can. But I want it back."

"Of course," said Henry. He flipped the frame over, popped the photo out and slid it into his bag.

Fitz mewed in protest, but Henry ignored him. He laid the empty frame on the desk.

"Call me when you have all that information together, Mr. O'Donnell, and as soon as I have that, and your check for my retainer, I'll get started."

"Oh, yes. The retainer." O'Donnell nodded, but his body language shouted, *oh, crap, the retainer.*

They shook hands at the front door of Superior Jewelers, and Henry heard the lock click into place as he left.

He walked several blocks back down Sherman, across Church, and a few more blocks, to pass the front of the two-story, brick-fronted building that housed Colonel Mustard's Books. Water was drying on the sidewalk near the planters full of geraniums.

He turned into the alley next to the store, then went behind the building where his burgundy red, imitation-wood-paneled PT Cruiser was parked. He unlocked the back door of the store.

Martine Boucher, his manager, was in the office, putting together their weekly book order. Soft voices came from the front of the store.

"How'd it go?" she asked, when he poked his head in, her Québécois accent worn smooth by years in the US.

"About as I expected."

"He want you to find out who robbed his store?"

"No," said Henry. "It's a personal matter."

"Oooh. Do I scent scandal?" Martine's eyebrows danced.

Henry gave her his best mysterious look. "Could be," he said.

Martine laughed.

"Do you need help down here?"

"No. All quiet right now," said Marine. "But we've got the Sisters in Crime event here tonight. It'll be crazy busy then."

"I remember. We have enough books?"

"I hope so. Our local writers have been especially helpful."

"Should be a fun evening," said Henry, heading toward the stairs that led up to his investigations office. "I'm looking forward to it."

"I'm getting Vietnamese food for dinner for everyone before the event," Martine called after him.

"Take the money out of the till," Henry called back.

"I already did," she answered.

Henry smiled and kept climbing.

Henry sat down in his non-leather ergonomic chair, bought on sale when an office supply store closed. He started his primary computer and opened his case software.

He still preferred paper, and one wall held three large filing cabinets where he kept his printed records. But, fully aware that he sat above a store filled with fire-starters, he had for several years backed up everything on his computer into the cloud.

He started a file on Tish, entering the date and amount of time he'd spent talking to Fitz. He'd keep a record of his time to document the loss when Fitz didn't pay him. He knew the retainer would be all the payment he'd ever see for this job.

The merchants that owned the stores near Colonel Mustard's gossiped, and Henry listened. It was, after all, part of his job. Fitz was scrambling to sell property to pay creditors, he'd heard, and there were rumblings that customers might sue him for loss of their jewelry.

With two fingers and impressive speed, Henry typed in the paltry information that Fitz had given him about Tish. He shook his head. He'd worked with spouses who were almost incoherent with rage toward their partners, but they'd been able to give him the basic information he'd needed to start his search, almost from the tops of their heads. But he'd never worked with a client who seemed to know or care as little about his spouse as did Fitz O'Donnell. Henry reached into his messenger bag and pulled out the photo the jeweler had given him. He looked at it for a long time.

Without a qualm, he folded it into quarters, obliterating Fitz, his award, and the award-winning actor, leaving only Tish's laughing face exposed. He creased it sharply and set it next to the 4" x 6" snapshot, encased in a silver frame, that sat next to his monitor. In it, Henry, college-aged and beardless, stood with his arm around a very pretty, laughing girl in front of a lake sparkling in the summer sun.

That perfect summer. Henry touched the framed photo gently.

Then Martine called. Book sales for the signing were already starting. Could Henry come downstairs?

Henry could.

CHAPTER 16

THE ARMENTROUTS AGAIN

Tish stopped telling her story and followed Kat's gaze. "Oh, no." She looked at Kat. "How on earth...?"

Kat shook her head.

"What? What is it?" asked Tim.

Tish pointed at the bright blue Nissan Cube pulling in next to the Buick on the far side of the lot.

"Remember those people we told you about? The ones who show up wherever we go?" asked Tish. "It's them."

"In that blue...vehicle?" asked Tim, nodding toward the Cube.

"Yes," Tish said.

"This is no longer funny," said Kat. "They're beginning to give me the creeps."

They watched as the Armentrouts got out of the Nissan and circled the Buick.

"I'm glad we put the top up," said Kat. "I'd be half worried they'd get in."

"How do they keep finding us?" Tish asked. She looked

at Tim. "They should never have been able to find us here. We haven't seen them for days."

"They could be tracking you," said Connall.

Kat started to scoff, but she saw the look that Tim fired at his son. Connall wasn't joking.

"We have to go," said Tish, pushing her chair back and reaching for her bag.

Jamie twisted back to the table from looking into the parking lot. The grin he gave his brother had sparks in it. Connall grinned back.

"Tracking you or not," he said, "we could give you a bit of help losing them. At least for a bit."

"We don't want to get you involved in this," said Tish.

"I agree with...Mary Pat," said Kat, as she started getting to her feet. "You're kind to offer, but..."

"We'd better hurry if we're going to get out of here," said Tish, as the Armentrouts started toward the café.

Maureen put her hand lightly on Kat's arm. "It's no trouble at all," she said. "The boys won't be a tick."

Jamie and Connall were already up.

"As Ma says, it's no trouble," said Connall. "We've gotten rid of more experienced annoyances than these. We don't have time to find a tracker if there is one, but we can give you a head start."

"Don't get caught," said Tim.

Connall grinned. "Have we ever?" he said, as the two young men headed toward the café door.

"What's going on?" asked Kat. She and Tish seemed to have lost control of the situation.

"It's all right, Katherine," said Maureen. "This is what they do. They get rid of the vultures that follow celebrities. This is easy for them. Sit down. It'll be fine."

Kat and Tish exchanged looks, but they heard the door of the café opening. Voices. The Irish accents were cut off by the door closing.

Escape was now out of the question.

"Follow our lead," said Tim quietly.

Uly and Erma Armentrout came into the covered patio, obviously looking for Kat and Tish.

"Well, this is our lucky day!" boomed Uly, as he spotted them. He hesitated slightly as he noticed the others at the table, then kept coming. "Why, if Erma hadn't spotted that big old Buick, we might have gone right on by!"

"Look at you," said Erma. "You're just making friends everywhere along the Route."

"Yes," said Kat. "As you can see…"

"Well, hello!" said Tim. "Mary Pat, Katherine, are these friends of yours and you not telling us?"

Kat spun around at the sound of Tim's caricature-ish Irish.

"Tim, stop," Maureen whispered fiercely to her husband. "You sound like that leprechaun on those terrible American adverts."

Deirdre was laughing, however. "Why don't you join us?" she said, waving the Armentrouts into the empty seats across from them that Jamie and Connall had vacated. Kat's head whipped in the other direction. "Any friend of Aunt Mary Pat's is a friend of ours."

"Well, thank you," said Erma, sliding around the table to sit next to Siobhan. "Come on, honey," she said to Uly, patting the empty chair between her and Deirdre.

"We're the Armentrouts, by the way," she added. She poked herself in the chest. "I'm Erma, and this," she draped an arm around her partner, "is Uly. Short for Ulysses, like General Grant. He was a great American hero."

"Howdy," said Uly, raising a hand.

"So, you all are family then?" asked Erma.

Kat noticed an edge in her voice.

Interesting, she thought, frowning slightly.

"Yes, we certainly are," said Maureen, with a touch of sweet venom, "whether or not there is a blood connection."

Did Maureen just say, Don't mess with me and mine? wondered Kat, even more surprised.

Erma missed a beat, obviously hearing the same hiss of warning as Kat. Then she turned to Kat and Tish, smiling.

"You all really should have come with us to the caves," she said. She looked at Maureen. "Have you folks been to the caverns? Meramec Caverns? It was the hideout of Jesse James, you know. The American outlaw? Where are you folks from?"

Kat itched to get away from these people, but the Geraghtys seemed content to settle into a conversation with them. It began to irritate her.

Then she saw Tim's eyes flick quickly to the parking lot and back.

While Uly told the family the outlaw history of southern Missouri, Kat picked up her iced tea and let her eyes slide slowly toward the parking lot. She realized the Geraghtys had maneuvered the seating so that the Armentrouts could not see Jamie leaning on his bike, arms and ankles crossed talking casually to Connall, who squatted down to disappear between the Buick and the Nissan's rear fender. A moment later, Connall popped up, then disappeared again closer to the front of the Nissan.

Follow our lead, Tim had said.

Suddenly, Kat knew what was going on.

She had to admire how smoothly it had been done, but

it made her wonder. Perhaps the Geraghtys lived a bit in the shadows, too.

Security, Maureen had said.

"Aunt Mary Pat," said Deirdre quietly on the other side of Tish. "I'm a bit embarrassed. I'm afraid I've had a...a wardrobe malfunction. Would you have a safety pin in your handbag?"

"Of course," said Tish, reaching for her purse.

"Would you mind going with me to the ladies' for a minute?" Deirdre added. "I may need a bit of help."

Kat was scrambling for an excuse to go with them when Maureen's hand rested on her arm under the table.

"The Irish have a soft spot for outlaws, too," she said, when Kat turned her way. Kat's blood curdled and slid to a stop.

Security.

She wondered wildly for a moment if Tish had told the Geraghtys everything while she was in the restroom.

Maureen, however, was talking to Uly. "But then, the English made outlaws of us all."

"Oh, I loved hearing all those stories about Robin Hood when I was a kid," said Erma.

For a moment, the conversation froze. Even Tim seemed at a loss for words.

They were saved by the server who brought out coffees and cupcakes and set them in front of Erma and Uly.

"Oh, thanks, hon," said Erma. "You'll remember to pack us up that box, now, won't you?"

"Yes, ma'am," nodded the server and headed back to the front.

"You know, something for the road sounds good," said Siobhan, pushing back her chair. "Katherine, didn't Mary Pat say something about sandwiches for later?"

Under the table, Maureen, squeezed Kat's wrist gently and released it. "It's slow right now," she said. "It might be a good time to get your order in. And if you'd refresh my coffee for me?" She handed Kat her cup.

Kat looked around the café, appearing to suddenly notice the lack of customers. "Good idea," she said, taking Maureen's cup, and nodding at the table in general. "I'll be right back."

"So, who's this Jesse person you mentioned?" Tim was asking Uly. "Is that the outlaw they made that movie about years ago? The one with...oh, what's the name of that American actor your ma was so keen on, Maureen?"

"Paul Newman."

"Oh, no," Erma was saying. "You're thinking of Butch Cass..."

Deirdre and Tish were waiting near the front door.

"Are the boys still by the motorcycles?" Deirdre asked Siobhan.

"They are," said Siobhan, grinning. "Looking like a proper set of villains. You'd best go, quick. Here, Katherine." She stretched out her hand. "Give me Maureen's coffee."

Deirdre hugged Tish. "You've got my number. Keep in touch," she said.

"I will," said Tish.

Her number? thought Kat, and was startled to get a hug, too.

Siobhan wasn't going to be left out. "Mary Pat, it's been grand meeting you." She hugged Tish. "Katherine, you, too."

Kat found herself hugged again. She couldn't remember the last time she'd been hugged in friendship. If ever.

"We can't thank you enough," said Tish.

Siobhan waved off her gratitude. "I'm afraid there's a

bit of the Devil in all of us," she said, smiling. "We like to let him out for a walk now and again. Now go. And be safe."

"Come on, Mary Pat," Kat told Tish. "We'd better go before Uly runs out of outlaws."

"No worries there," said Siobhan. "Tim will keep him talking. That man can talk the paint off the wall."

Tish squeezed Deirdre's hand once more, then she and Kat slipped out and around the side of the café to the parking lot. Kat glanced inside and saw Uly's arms waving, no doubt describing some kind of gruesome shootout.

"Jamie did a quick look," said Connall, when they reached the car, "but we couldn't search properly for a tracker, at least not here," he added, nodding toward the back patio of the café.

"I really can't imagine they're clever enough for that," said Kat.

"Doesn't take clever. Just takes a credit card and the Internet," said Jamie.

"You'd better go before they come looking for you," said Connall. "We've bought you some time, but if they've a tracker on the car, they'll find you again. As soon as you can, you'd best look around the body to see if you can find it."

"They won't see you from where they're sitting," said Jamie, "but they will hear that big engine fire up." He swung a leg over his red Ducati Multistrada. "So…"

Connall climbed onto his gray BMW K1300 GT.

"When you get ready to start the Buick," he said, "give us a sign. We'll rev our engines so no one will hear the car."

Kat turned toward the Buick and stopped. The Cube was canted sideways on two flat tires.

Tish noticed the flats as well and laughed. "Erin Go Bragh!" she said.

Jamie raised a finger to his forehead in salute.

Kat slipped behind the wheel of the convertible and nodded at the brothers. The big bikes roared in unison as she turned the ignition key.

The Buick rolled out of the parking lot, unnoticed by the group in the patio.

CHAPTER 17

THE PAWN SHOP BY THE SIDE OF THE ROAD

Tish, with her superior directional sense, got them out of Sullivan and rolling southwest through the Missouri summer, past a jumble of small businesses, old boarded-up motor courts, homes, and light industry. They had the road mostly to themselves, though I-44, not thirty feet to their left, buzzed with light traffic.

"It was good of the Geraghtys to help us get away from Uly and Erma," said Tish, breaking the silence. She gave an exaggerated shudder.

Kat was—grudgingly—grateful, too, but she was also irked.

"Maybe they wouldn't have had to help us, if you hadn't decided to bond with them," she said irritably.

"What do you mean?" said Tish, obviously surprised by Kat's tone.

"I just don't understand this...this...compulsion you have to make friends with everyone you meet. It doesn't seem to matter who it is. I've seen you chat up hotel registration clerks, the waitresses at diners—even the check-out clerks in grocery stores."

"It doesn't cost anything to be friendly, Kat," said Tish, irritation in her voice.

"Tish, when you do that, you put us at risk. We were sitting ducks there at the café. We're safer when we keep moving."

"Well, excuse me for living, but it felt good to act normal for little while, and just talk to friends about silly stuff."

"They aren't friends. They're just people we met on the road."

Tish looked at her.

"It's just an expression, Kat. Why does it bother you so much?" she asked.

"I just don't like the thought of the Armentrouts finding us again," said Kat. She would not acknowledge jealousy, even to herself.

"Do you think Connall was right, then?" Tish asked, with less irritation. "Do you think Uly and good old 'Erm' are tracking us?"

"It would explain how they found us off the beaten track in Sullivan, not to mention St. Louis."

"True. *We* almost couldn't find us in St. Louis. And we were there. Maybe we should put our own tracker on the car so we can find ourselves."

She knew Tish was trying to get her out of her crabby mood, but Kat didn't feel like being jollied. She didn't rise to the bait.

"My question would be why?" said Kat. "Why would people like the Armentrouts want to follow us?"

"Couldn't possibly be what we have in the trunk," said Tish with asperity.

"They couldn't possibly know *what's* in there," said Kat.

"Maybe they opened the trunk sometime in Illinois? In Pontiac? That's where they first found us."

Kat shook her head. "When they first saw Beauty, she was surrounded by all those photographers, remember? They couldn't have done it then. After they invited themselves to our table at that restaurant, we stashed her overnight in that little garage a few blocks from the courthouse square."

"I remember. The owner charged us $100 for that."

"Sure. But it means the Armentrouts couldn't have found her there. Even if they had, the trunk was empty by then. We had the 'inventory' with us in the apartment."

"If they couldn't find the car to empty the trunk, then how could they find it to plant a tracker?"

"I have no idea," said Kat.

"Then you think this is just a coincidence?" asked Tish.

"I'm not sure I believe in that much coincidence," said Kat.

"Coincidences never are," her father always told her. "Being suspicious of coincidence is how you stay alive."

"So, you think we should search the car?"

Kat nodded. "Beauty has any number of places to hide a tracker, but I think we should try. We'll do it tonight when we stop."

Suddenly, Kat slowed the car. On their right there was a small Pentecostal church. Between it and a tavern, there was a large, hard-packed gravel and grass area obviously used for parking.

Kat used the lot to turn around, and go back along the Route.

On the eastern side of the empty church was a gray, windowless cement-block building. Out front, twin red signs simply read: Guns and Pawn. The parking lot was littered with assorted trucks, most with a lot of miles on them.

"Holy cow," said Kat, slowing. "I haven't seen an El Camino in decades." She turned into the lot.

"No," said Tish.

She wasn't talking about the Chevy.

"We have to get rid of the Clapham Collection somewhere," said Kat, pulling around the back of the building.

"Here?" asked Tish in disbelief.

"We'll never know until we try." Kat reversed, turned around, and parked the Buick alongside the building, facing Route 66. "Here, they probably won't look too closely at our IDs."

Tish looked toward the interstate, where traffic whizzed by. Closer to them, the service road that had once been Route 66 lay empty and quiet. There was no one at the church, and behind them a stretch of woods was tangled with undergrowth.

"Kat, I'm not sure this is a good idea..."

But Kat had already contorted herself to drape her small frame over the back of the front seat. Her rear end was in the air as she reached into the backseat footwell. She dragged the red Dolly Parton wig out of the bag they kept handy for quick adjustments to their costumes.

"We'll just go in and look around," she said breathlessly, as she righted herself behind the wheel again.

"For guns?" asked Tish sarcastically.

"Sure. We can start with that." Kat pulled on the wig, adjusting it with a practiced hand. "If they have any jewelry at all, we'll try to shift the diamonds."

"I don't know..." said Tish.

Kat reached inside the tight black camisole and hoisted

her breasts higher, bringing up the lace edge of the sheer push-up bra to show over the neckline.

"Look, Tish. You dressed me this morning for a stop just like this." She waved her hand at the skimpy top and the seductive bra. "This was all part of the plan. You can't back out on me now."

Kat took a hand mirror out of her purse, reapplied red lipstick, and fluffed the wig. She stuffed a piece of gum in her mouth and looked at Tish.

Tish sighed.

"So, is this the story we tried out in the pawn shop in St. Louis?" she asked.

"I think it will work here," said Kat. "You're Terry. I'm Kitty."

"For the record, I hate doing this," said Tish.

"I know," said Kat. "For the record, so do I," she admitted, then grinned. "But you are so good at it."

Tish snorted. "Great. I get to mid-life and discover I'm a good con woman. You can put it on my headstone."

"It'll be fine," said Kat. "A quick in and out if it's too weird."

Tish pulled her gray wig out of the glove box, put it on, and borrowed Kat's mirror. She took a couple of deep breaths, adjusted the glasses on the lanyard around her neck, then picked up the sweater that lay on the seat between them. "Okay," she said. "Let's go."

They stepped out of the Buick into the humid Missouri summer.

An aggressive buzzer went off as they opened the door into a room that was dark in contrast to the bright sunshine outside. Tish, walking behind Kat, noticed how small Kat's waist was compared to her tight and well-curved butt. Kat had always worn suits at the store, and it struck Tish for the first time that, although her figure had been hard to hide, Kat *had* hidden it as much as possible.

Looking at that hour-glass figure now, Tish felt jealousy and envy rise. *I wonder if she starves herself*, she thought. *She certainly hasn't been eating much on this trip.*

She immediately felt guilty, knowing they were using Kat's figure as a distraction. And knowing that Kat *knew* they were using her.

The store spread out to their left and right. There were guns on all the walls, guns on racks in the center of the room, guns in cases. The cases not holding guns held ammunition and knives.

A dozen men were scattered around the room, loud voices talking and laughing. But the room went silent when the women walked in. All eyes swung toward them, like turret guns on a tank. Tish thought her heart would stop.

Kat didn't appear to notice. She scanned the room, snapping her gum—*How does she* do *that?* wondered Tish— then moved to the right where there were three cases holding jewelry.

Tish followed, nervousness rising. She tried to calm down, then realized nervous timidity was part of this character.

I'm a character, thought Tish. *A character on a stage. This is just stage fright. That's all.*

Nothing to do with all the men and all the guns and all the eyes on them.

Nothing to do with that at all.

Kat's behind swung as she sashayed to the counter, dragging her fingers along the edge of the germ-coated, finger-smeared glass that hadn't been cleaned in at least a year. She stopped, folded her arms, and leaned forward on the case, pushing her cleavage up further.

Some of the gun conversation near the back of the store started up again, but from the corner of her eye, Tish saw a number of men grinning and nudging each other. A couple of them frowned, making Tish more nervous.

I'm a character, she thought. *I'm playing a role.* She gripped her handbag and began flipping the lock on it. Up. Down. Up. Down.

It didn't take long for the pawnbroker to wander over like he was doing them a favor.

He wasn't much older than Kat, his regular features and sun-darkened skin were marked with old acne scars, his gray-spattered hair was shorn in a brush cut. He was wearing camo pants and a khaki shirt that covered a burgeoning waistline.

Kat pretended not to notice him.

He stuck his thumbs behind his belt and rolled his shoulders back.

"See anything you like?" he asked.

There was scattered snickering around the room.

"I see you sell jewelry," said Kat, not looking up.

"Good eyes," said the pawnbroker.

More snickering.

Tish hunched her shoulders and kept playing with the lock on her purse. Up. Down. Up. Down.

"Well," said Kat, glancing up, "if you sell, maybe you buy?"

"What do you have to sell?" asked the dealer.

The snickering was joined by a couple snorts from the other side of the store.

Kat stood up slowly, put her hands on the edge of the counter, and rolled her shoulders back deliberately mimicking the dealer's move earlier. The spandex in the black camisole strained.

Now who's the good actress? thought Tish.

Rude comments and a couple guffaws from the watchers around the room.

"Diamonds, interest you at all?" asked Kat, and snapped her gum.

CHAPTER 18

TERRY AND KITTY

The snickering died away. The gun conversations in the back got a little quieter as ears strained to hear.

The dealer's mocking grin faded a bit.

"What kind?"

"Well, we don't rightly know. Terry, get them out and show the man."

The purse lock went flip, flip.

"Kitty, I'm not sure about this..."

"Honey, Mom's gone. We can use the money."

"Well..." Reluctantly, Tish opened her purse, slowly drew out a plastic baggie with a mess of diamonds in it and held it out.

The dealer took the baggie, looked at it, then looked at Kat.

"Your *mom's*," he said, disbelief in his voice.

"Yes," said Kat, staring back at him.

"Just the diamonds. No jewelry."

"Well, there was," said Tish.

"Was?"

"Mama melted it down," said Kat.

"But kept the diamonds." More skepticism from the dealer's side of the counter.

"Well, she couldn't very well wear them, could she?" said Kat, beginning to lose patience.

"Why not?" asked the dealer.

"If you'd known Mama, you'd know," said Tish. "She hated show. Didn't even have precious stones in her wedding ring. Said all that sparkly stuff was just showing off. She had a real low opinion of it all."

"So, where'd she get all the diamonds, then?" He was still skeptical, but Tish could see him thinking: If the diamonds were hot, maybe he could get a good deal.

Well, the diamonds are *hot*, thought Tish. *And we are definitely going to give him a deal.*

"Well, her aunts..." Kat started to say.

Tish took over the story, as they'd planned. For this story, she'd be the more believable sister.

"All they had was boys, you see," said Tish, her hand now toying with the buttons on her sweater. She stopped, as if it was obvious.

"Yeah? So?" said the pawnbroker.

"So," said Tish, "when the aunties' time came, well, Mama was the only girl, see? She ended up with all that gaudy stuff. Her aunties just loved it all, you see. But Mama pure hated having it. When she prayed about it, God told her it was a test, you see. Of her purity of heart..."

"Terry, honey, the man doesn't need to know this..."

"Oh. Oh. I'm so sorry," said Tish. She looked down and fiddled with her buttons some more. "Sorry..."

"It's okay, honey," said Kat, patting her arm.

"So, why didn't she just sell the jewelry?" asked the dealer.

"Well, she couldn't, could she?" said Tish.

"She couldn't?" he asked.

"It'd be making a profit from the devil's work," said Kat. "Devil's work."

"All that showy, gaudy stuff," said Tish, tugging at her sweater.

The dealer looked at Kat. "But she melted the gold down."

"For her crucifix, of course." Tish pointed to the cross at her own throat.

"I'm not following," said the dealer. He clearly thought Tish was a few bricks short of a load.

"Her *crucifix*," Tish repeated, looking up at him like he hadn't the brains of a frog. "Honoring Our Lord. She wore it every day. To remind her of the sacrifice He made, and of all the greed and avarice in the world. Even in her own family."

Avarice that Tish saw light up in the dealer's face.

"So, what happened to the cross?" he asked.

Tish drew back in shock. "We buried it with her, of course." Her eyes teared up.

Kat patted her hand. "It's okay, honey," she said again.

The store had gone quiet, and while Tish tried to get hold of herself, Kat made a show of comforting her.

The pawnbroker picked up the baggie from where he'd laid it on the counter and poured the diamonds out onto a sheet of paper. He stirred them around with a stubby finger.

Kat and Tish had mixed as many small stones in the lot as they thought they could get away with, but they'd salted it with enough quarter and half-carat diamonds to make it interesting. There was even a three-quarter carat pear-shaped diamond in there, though the quality was lower than that of the other stones.

"How much do you want?"

"We don't know, really. Maybe two, three thousand?" said Kat, taking control of the negotiations. "Couple of these are pretty big." She nudged at the largest stone with her finger. "And diamonds, they're pretty expensive, right?"

They knew the quality of the diamonds wasn't the best, but Tish was pretty sure that a pawn dealer or jeweler could get at least five thousand dollars when they were resold.

The broker hemmed and hawed, shoved the stones around some more. "I can maybe give you $1500," he finally said.

Tish gulped and gasped as if she were overcome with emotion again. But Kat, made of sterner stuff, asked him, "Can you maybe make it $2500? We need to fix the roof on Mama's house, so we can live in it."

More poking of the stones, more thinking, scratching his chin.

"I can maybe go a bit higher," he finally said. "But $1800 is the most I can do. If you look around," he said, waving his arm to the rest of the store, "you can see we don't sell much in the way of diamonds."

"No, no, we can see that," said Tish glancing around. She was startled to see that a couple of the gun customers had sidled over closer to them during their conversation with the broker. They acted like they were looking in the closest gun case, but when Tish looked their way, it was obvious they'd been watching the diamond transaction closely.

Tish's nervousness, which had abated a bit as she'd gotten into her role as shy Terry, came rushing back.

She turned to Kat. "Kitty, I think the man's doing the best he can."

Kat gave the broker a dark look. "Maybe," she said, and

turned to Tish. "But if you think it's okay, then we'll say yes."

Tish gave her a shaky nod.

The dealer hurriedly pulled a dog-eared notebook from under the counter. "If you'll show me some ID," he said to Kat. He scribbled down the name and address on the fake ID Kat had created, then handed her $1800 in hundreds.

Looking him straight in the eye, Kat folded the bills in half, then in half again, and stuffed them into her cleavage.

"We thank you, mister," she said, and held out her hand to shake.

Tish nodded again, and they quickly headed for the door.

Just as Kat pulled open the door, Tish asked her timidly, "You sure Mama would approve of this?"

"Honey, we had no choice," said Kat.

Once outside, they darted quickly around the building, got into the Buick as fast as they could, and headed for Route 66, now a service road running back to Sullivan along the interstate.

Kat immediately turned to the left.

"Wrong way," said Tish. "We have to go the other way."

Kat glanced into the rearview mirror.

"This time, I'm right," said Kat. "Trust me."

CHAPTER 19
THE SCENT OF MONEY

"But Kat," said Tish. "We're heading back toward Sullivan."

"I know," said Kat, glancing past Tish. In the right-hand sideview mirror—an upgrade Tish's father had added, and for which Kat was grateful right now—she saw the El Camino slide out of the pawn shop parking lot and turn east. Right behind them.

"But why?"

"Because we're being followed."

"What?" Tish's head snapped around. "Mother of God. Who is it?"

"It's the two nosy Nellies who were too interested in our conversation with the pawn dealer. I saw them come out the front door when we pulled out of the lot."

"Mother of God," said Tish again. "What do we do?"

Kat's only answer was to put the pedal down.

There were few cars on the Route, and traffic on the interstate was thin. Kat's intent gaze shifted constantly between the road in front of them and the rearview mirror.

Tish kept her eyes riveted on the side mirror. The fingers of her right hand dug into the arm rest on the door.

As they got closer to Sullivan, roads began to branch from the Route away from the interstate.

"Can't we turn down one of those roads?" asked Tish.

"We don't know where they go. We could get trapped. I think I've got a better idea."

If it worked.

Kat was watching the road rise and fall, and as it did, the El Camino occasionally fell out of view. If she remembered the road right, she hoped to be able to use that to her advantage, but her timing had to be perfect.

She recognized a landmark. Then another. The road rose slightly in front of them. Kat gunned it. The Buick flew over the rise, bottoming out on the other side.

Tish yelped.

Kat flashed a glance in the rearview. No sign of the El Camino.

At the next corner was an old, abandoned, U-shaped motor court. Without warning, Kat swung hard left onto the side street, crushing Tish against the passenger door. Kat spun the wheel left again and, spitting gravel, swung the Buick in behind the motor court, out of sight of the Route. She hit the brakes and threw the gearshift into PARK. As the dust cloud rolled past the car, Kat tore off the Dolly wig and flung it into the back seat.

"Kat! I know it wasn't expensive..."

"Stay here and keep the engine running."

She threw herself out of the car and ran back to peer around the end of the building, her heart hammering.

Good. There was enough grass in the old parking lot that the little dust they had generated was already settling.

Tish came up behind her. "What are..."

Kat jumped and pushed Tish out of sight. "I told you to stay in the car!"

Tish dug in her heels. "What are you doing?"

"Keeping us out of trouble," said Kat. She turned back to the corner of the building in time to see the El Camino roar by heading east toward Sullivan.

Kat's breath whooshed out.

"Let's get out of here," she said, running back to the Buick with Tish close behind her.

Twenty seconds later, Kat was skidding out of the motor court parking lot.

"Why would they follow us?" asked Tish once they were back on Route 66 heading west.

Kat was picking up speed, eyeing the interstate that lay not thirty feet away to her left across a shallow swale covered with browning grass and weeds.

"Maybe they think we have more diamonds," she said. "My guess, though, is they want the money I have in the bank." Kat pointed to her cleavage where eighteen one-hundred-dollar bills were getting damp. "Who knows? Maybe they want to dig up Mama for the gold. Whatever the plan, I'd bet this roll of cash that that pawn dealer is in it with them."

"What happens when they can't find us?" Tish asked.

"They'll give up," said Kat. "They'll stop at a tavern, swear a bit, and forget us."

"You're sure?" asked Tish.

"Yes, I'm sure."

But Kat wasn't sure enough that she was willing to pass in front of the pawn shop again. One of the guys in the El Camino might phone the pawn dealer when they realized they'd lost the Buick.

She accelerated and said a quick prayer to the Virgin Mary. If this didn't work, they'd be finished.

"Hang on," she said to Tish.

"Why? What are you... *Kat!*" she shrieked, as the Buick ripped across the eastbound lane of Route 66 and dove down the incline onto the grassy swale between the service road and the interstate.

Kat hit the gas hard. The 300-horsepower, V8-engine roared. Four steel-belted, white-walled tires dug into the (mercifully) dry ground and launched 4500 pounds of American-made steel over the edge of the interstate to bounce in neatly behind an 18-wheeler heading west. The car slewed a bit, but Kat wrestled the wheel and straightened it out.

The shrieks and curses from the passenger seat kept coming.

"Whoo-hoo!" yelled Kat. "Oh, you Beauty!"

"You're out of your god-damned mind!" screamed Tish. "You're going to kill us!"

Kat's moment of self-congratulation was brief. Coming up fast on their right, across the median and Route 66, Kat saw the pawn dealer step out of his store, followed by a couple more of the guys who'd been paying too much attention to them.

The broker was holding a phone to his ear.

Kat knew in her gut that the two hooligans in the El Camino were telling him what kind of car Kat and Tish were driving. She couldn't chance them being seen, even at this distance. After all, Beauty was distinctive.

She glanced back, yanked the Buick left, and punched the accelerator to bring them alongside the 18-wheeler where they were hidden as they passed the pawn shop.

Tish's stream of expletives continued un-self-edited.

Intent on staying hidden, Kat didn't, at first, register the black Navigator coming up fast behind them. The smoked windows hid the driver.

When she did see it, it was all Kat could do to hold back the scream that threatened to rise up from the base of her spine, driven by the bone-melting fear she'd bottled up for almost forty years.

"Shit, shit, shit," she muttered through clenched teeth.

"What? What is it?" said Tish, her penance-earning stream of profanity stopping long enough for her to crane around to look behind them.

Kat didn't answer. She just pushed the accelerator down to the floor. As she glanced back, preparatory to changing lanes, the Buick kicked up a good-sized stone that arced through the air, as if in slow motion, and hit the Navigator's windshield dead center.

The rear bumper of the Buick had barely cleared the grill of the 18-wheeler when she pulled to the right without signaling.

The SUV shot past them, but not so fast Kat couldn't identify the plates.

Illinois.

The truck driver laid hard on his horn, signaling his displeasure, but Kat was already pulling away from him. She was careful not to gain on the Navigator, though.

Not hard, as the Lincoln was already three-quarters of a mile away.

For the next few miles, Kat was sure she could hear her heart pounding even over the air thundering in the windows.

"Are you planning to slow down before we get to Oklahoma?" asked Tish, her voice brittle.

"Oh," said Kat, letting up on the accelerator.

As one mile, then another clicked away, and the speedometer dropped, Kat felt Tish's brown eyes—flashing red, she was sure—boring into the side of her head.

"You know," said Tish finally, "I may not like this car. But it is still *mine*. And it is still worth a hell...a heck of a lot of money. Or it was," she added.

"Sorry," said Kat. She patted the dashboard. "Sorry, Beauty, you amazing old girl, you." She flashed a glance at Tish. "Sorry," she said again. "But it was the only way to be sure they couldn't follow us again."

More silence in the car as the expansion joints in the highway thumped quietly beneath the wheels.

"That wasn't why you almost drove that trucker off the road," said Tish.

"I didn't almost dr..."

"Kat, you have to stop freaking out every time you see a black SUV."

"I didn't 'freak out.' Stop saying that."

"Yes, you did."

"No, I didn't. He was coming up behind us too fast. I had to get out of his way."

Kat didn't have to look to know that at least one of Tish's eyebrows was up near her scalp. The word "liar" hung unspoken in the wind buffeting around the wing windows.

"You do know you'll have to confess all those words you said back there," said Kat finally, hoping to change the subject.

"Not to mention my thoughts of murder," said Tish.

"Do you have to confess those?"

"I'm certainly not going to ask advice of a priest," said Tish. "That would lead to too many explanations neither of us want me to make."

"True," said Kat, chastened. "Look, I'm sorry. Maybe it was the wrong thing to do. But it's done. I won't do anything like that again."

Please, Holy Mary, make it so I don't have to do it again, she prayed swiftly.

Tish's eyebrows were still up near the Buick's headliner.

Best to get her mind on something else, thought Kat.

"Those guys may not be able to follow us now, but it might not be a bad idea if we left Route 66 behind us for a while," said Kat. "Why don't you dust off those super-powers and see if you can find us some nice, deserted back roads that get us to the next sizable town by other means."

"That would be Cuba."

"Then Cuba it is."

As Tish got out her phone and began searching maps, Kat hoped that Cuba would be big enough to hide them from everyone who seemed to be following them.

CHAPTER 20
THE FRIENDSHIP
STRESS TEST

Tish, trusty phone in hand, led them off the freeway and onto country roads that curved through woodland. Dappled shade flickered over the Buick's hood. The trees breathed a cool sigh over them, as if the leaves still held some of the morning's freshness.

Occasionally the road passed through pastures populated by butterflies stunned almost motionless by the heat in the open fields. Custom-built homes, surrounded by sheared lawns where the random horse or llama grazed, alternated with manufactured homes flanked by large equipment and accessed by rutted dirt drives.

As Tish led them through a variety of turns, the well-maintained, double-wide roads would sometimes give way to narrow lanes where the asphalt was delaminating and crumbling at the edges. They were almost the only car moving through the summer afternoon. At one point, Kat simply stopped in the middle of the road and put the top down again. Tish didn't argue.

They were rolling languidly down a narrow strip of pitted asphalt when Tish called out.

"Stop! Stop!"

The Buick rocked as Kat braked.

"What?" asked Kat, looking around them. Then she frowned. "Why are we stopping here?"

"There." Tish pointed back over her right shoulder to a tiny overgrown cemetery. It was embraced by a stand of trees and fronted by a cast-iron arch with *1873* written at the top in old-fashioned numbers.

"I told Deirdre I'd check any small cemeteries we happened to stumble across."

"You *what?*"

"I'm sure the Geraghtys will never get back here. Wherever here is."

"Tish, this isn't a scavenger hunt for corpses. We can't stop at every country graveyard..."

"You don't have to get so testy. It won't take ten minutes and there's a pullout right there."

"That's hardly a pullout. The Armentrouts couldn't even fit their blue juice box in that. But that's not the point. We need to keep going, or we'll never get to the next town, whatever it's called..."

"Cuba. It's called Cuba."

"Whatever. We can't keep stopping for some goose chase because you prom..."

"Fine," said Tish, feeling stubborn. She shoved open the door. "Stay parked here in the middle of the road. I'm going back," she said. She slammed the passenger door, rocking the car, and marched back along the shoulder of the narrow lane.

Maybe it was just petty revenge, but Tish was going to do something for the Geraghtys who'd helped her feel, just for a short while, like this was a normal vacation.

"Let *her* be pissed off for a change," she muttered, then thought, *and to hell with worrying about another Hail Mary.*

A moment later, she heard the Buick reverse. Kat backed up past her and into the wide, weedy spot in front of the cemetery. The nose of the big car poked out onto the crumbling asphalt.

Kat got out as Tish caught up and eased around the car.

"Coming then?" said Tish.

"Not me," said Kat. "I don't like graveyards."

"Afraid of ghosts?"

Kat gave her a look and said nothing.

"Fine. Stay here and pout then," said Tish, and walked up the grassy, overgrown path that led to the cemetery's entrance.

She walked carefully, using her foot to shove aside the weeds and grass shrouding the headstones. Insects buzzed. A cardinal's call cut through the chattering of the sparrows and finches. Mosquitos whined by, thirsty for blood. The Buick's engine ticked loudly as it cooled.

"There's a bunch of children's graves up here," she called to Kat, who was leaning on the Buick's trunk. "They're all the same year. Must have been an epidemic around here."

"Well, that's a reason to go sightseeing."

"Okay, look," said Tish, looking back to Kat. "Maybe you're not big on history, but you don't have to be snarky about it. These were children someone loved."

"You're right. I'm sorry."

She didn't sound all that sorry, but a bit mollified, Tish finished moving around the headstones, although she already knew there were no Geraghtys here.

"No Geraghtys," she said to Kat when she got back to the car. "The family or extended family of Baumans."

"Fine. Can we go now?"

"What do you have against cemeteries?" Tish snapped.

"Maybe they remind me of where we could end up if we don't keep moving," Kat snapped back. "Are you ready?"

"What is the matter with you?" asked Tish, digging in her heels. "It was a five-minute stop. I thought it would be a nice thing to do for friends."

"Tish, you just met them in a coffee shop. I told you. They're not *friends*. You don't pick up friends like…like… lint," said Kat. She stopped, crossed her arms, and looked away.

"That's exactly how you find friends, Kat. You talk to people. You find things in common. You laugh together. You eat together. You help each other."

"They live on the other side of an ocean. What's the likelihood that you'll ever see them or hear from them again?"

"It doesn't matter," said Tish. "Friendships are not about transactions—you do this for me, I'll do that for you."

"That's what you just described."

"How is laughing together a transaction?" shot back Tish.

Kat said nothing.

"They helped us, Kat. They didn't have to do that."

"Yeah. Well… It doesn't mean we have to pay it back."

"Maybe I want to. Maybe I want to do something nice for someone."

"Maybe we should do something nice for us, Tish. Like get us on down the road." Kat waved an angry hand at a mosquito that flew at her face.

Tish paused. Thought. Took a breath.

"What *is* it, Kat?" she asked.

"What's what?"

"What's upset you so much? We were having fun when we drove into Sullivan. I thought you were enjoying the Geraghtys' company as much as I was. Now, all of a sudden, you're angry."

Kat's mouth worked, pulling lips in, biting them. Tish had the feeling she was trying not to cry.

Kat? Cry?

Kat lifted her shoulders in a shrug that wouldn't have deterred a mosquito and continued staring into the woods.

"Use your words, Kat," Tish snapped again.

Kat flashed her a blue glare. "Don't treat me like a petulant child."

"Then talk to me," said Tish. "Friends talk to each other when they're upset about something."

"Do they? Isn't that how friendships end?"

"Why don't we try it and see?"

Tish heard the nasty edge in her voice. As Kat opened her mouth, Tish put up her hands in a "time out" sign. Kat's middle finger started to tap against her arm, but she stayed quiet.

Tish took a deep breath. "I'm sorry," she said. "Now *I'm* getting angry." She slapped at her ear. "Partly because I'm hot, sweaty, and the damn... stinking mosquitos are using me as a filling station."

She took another breath, looked at Kat.

"Look. You're upset. Or..." Insight hit Tish hard. "Or maybe you're scared. I know I am."

"Then why are we hanging around here looking at dead baby graves rather than getting farther down the road?" asked Kat. She stopped suddenly and put up a hand. "Sorry. The remark about the dead children was uncalled for. Maybe I'm hot and sweaty and bug-bitten, too."

Tish recognized the olive branch.

"Kat. Please. I need to stop being scared once in a while," she said. "I need to feel...normal. I want to forget, at least for little snatches of time, that literally overnight I lost everything. My toad of a husband. My store. My home, my community. I want to forget that my kids are greedy, covetous, selfish little sh... That Luke is 3000 miles away. That we have a trunk full of stolen diamonds.

"Now you don't even want me to be kind to people who befriended us. They didn't have to help us with the Armentrouts, you know."

"I know," said Kat quietly.

"You said this could be like a vacation," Tish continued. "But every time I try to enjoy it like one, you remind me how close we are to death. I know it, Kat. I know that. But I just need ten minutes—or even fifteen minutes—at a time when you're not reminding me that someone might want to kill us, or that we might end up in prison. Once in a while, I want the fun you promised me. Like the Segways in Forest Park in St. Louis."

A smile whispered around Kat's mouth. "Mario Patrice Speedracer."

Tish laughed. It was a bit forced, but it *was* a laugh.

"Yes, like that. I want jokes. Laughing. Laughter helps keep me from being frightened, Kat. And Jamie reminds me of Luke." Her voice broke.

Kat took a deep breath. Tish watched the anger drain out of her.

"You're right, Tish," said Kat. "I did promise you a fun road trip. But...we do need to keep moving. Please?"

"Sure," said Tish. "Look, I know we have to sell the inventory. But we've done enough for today, haven't we?"

Kat huffed a laugh. "I'd say so."

As Kat turned toward the car, Tish put a hand on her arm. "We have to work together, Kat, and we need to trust each other. So, I need to understand. If I've upset you, then I want a chance to apologize. If you're scared—if it's those cars—then tell me. It can help, sometimes, to talk about what scares you."

Because if it scares you, she thought, *maybe I should be more scared than I am.*

The naked look on Kat's face told Tish she'd hit home.

A mosquito whined into her face. Tish slapped again.

"But maybe we should drive right now and keep these things from eating us alive?"

Kat nodded.

"Sure," she said. "Let's drive.

CHAPTER 21
CUBA

It was late afternoon when Kat and Tish rolled into Cuba, a tidy small town where murals covered the walls on the buildings in the center of town, and telephone pole banners proclaimed it Route 66's Mural City. They'd found a couple more backcountry cemeteries along their way, and Kat had stopped—without prodding from Tish—so that Tish could look through the headstones for the Geraghtys.

Tish was grateful for the peace between them as she searched her phone.

"There's an old motel here in Cuba called the Wagon Wheel. It's an original," she told Kat.

"Do you think the Armentrouts will stop there?

"Only if Jesse James stayed there."

"Did he? Is it that old?" asked Kat.

"No," said Tish. "But Bonnie and Clyde did."

"Are you serious?" Kat gave her a shocked look.

Tish started to laugh, collapsing against the passenger door.

Kat grinned sheepishly. "Okay, okay. You got me."

"Oh, your face," said Tish breathlessly.

"So, where is this relic?" asked Kat. "We can at least drive by. See if there's some place we can hide the car."

"Maybe we won't have to," said Tish, wiping tears away. "Bonnie and Clyde actually stayed in Joplin. Maybe Uly and Erma will go there. Oh! It's there." Tish pointed.

Off to the left was a stone house with antique gas pumps in front. Set behind it, in a carpet of grass, still emerald-colored before the summer heat burned it dry, was a semi-circle of similar small stone buildings.

"It's like driving back into the 1950s," said Kat, as she swung into the driveway. "Beauty will feel right at home."

Twenty minutes later, the Buick was parked out of sight of the road, and Kat and Tish were dropping their luggage in a small, wood-paneled, two-room suite in the back of the motel. One room was a tiny kitchenette with a stand-up table. Through squeaky swinging doors, they found two queen-sized beds that took up almost the entire space, with just enough room left for a sink. A separate, closet-sized room housed the toilet and shower.

"Oh, it's like the summer cabins they used to have on the Great Lakes," said Tish, wistfulness in her voice.

"I remember those," said Kat.

"It makes me wish we could spend a few days here. If we got some groceries, we could make our own dinner. It would be fun."

"Or we could just go to the restaurant next door."

Tish sighed. "You're probably right. I don't feel much like going out again to find a market, anyway."

"I'm going to get a quick shower first," said Kat, starting to strip off her clothes. "I'm feeling a bit grungy."

Tish went back through the swinging doors and settled

into one of the chairs that sat outside the door to their room. A small breeze rippled the leaves of the trees across the strip of gravel running in front of the room. As she heard the shower start running, she pulled out her phone to text Deirdre.

Checked three cemeteries, she wrote, adding their names and locations. *No Geraghtys. Sorry.*

No worries, came the quick answer. *Three less for us. Will please Jamie.*

Thank the boys again for their help, tapped out Tish. *Much appreciated.*

She got a "thumbs up" in response.

She was about to text Luke when the phone rang in her hand.

"Okay. Thanks," said Tish and broke the connection as Kat came out the door. Instead of her usual all-black attire, Kat was wearing the lavender V-neck T-shirt and dark purple wrap skirt that Tish had convinced her to buy in St. Louis. They made the burgundy highlights in Kat's hair stand out.

"Feel better?" said Tish.

"I did," said Kat, her face blank. "Who were you talking to?"

Tish was annoyed by the blush rising to her face. Sometimes Kat made her feel like a child caught snitching cookies before dinner. "The attorney Jesse recommended."

"Attorney?"

Tish stood up and faced Kat.

"Yes, Kat. The attorney. The one you urged me to hire yesterday. The one to start the divorce and to run interference with the police. Remember?"

"When did you contact Luke?"

What the hell...heck? thought Tish. *Why should I be ashamed?*

"I text him every night. To let him know I'm okay, all right?"

Kat looked at her silently. Tish saw her struggling with anger.

"He's my *son*, Kat. He's all the family I have left."

Slowly Kat nodded.

"You clean up nice," said Tish, trying to change the subject, but Kat wasn't having any of it.

"Does he know where we are?" Kat asked.

"Of course not," said Tish, belatedly remembering she'd told Luke the fire hydrants were in Sullivan, Missouri. "He just knows I've left Fitz."

"Is he okay with that?"

"Are you kidding? He's thrilled."

The skin around Kat's eyes wrinkled softly. "I always liked Luke," she said.

The tension eased out of Tish's shoulders.

"Shower's yours if you want it," said Kat.

"I do," said Tish. "I'll be quick. I'm hungry."

Thirty minutes later, she rejoined Kat, feeling refreshed in lemon yellow linen slacks and a Hawaiian-print camp shirt.

"You're right," she said, as she stepped outside. "That feels much better."

"You look like a woman on vacation," said Kat, and Tish relaxed more.

The two women walked around to the front of the motel, passing some old-fashioned, shell-shaped metal chairs on the lawn. Tish was telling Kat what she'd discovered online about the murals of Cuba, when there was a shout from the front of the restaurant.

"Aunt Mary Pat!"

They looked up to see the Geraghtys' six motorcycles ranged in front of the screened porch of the restaurant, and Deirdre waving wildly at them.

CHAPTER 22
BIKES AND BARBECUE

"Oh, crap," murmured Kat. She'd been sure they wouldn't see the Geraghtys again.

"Shut up," said Tish under her breath.

"I can't believe we're seeing you again so soon!" said Deirdre, walking up to Tish and giving her a hug. "This is a treat!" She stepped between Tish and Kat and threaded an arm through each of theirs. "You have to join us," she added, pulling them into the screened porch of the restaurant.

"Thanks, but we couldn't intrude again," said Kat, and saw the flash of anger in Tish's face.

"Don't be foolish," said Maureen, who had jumped up to hug each of them. "It's no intrusion. There's plenty of room. The boys are fighting over how many family packs to get, so we'll have more than enough food. And we owe you dinner, at least, for checking on those cemeteries for us."

"If you put it that way," said Tish, "We'd love to." She didn't meet Kat's eyes.

"Yes," agreed Kat, forcing a smile. "We'd love to."

She even sounded as if she meant it.

"Shove over, Jamie," said Deirdre, pushing his shoulder. "Grab another chair. Let Katherine sit down. Mary Pat, there's room across the table there."

"We thought you'd be farther down Route 66," said Tish, as she sat down.

"Do you have any idea how many cemeteries there are in Missouri?" said Jamie in a pained voice.

"We'd hoped to stay at that place next door," said Maureen, nodding toward the Wagon Wheel and ignoring her son. "But we need four rooms, and they only had two left. Tim got us rooms at some cold chain over by the highway, but we wanted to try the barbecue here first."

"I wanted to try the beer," said Jamie.

"But he's still too young," said Connall, laying a hand on his brother's shoulder.

Jamie shook his head, then leaned on an elbow and looked sideways at Kat. "You do know the alcohol laws in this country are demented, right?" he said.

Kat couldn't help smiling. Tish was right. Jamie's winsome manner was a lot like Luke's. "I'm afraid no one asked me," she said.

"Still. If I were a Yank, now, I could vote. I could join the army. But I couldn't drink. What kind of mad logic is that?"

"You'd not be drinking and getting on that motorcycle in any case," said Maureen. "Ma's law."

Jamie didn't take his eyes from Kat.

"Never travel with your ma," he said.

"So, where'd you hide that big car?" asked Connall. "We'd never have known you were here."

"It's behind the motel over there." Tish pointed.

"You're staying there?" asked Siobhan excitedly. "Would it be too much to ask to see your room? I'd like to be able to write about it. We're hoping to stay in a few of these old places, wherever we can."

"Sure," said Tish. "We can go over there now if you want."

"Brilliant," said Siobhan, getting up. "Tim, I want that stuffed potato. Come on, Mary Pat."

Kat watched them go, hoping Tish remembered to guard her tongue. No matter how much Tish might think of them as friends, the Geraghtys were still strangers. It would only take one moment to confide their secret, and...

"So, have you seen your stalkers?" Connall asked Kat. "The older folks. I can say that now that Gran has gone."

"No. What happened after we left?" she asked curiously.

"They weren't best pleased when Deirdre and Siobhan came back to the table without you," said Maureen grinning.

"Even less so when they found that we were leaving, too," said Tim. "The language they used, when they saw their flat tires, I think Siobhan is putting in her next book."

"We probably have a bit of time until our food gets here," said Connall. "Shall we look at your car, see if we can find that tracker?"

Kat hesitated. It couldn't hurt to have Connall and Jamie check the car, she argued with herself, but it would make them more beholden to the Geraghtys.

"It's no bother," said Connall, misunderstanding her hesitation.

Kat decided.

"Thanks. I don't really think the Armentrouts can have hidden a tracker on the car, but it would set our minds at ease if you'd check."

Swell. Now I'm *asking them for help*, Kat thought.

"I'll just get the sweeper, then. Jamie. Coming?"

Jamie produced a long-suffering sigh. "If I don't, you might have to crawl under the car yourself."

"Ah, right. I knew there was a reason I might need you," said Connall.

Kat walked over to the motel with the two younger men and watched as Connall ran his hand inside the wheel wells, along the grill, and under the hood. Jamie walked around Beauty with his electronic gizmo. Tish and Siobhan came out of the room just as the sweeper began to buzz.

"You have it?" asked Connall.

"Looks like," said Jamie, sweeping closer to the rear bumper on the driver's side.

Connall reached inside the curve of the bumper and ran his hand back and forth. He brought out a small box, the size of a matchbook.

"That's it?" asked Kat.

"That's it," said Connall.

"The Armentrouts really *are* tracking us?" said Tish, her eyes wide.

"Someone is," said Connall. "They're the ones keep showing up. It's a good chance they're the ones who planted this."

Kat looked at Tish. The unspoken question hung between them: *Why?*

"What do we do now?" asked Kat.

A grin lit Jamie's face.

"Oh, now we have some fun," he said.

"If you want us to," added Connall.

Another look passed between Kat and Tish. They nodded at the same time.

"First, we turn it off," said Connall.

"Won't they know?" asked Tish.

"Of course," said Jamie. "They'll think it either ran out of power, it was found or fell off, or there's a glitch. That's where the fun starts. And the cursing. On their part."

"What do you mean?" asked Kat.

Jamie grinned wider.

"I take it for a ride," he said. "Find it a new home."

When the women looked puzzled, Connall explained.

"He'll stick it on a delivery van or long-haul lorry," he said.

"So, Uly and Erma will follow the truck instead of our car," said Kat.

"Exactly," said Jamie.

Kat laughed. "I like your idea of fun."

Maybe Tish was right. Maybe the Geraghtys *were* friends, after all.

Jamie pocketed the tracker as they walked back to the restaurant. They were just in time to see the food being delivered to their table.

"Ah. The cat got the canary," said Tim to Jamie as his son sat down. "I see the feathers on your lips. You found a tracker."

"That we did," said Jamie, pulling it out to show his father.

"It just doesn't make sense that they would track us," said Tish.

"Maybe it does, Mary Pat," said Tim. "In Europe, there's a strong market for big American classics, like your Buick. Could be they're after the car."

"They *did* seem determined to buy it," said Kat, turning to Tish. "And a bit put out that we—you—wouldn't sell it."

"Maybe if they can't buy it, they're thinking to steal it," said Tim.

"Stealing it would be cheaper," added Connall.

"Maybe," said Tish. "But Tim, you've seen them. I can't believe they're car thieves."

People would say we don't look like jewel thieves, either, thought Kat.

"You can't always tell by looking," said Maureen, as if she'd heard Kat's thoughts. "You'd be surprised by some of the corporate thieves we've run into."

"Excuse me." Deirdre glanced up at the server setting plates in front of her. "We were wondering earlier—Americans come to Ireland all the time to hear Irish folk music. Is there any place close by where we can hear American folk music played in its natural habitat?"

"Well," said their server, landing the last plate, "there's the Crossroads Café at the highway junction. It's open mic tonight. I don't know what you'll get," she said, "but I guarantee it will be authentic. They have turtle races, too."

"Turtle races?" said Jamie. "You're having me on."

"Nope. People put their racing turtles in a big circle chalked on the floor. The first turtle to reach the edge of the circle wins. People place bets on their favorites, just like in horse racing."

Deirdre laughed.

"Brilliant!" said Jamie.

"I'm in," said Siobhan. "I've never heard the like."

"Will you join us?" Maureen asked Kat and Tish.

"Absolutely," said Tish, delight written on her face. "Won't we?" she added, looking at Kat.

There was a silent plea on Tish's face.

"Sure," said Kat. "It sounds like fun."

CHAPTER 23

AT THE CROSSROADS CAFÉ

Kat and Tish felt comfortable leaving the Buick hidden behind the motel, now that the tracker was disabled. They climbed—Tish a bit hesitantly—onto the big bikes behind Deirdre and Maureen. Less than five minutes later, Kat was grinning ear to ear when she dismounted at the Crossroads Café.

"I haven't been on a motorcycle since high school," she said to Deirdre, as she took off her borrowed helmet. "I'd forgotten how much fun they are. Even if they do have only two wheels." She looked over to Tish, pulling her arms from Maureen's waist.

"What did you think?" she called, as her friend freed herself from her helmet.

"Definitely faster than the Segway," laughed Tish.

"Segway?" asked Jamie. "Those motorized skateboards?"

"They're not that bad," said Tish.

"They can hit six miles an hour," said Kat with a straight face.

"Ah. You're right." Jamie nodded. "Skateboards are faster."

Tish lifted the hair from the back of her neck. "The wind on the bike felt wonderful," she said. "But it feels even muggier, now that we've stopped."

"I've got scissors and clippers with me," said Deirdre. "Just say the word."

"You travel with hair scissors?" said Tish.

"I'm the only thing keeps Tim from looking like an old rocker," said Deirdre.

"As long as he never looks like Mick Jagger, I'm content," said Maureen, taking off her helmet.

"Are you sure you're my daughter?" asked Siobhan.

"Stones fan?" asked Kat.

"She was the first member of their fan club," said Maureen.

"Second. My friend Evelyn was their first," said Siobhan sadly.

"It's been a mark of shame for her ever since," said Maureen, chuckling, and gave her mother a one-arm hug.

Connall held the door as they trooped inside.

The Crossroads Café was clearly the center of the community. Murals depicting the sights all along Route 66 lined the walls, like they covered the walls of many businesses outside. The largest room was lined with booths. Free-standing tables filled the center of the floor. At the far end, a small, raised stage held a couple chairs and three microphones on stands. A guitarist and fiddler tuned up as the washtub bass player watched them idly.

"I didn't think those were real." Deirdre pointed at the bass. "Siobhan, look…"

"I have to talk to them," said Siobhan. She took her pad

and camera out of the bag she had strung across her body and followed Deirdre to the stage. They were soon engaged in conversation with the band.

"Is it all right if we move these?" Maureen asked a passing server laden with food, as she pointed at a cluster of tables. "We'll put them back."

"Go for it," he said.

"The usual for those of us driving. But for those not? First round's mine," Tim said to Kat and Tish. "Mary Pat, what's your pleasure?"

"Well, I... Well, I..." said Tish. "Wow. It's been years since I've had anything but wine. But tonight, I feel daring." She turned to Kat. "Luke used to talk about some kind of tea?"

"A Long Island Iced Tea?" said Kat.

"Yes! Long Island Iced Tea, please," she said.

"Are you sure?" said Kat, "They're pretty strong..."

"I'm over 21," Tish told her, rather sharply.

Kat held up a hand. "Just saying... A Coke for me, please, Tim."

As Tim and Connall headed toward the bar, through a door on one side of the main room, the knocking sound of pool balls and the pinging of pinball machines came through another door next to the stage.

"Ah. Pinball. Music to my ears," said Jamie turning toward the sounds and cracking his knuckles.

"Oh, you think you're good, do you?" asked Tish.

"Is that a challenge?" asked Jamie.

"It most certainly is," she said.

"You play pinball?" asked Kat.

Tish turned to her. "Who do you think taught Luke?" she asked.

Kat lifted her eyebrows, remembering how Tish had described the Halloween costumes she'd designed for her children. "You were definitely the cool mom on the block."

"Now you'll be the cool auntie," said Jamie. "I promise I will be easy on you."

"No need," said Tish. "I won't be easy on you."

"Let's get some change, then, and you can put your money where your mouth is," said Jamie, nudging her toward the bar.

"Coming here was a wonderful idea," said Siobhan, as she and Deirdre returned to join Kat and Maureen at the table. She began to give them a bit of background on the band that was about to play.

Tim and Connall came back and dealt out the drinks. Jamie and Tish were right behind them, Jamie sorting the coins in his hand.

"I'm just saying a bit of money on the side will help focus our attention," he said to Tish.

"I'd hate to be responsible for taking your allowance," said Tish.

"Those are fighting words, they are."

Tish scooped up her drink and sipped.

"How is it?" asked Kat.

"Good," said Tish. "Stronger than I expected for something named 'iced tea.'"

"Don't let it go to your head or Jamie will beat you," said Kat. "Then what would Luke say?"

"Come on, then, Auntie," said Jamie, tapping Tish's shoulder. "Let's see what you've got."

Tish set her large shoulder bag on the table next to Kat and rubbed her hands together. "You're on," she said, picked up her drink, and followed him into the game room.

"This I have to see," said Connall. "Dee?"

"Oh, I'm with you," said Deirdre, getting up.

"I'm with you, too," said Tim, and the three of them followed Jamie and Tish.

"So, who's your money on?" Siobhan asked Kat, as they walked away.

"I've learned never to bet against Ti... Mary Patrice," said Kat. "She never fails to surprise me."

At least that, she thought, *is completely true.*

"Who is Luke?" Maureen asked.

As the emcee announced the start of the open mic event, and introduced the first band, Kat realized she was going to have to make conversation.

Stick as close to the truth as possible, and let the others do most of the talking, she thought.

As long as they didn't ask about the family connection between Tish and her. For that, Kat had no answer.

"He's Mary Patrice's youngest," Kat explained, as the small trio started to play bluegrass tunes. "She has three. Two sons and a daughter."

"They're quite good," said Siobhan, nodding toward the band.

"They are that," said Maureen, who was gently tapping her fingers against her thigh. She turned back to Kat. "We've just got the two boys, if you don't count the devils inside them."

"Have you always ridden motorcycles?" Kat asked her in order to head off any questions about *her* family.

"Tim and I met in a motorcycle club in college," said Maureen, "and the boys could ride almost before they could walk."

"Did you learn from Siobhan?"

"Good heavens, no," said Siobhan. "I didn't start riding until after the breast cancer."

Kat froze. It was like Connall's innocent question about Tish's reasons for taking Route 66. Siobhan's question hid a landmine.

"I'm sorry," said Kat. "It's none of my business."

"No need," said Siobhan. "It's old news. After I had the mastectomies and Colm left, Tim bought me a small Honda. Maureen insisted I learn and join her group of women riders. It was the best thing for me. Riding with them saved me." She calmly took a drink of her soda.

Against her will, Kat felt her eyes shoot down and back again. Siobhan smiled understandingly as Kat blushed.

"I'm sorry," said Kat. "I didn't... I mean..."

Siobhan laughed. "Not to worry. Most folks look when I first tell them."

"You had a...mastectomy?" The word stuck in Kat's mouth.

"I did," said Siobhan. "A double. Today, it probably wouldn't have been done. But at the time, mastectomy was pretty much the only way. Women have more choices now. Less radical choices."

"I wouldn't have known," said Kat.

"It's the prostheses," said Siobhan. "They look pretty good."

"She wasn't going to get them," said Maureen. "She said she was forty-five, her husband was gone, her kids were grown. What did she need with breasts?"

"Forty-five?" said Kat softly. She felt sick.

"This one," Siobhan patted Maureen's arm, "and our women friends talked me into it. I'm glad they did. I know what's missing, of course," said Siobhan. "But with my clothes on, no one else does. I find it gives me a bit more confidence when I meet strangers. Foolish maybe, but that's the truth of it. Besides," she chuckled. "I improved a bit on nature. Not a lot, but enough."

"You didn't consider reconstruction?"

"I considered it," said Siobhan. "Briefly. But I'd done enough surgery. And I didn't like the idea of all that," she waved a hand at her breasts, "foreign stuff, silicone, under my skin. So, I chose the built-out bra."

"But the surgery?" said Kat. "I'm forty-five now. I can't imagine..."

She didn't want to imagine.

"I'm not sure I could go through with something that... that..." She couldn't bring herself to say *disfiguring*. "How could you stand it?"

"My women friends," said Siobhan again. "And my family. They got me through."

She squeezed Maureen's hand. "They helped me see that what I lost wasn't a patch on what I still had. My grandchildren. Traveling the world with them. My work."

"Seeing the look on Da's face, outside the pub that night, when you swung a leg over that big old BMW," said Maureen.

Siobhan produced a wicked smile. "You could be right."

"But what if you had been alone?" persisted Kat.

Siobhan gave Kat a look so long the band finished the set.

"You're only as alone as you choose to be," said Siobhan quietly, under the applause.

"You must have been afraid," said Kat. She felt tears rise in her eyes. *Damn, damn, damn,* she thought, and blinked them away.

"Oh, sure," said Siobhan. "Plenty of times. Even now. Every time I go in for a check-up or feel a twinge."

She gave Kat another long look. "You can't let fear rule you, Katherine. It will poison your life."

Kat was opening her mouth to say something—she had no idea what—when Connall came back, and put his hand on Maureen's shoulder.

"That, Ma," he chortled, "was a beautiful thing to see."

CHAPTER 24

TEA AND TURTLE RACES

Tim and the two pinballers were right behind Connall and Deirdre.

"It was, love, it was," agreed Tim, grinning broadly.

"It's shameful," said Jamie. "My own blood gloating over my humiliation."

"She beat him?" Maureen asked Tim.

"She did most resoundingly," said Tish, drifting up and setting down her empty glass. "Four out of five."

"I think she gave him the first one so he'd be overconfident," said Connall.

Tish reached up to tap her nose and almost missed. "On the nose," she said.

"Oh, my," said Maureen, smiling.

"She said only wine before tonight?" asked Siobhan.

"She did."

"She'll have a head in the morning," said Siobhan.

"I believe she will," agreed Maureen.

Kat took a closer look at Tish and realized Siobhan and

Maureen were right. Her friend was drunk. She would definitely feel it in the morning.

"It's the American machines," Jamie was saying. "They're rigged against the Irish."

"Ladies and gents," interrupted the emcee, as the 1950s song, "The Hokey Pokey," began to play over the sound system. It was met by cheers and applause. "It's now time for the first heat of the Crossroads Café's weekly *Hokey Pokey Speed Race!*"

Throughout the main room—more crowded now as patrons came in from the bar—people were standing, singing, and doing the Hokey Pokey. Even a few pool players, cues in hand, were "shaking it all about."

It was clear to Kat that Tish wasn't the only one having a good time.

"Oh! I have to see!" said Tish, rooting through her big purse. "I put five dollars on…" She looked down at her betting ticket. "Number 74. Ruby!"

She slung her bag over her shoulder and turned away from the Geraghtys' table.

"Tish, maybe you should si…" Kat started to say, but Tish was weaving her way toward the chalked ring on the floor near the stage.

"Ruby! Ruby!" she chanted, as she took a few fancy steps, waggled her fingers in the air and turned around.

"You'd better go look after her," said Maureen to her sons, nodding toward Tish. "Maybe you'll do better betting on the turtles," she added to Jamie.

"I don't think it's my night," he said.

"Come on, brother. I'll spot you a dollar so you can bet on a turtle." Connall tugged him away.

"At least Mary Pat is still upright," said Tim. "It could be worse."

You have no idea, thought Kat.

At least Tish could only bet five dollars. The "inventory" suitcase, holding more than a million in cash, was locked in their room at the Wagon Wheel.

"Come on," said Maureen, pulling Kat to her feet. "We can't miss this."

There were six turtles in the race, each with a number sticky-noted to its back. A chalkboard on the stage listed their names next to their numbers. They were corralled in a low enclosure, about six feet in diameter, that surrounded a dot in the center of the chalked circle. One of them, number 6—named Speedy, Kat was amused to see—was asleep. Its head and all its extremities were tucked firmly into its shell.

It was clear why Tish's favorite, number 74, was named Ruby. About half again the size of Kat's hand, it had green and yellow markings on its skin and shell, and a red slash of color behind its eyes.

"Isn't she pretty?" Tish gushed, as Kat slipped in next to her tipsy friend. "She's a red-eared slider. Isn't that a sweet name?"

Still shaken as she was by Siobhan's confession, Kat couldn't help but smile and discover, to her surprise, that she was glad they'd come.

"I think you've chosen a champion, Mary Pat," said Connall, standing on the other side of Tish. He pointed toward Ruby, who had started to move toward the outer chalked ring and had her head butted against the aluminum corral. "She looks alert. Ready to race. She's done this before, do you think?" he added, sounding like a sports announcer.

"She's definitely a winner," said Tish, nodding. "I have a good eye for turtles."

Kat grinned more broadly.

"Did you like the Long Island Iced Tea?" she asked innocently.

"Oh, it was so *good*!" said Tish. "I asked Tim to get me another." She leaned into Kat. "But I think he forgot," she added in a voice that was supposed to be a whisper.

Kat caught Tim's eye. The Irishman winked.

"Well, maybe you can have one another time," said Kat. "Right now, you'll want to keep your wits about you for the race."

"Oh, yes," said Tish. "You're right." Tish made another swipe at her nose. This time she did miss and almost poked herself in the eye.

"Who did you bet your dollar on, Jamie?" Maureen asked her son.

"The big bruiser over there," he said, pointing. "Number 14. He's called Rocky."

"Slow," said Tish, knowingly. "Bigger means slower."

"Bigger means older and smarter," said Jamie. "You'll see. He'll outsmart the rest of them."

"Seventy-four loves me more! Seventy-four loves me more! Seventy-four loves..." Tish began chanting.

Kat shook her head and smiled to herself.

The turtles, except for Speedy, had edged outward and, like Ruby, had their noses pressed against the corral. Rocky was edging his way sideways along the twelve-inch-high aluminum wall.

"Betting is now closed!" said the emcee. "Owners will step out of the ring."

One middle-aged man in a T-shirt leaned over and gave Speedy a final gentle prod in the shell. There was no response. The audience laughed. The turtle's owner stood up, raised his eyebrows, and shrugged, hands out.

"Busy night," he said to the crowd around the circle and winked. There were hoots and applause.

"Everyone, get ready!"

Two men wearing Crossroads Café T-shirts stepped toward the corral.

"Get set!"

They bent down and gripped the edges of the turtle corral.

"Aaand…"

As the corral wranglers lifted the enclosure and moved away, the emcee brought down a gavel on a block of wood.

"Let's turtle!" shouted the crowd.

Ruby began a determined waddle toward the chalk line. Rocky, startled by the sudden disappearance of the aluminum palisade, turned away from his side of the circle and began to scuttle to the far side. Almost immediately, he ran up against the solid form of Speedy, still immobile in the center of the circle.

"Go around him, you daft animal!" shouted Jamie at his favorite. Connall and Tim were laughing.

"Ruby! Ruby!" yelled Tish, pumping a fist.

Siobhan had knelt on the floor, her family standing protectively behind her, and was taking pictures.

Rocky got a clawed toe up onto Speedy's shell but slipped off again. He tried again, this time gaining a bit of traction. Speedy slept on. Ruby's waddling pace increased.

Kat started to laugh. "I never really believed a tortoise could outrun a hare," she said, "but now I see it's possible."

"I suspect turtle doping," said Jamie.

"Oh, stop whinging," Deirdre told him.

"He hasn't lost yet," Jamie said, as Ruby crossed the chalk line.

"He has now," said Connall, putting his hand out. "Pay up."

Around the room there were groans, laughter, and cheers.

"I won! I won!" cheered Tish, clapping.

"You'd better go collect your winnings," Kat told her.

"Oh! Yes! Maybe there's another race," said Tish. "I could double my money."

"It doesn't pay to be overconfident now, Mary Pat," said Maureen, raising a finger warningly.

"Best to quit now, Auntie," said Jamie, as he dropped a ten-dollar bill into Connall's hand. "I feel my luck beginning to turn."

"We'll see," said Tish and hurried away.

Connall pocketed his winnings from Jamie, then held a business card out toward Kat, as they all moved back toward their table.

"You shouldn't have any more trouble with your stalkers," he said. "But if you do, give me a call. We have some tricks you could try."

Kat looked at the card, then up at Connall.

"Won't you all be off somewhere?" she asked.

"We have all summer, remember?" said Tim. "We've rented a house near a river in Joplin…"

"Carthage," corrected Maureen.

Tim turned a thumb toward his wife in affirmation. "Carthage. We'll be there for a little over a week. It's time to pay the piper. We have some work to do."

"I'll be searching for cemeteries while they work," said Deirdre, rolling her eyes at Maureen. "I have my orders."

"Twenty dollars!" said Tish, rushing up. "Ruby won twenty dollars for me! I knew she would when I looked into her sweet little black eyes."

"Maybe we should have another go at pinball," said Jamie. "It would give me a chance to earn back some of what I lost tonight."

"It wasn't more than ten euros," Connall told his brother. "Quit carrying on so."

"Much as I hate to put an end to this," said Maureen, "it's probably best we all be going off to our hotels. Connall, help me put these tables right?"

"No more races?" Tish looked bereft. "But I might win again."

"You won't think that tomorrow morning," said Kat. "We'd better get you to bed."

"Okay, then," said Tish, pouting. "But I want to say good-bye to Ruby."

"Do you think she'll be okay on the motorcycle?" Kat asked Maureen, as Tish moved deliberately into the crowd of well-wishers around the turtle racers.

"She'll be fine," said Maureen. She squeezed Kat's wrist lightly. "She's a bit pissed, but I've carried friends who were totally wrecked and gotten them home safely."

They'd just finished putting the tables and chairs back where they belonged when Tish hurried back.

"Okay, I'm ready to go. We should go, now," she said in a rush.

"Well, all right," said Maureen laughing. She took Tish's arm. "You're behind me again."

CHAPTER 25

HENRY INVESTIGATES

"Why are you calling *me*?" Carlisle demanded.

"I'm talking to everyone in the family, Mr. O'Donnell, trying to get an idea of where to find your mother," said Henry.

He yawned. The Sisters in Crime event the previous evening had gone on long after closing. They were a great group.

"I'm the one who recommended you, remember?" Carlisle's voice buzzed like an angry wasp through the phone's speaker.

"Of course, Mr. O'Donnell, but if you could take a moment and think... Who might your mother have gone to when she left?"

"How the hell should I know?"

Henry rubbed his forehead just above the bridge of his nose. He glanced at the photo of Tish that Fitz had given him. Times like these, he wondered why he did this kind of work.

"Friends? Family? She must have mentioned someone."

"Really, Fox. Do you pay attention to *your* mother yammering on?"

Yes, well, that was a path best not followed, Henry thought. He'd forgiven his parents, for the most part, but still...

"I really resent this interrogation," said Carlisle.

"I'm sorry you think I'm interrogating you, Mr. O'Donnell. You did me the honor of recommending me to help your father." Henry cringed at the groveling tone in his voice, but it usually paid to massage egos like Carlisle's. "I owe it to you both to be as thorough as I can be."

"Okay, fine," said Carlisle. "I don't know where my mother would have gone. As far as I know, she has no friends. No other family. She doesn't do anything. She's just *there*. You know what I mean?"

"All right, sir. One last thing. Do you have your mother's phone number?" Fitz hadn't included it on the form Henry had given him, and Fitz hadn't yet returned his phone call asking for it.

"Why would I? We don't have anything to talk about."

"Do you have your brother's phone number?"

"God no. Madison might have it."

"Thank you, Mr. O'Donnell. That's all."

Henry was barely able to break the connection before Carlisle cut him off.

He leaned back in his chair, rubbed his temples, took a sip of his lukewarm coffee, and made his next call.

"Ms. Mountjoy, my name is Henry Fox. I'm a private investigator your father hired to find your mother."

"Why?"

"Why?" asked Henry, taken aback by the hostility in Madison's voice.

"Yes. Why does he want to find her? I mean, what did she ever do for him? Or me?"

For a moment, Henry was at a loss for words.

"Your father needs her to sign divorce papers so he can remarry," he finally said.

"Oh, like I'm going to let that happen," said Madison. "If he wants to screw her, who cares? But I'm not going to let that little gold digger gouge all his money out of him. She's younger than Luke, and *he's* only 25!"

Henry paused in the middle of framing his next question.

"Your younger brother is 25?"

"Disgusting, isn't it? The thought of my parents doing it." Henry could feel her shudder through the phone. "I mean, I was eight. What if I'd walked in on them? To think of my father and that little slut..."

Madison made gagging noises.

"It must be distressing for your mother, too, I'm sure," said Henry.

"She wasn't so distressed that she forgot to take my jewelry with her, the selfish bitch," said Madison.

"Your jewelry?" asked Henry, a bit confused.

"All the stuff she had hidden in her closet. She was always having our jeweler make things for her on the sly. I *thought* she was making it for me. For when she died, though why she expected me to wait that long, I don't know. But now she's gone and taken it. *My* jewelry!"

Ah, he thought. *That jewelry.*

He shook his head.

Knowing the answer before he asked, Henry said, "Do you have any idea where your mother might have gone when she left?"

"Who cares?"

Unbelievable, thought Henry. *The venom.*

"Friends? A holiday home?"

Madison snorted. "Friends? My mother? She has no life."

"Can I assume, then, that you don't have a contact number for her?" said Henry, wanting to end this call as soon as possible.

"Not anymore. As soon as she walked out and took all my jewelry, I deleted her number from my phone."

"Do you have a number for your brother, Luke?"

"Why? He won't know where she is."

"He might have her number."

A big sigh. "Hold on."

He did, while Madison scrolled through her contacts, then rattled off Luke's number.

"He's out in Oregon some place," she added, like it was another planet.

"Thank you, Ms. Mountjoy," said Henry, and hung up.

He threw himself back in his chair, ran his hands into his hair, and blew out a breath. He looked again at the picture of Tish next to his computer.

"Wherever you are," he told it fiercely, "keep going."

Henry came up the stairs reluctantly. He'd made a fresh cup of coffee, talked to Martine and his other staff members to remind himself that there were kind, normal people in the world, and sat at his desk again. He was dreading this last call.

"Luke O'Donnell?" he asked, when a male voice answered the phone.

"Nope. That would be my husband, Luke O'Donnell Fonseca. May I ask who's calling?"

"Henry Fox. I'm a private investigator in Evanston."

"May I ask what this is regarding?"

"I'm looking for his mother."

"Ah. One moment."

One minute. Two. Five.

The husband either had to go a distance to find Luke or there had been a conversation about his call. Henry had been told Luke's husband was an attorney.

"Luke Fonseca," said a pleasant male voice.

There were faint noises in the background. Luke had put him on speaker.

Ah. Domestic legal advice, thought Henry.

"Mr. Fonseca, my name is Henry Fox. I'm a private investigator here in Evanston. Fitz O'Donnell hired me to find Tish O'Donnell. I'm hoping you can help me."

"You can call me Luke, Henry. And as far as I'm concerned, my mother can remain unfound."

Oh dear, thought Henry. *Another one.*

"Why is that?" he had to ask.

"Because I couldn't be happier that she's left. She should have gone years ago, the way he treats her."

"How is that?"

"Like she's stupid, which I guarantee you she's not. She's smart, funny, and a brilliant jewelry designer, though my dad won't admit it. I don't understand why she married Pop in the first place."

I don't either, thought Henry.

"Much as that might be true, Luke, Mr. O'Donnell needs your mother's signature on divorce papers so he can marry Hilary Schoenmeyer."

Luke laughed. "Yes. I heard about that. I can't believe he's really going to marry her. The upside is that it's got my sister really wound up."

"Oh?" said Henry.

"Oh, yeah. She's sure the girlfriend... Hilary? That Hilary will only stay until the insurance company pays out on the robbery before she divorces Pop and takes half or more of the money with her. If she doesn't take the store and the house as well."

"You know about the robbery, then?"

"Yeah. Maddie Mags told me."

"Maddie Mags?"

"Madison. The sister formerly known as Mary Margaret or Maggie."

"I'm sure she's just as concerned as you are that a younger woman might be taking advantage of your father..."

"Me? I'm not concerned," said Luke. "I hope she takes everything. It would serve him right. Maggie's only concerned that she'll lose access to the Bank of Fitz and the inheritance she thinks she so richly deserves. She's already frothing because Mom took all her jewelry when she left."

"But I understood that Mr. Mountjoy was well off."

"Teddy? Yeah, he's got money. But he's smart enough to hang onto it. He keeps Mags on a short leash, financially. She probably knows he'll dump her someday and she'll need Pop's money. That's why she's panicked."

"But what about your mother," said Henry.

"My mom? You mean what happens if Hilary takes it all?" He laughed. "Hilary will have to be happy with what's left. My mom will have a great attorney."

"Do you have any idea where your mother might have gone when she left, Luke? Friends? Other relatives, like cousins?"

"Henry, you're only doing your job, but even if I knew

where Mom was, I wouldn't tell you. You're working for my dad."

"Would you have a contact number for her?"

"Same goes, Henry. I won't have you calling and bothering her, not for my dad."

Ah ha, thought Henry. *He didn't say he didn't have a contact. He just won't give it to me.*

"You know, Luke," said Henry, curious to see what Tish's son would say, but hating himself for asking, "your father has raised the question that your mother might have been involved in the robbery that took place at the store. Do you think…"

"*What?*" said Luke, his outrage vibrating through the connection all the way from Oregon. "She didn't… That's insane. My mother would *never* do that. You do know the store should have been hers, don't you? But her father gave it to my dad. Pop never even made her a partner."

Henry winced.

"Hmm," said Henry. "The police might think that's a good reason to stage a robbery—to get what she thought was hers."

"Shit," said Luke. "Yeah, I can see that." He paused. "Can you hold on a moment?"

The background noises disappeared. Henry was sure he'd been muted. He could almost see Luke's husband, hands waving frantically to get him off the phone so they could have an intense discussion.

"I don't suppose you can forget I said that?" said Luke, coming back on the line suddenly.

"Said what?" asked Henry.

Luke laughed weakly.

"Luke, I may work for Mr. O'Donnell, but as far as I know, there's no evidence your mother committed a crime, and no reason to think she's involved. I get the feeling the police don't believe it either."

"So, you can't force her to go back to Evanston."

"No, Luke. I can't. And at this time, I'm not obliged to tell the police or your father where she is when I locate her." *Probably not how O'Donnell and the police would see it,* he thought, *but…* "My only obligation is to find your mother and deliver your father's message: that he wants her to return to sign divorce papers so they can both get on with their lives."

"That's it?"

"That's it.

There was a pause. Henry could almost hear Luke thinking it over.

"Well, I can't tell you where my mother is, and won't give you her number. So, I can't be of any help to you."

"If you hear from her, perhaps you'll give her my number and ask her to call me?"

"You can give it to me," said Luke, "but I make no promises."

"Thank you for your time," said Henry, after he gave Luke his contact information.

He wondered, after he broke the connection, what Tish would do when—or if—Luke gave her the message.

Luke dropped the hand holding the phone. He stared at Jesse, who'd listened to the entire conversation.

"I thought you said your mom wasn't in trouble."

"That's what she told me," said Luke.

"Well, I'm glad she'll have Felicia Denham in her corner. Because it sounds like she may be in trouble now."

CHAPTER 26
TISH AND THE TURTLE

Kat woke to the sound of Tish throwing up in the bathroom. She tossed off the sheet and went to hold Tish's hair back.

"I'm going to die," said Tish into the toilet bowl.

"No, you just wish you would. We'll stop and get you a Coke on the road," Kat told her, not unsympathetically.

Tish lost more of the previous night into the basin. "I didn't think you were so mean."

"It will make you feel better. That and a couple aspirin."

Tish gagged again.

"I didn't realize that being 'normal' for you would include tossing your innards up," said Kat, less sympathetically this time.

"Shut up."

Kat smiled.

With Kat's help, Tish staggered to her feet and rinsed her mouth out in the sink in the room.

"If you think you're okay, I'm going to get a shower," said Kat, after she helped Tish back to bed.

Tish nodded and winced.

When Kat came out again, Tish was sitting in the same place, eyes closed.

"How are you doing?" she asked.

"Awful," said Tish. "Why is it so bright in here?"

"Do you think you can manage a shower? It might help."

"Death will help."

"You'll be better in a few hours. Here." Kat handed Tish a glass of water and two aspirin. "Drink a lot of water. You need to get hydrated again."

"I'll just throw up again."

"I don't think so. I doubt you have anything left."

Tish took a sip, and another as Kat towel dried her hair and fluffed it into place.

Tish finished her water slowly, then moved gently off the bed.

"I think I'll try that shower."

As she dressed, Kat heard something scratching in Tish's purse.

She froze.

"Oh, hell," she muttered. "I hate mice."

But in Tish's condition, Kat knew she was the better person to deal with stowaway livestock. She carefully opened Tish's large bag.

Two beady eyes looked at her from a reptilian face. The sticky note was still glued to its back.

Tish stepped out of the bathroom.

"Tish. You took the turtle?"

"I did?"

"Well, *I* didn't put this in here."

She held the open bag toward Tish. The turtle looked up at Tish.

"Oh." Tish closed her eyes. "I remember. I went to say

good-bye. She looked at me so sadly, like she hated me to go…"

"Tish, you stole someone's turtle. In Missouri, that may get us shot."

"Maybe we can just let it go?"

"No. You heard what that waitress at the restaurant said. These are people's 'racing turtles.' They're pets. We can't just let it go. We have to take it back."

A storm of panic washed over Tish's face. "I can't tell them I took it!"

"We'll tell them we found it in the road."

"Will they believe us?"

"We can only hope," said Kat, who had passed through anger to annoyance and was heading toward amusement. "But you'll need to get a new purse."

"Why?"

"Your friend peed in this one."

Tish looked like she was going to throw up again.

They finally finished dressing, Tish groaning throughout the process. Kat let her sit in the front seat of the Buick while she packed the car. Then they drove down to the Crossroads Café. Fortunately, it was open.

"I can't go in there," said Tish. "They might remember me."

Kat sighed, lifted the turtle out of Tish's handbag, and went into the café.

"Hi! Just one?" asked the woman at the counter.

Kat hefted the turtle.

"Actually, we were heading out of town and saw this outside at the curb. We were here for the races last night and wondered if it belonged to someone?"

"Oh, my goodness that's Ruby, Ray's racing turtle! He was so frantic last night trying to find her."

"Can you see she gets home?" asked Kat.

"Of course. Thank you for doing this. I'll call him now. I know he'll want to give you a reward."

"Not necessary," said Kat. "Happy to help." *More than happy*, she thought. "But my friend is a bit hung over. If I could get a Coke and some toast to go? We're getting a late start this morning."

"Of course. On the house."

"No, no," said Kat. "I'll pay for it. And maybe a coffee for me?"

The woman turned and shouted toward the kitchen. "Jonah! Can you come get Ruby? Someone found her!"

A young, bearded man came out to the counter.

"Hey, girl," he said, taking the turtle. "We were worried about you."

"Can you find her a box and call Ray?"

"Sure," said Jonah, and carried the turtle away.

"Then bring back a coffee, Coke, toast, and a couple of Josie's cinnamon rolls. To go," she called after him.

Tish woke when Kat got in and started the car.

"What did they say?" she asked.

"They wanted to give me a reward for returning the turtle. Maybe this is a new scam for us. You steal a turtle. I give it back. We get a free breakfast." She nodded at the bag on the seat between them as she pulled from the curb.

She glanced up. Tish was glaring at her.

Kat laughed.

"Eat your toast and drink your Coke. You'll feel better," she said, grinning.

CHAPTER 27
DEVIL'S ELBOW

Instead of eating, Tish fell asleep, leaving Kat to the road and her thoughts.

It was already hot, but the big car was cooled by what her father had jokingly called its "four-sixty" air conditioner: Open all four windows and go sixty miles per hour. As a child, Kat had thought this hilarious.

The memory warmed her.

Whenever she and her father were on the road, especially after her mother had died, he'd told her stories about Route 66 and the other highways he'd driven, the things he'd seen, the breakdowns he'd had, the repairs he'd made. They were great adventures, and he'd shared them all with Kat. She'd absorbed his tales like a plant absorbs water, and they'd been almost as vital to her.

She'd been a vintage car junkie even then, just like her dad and the other mechanics at the garage.

We weren't much different from the Armentrouts, she thought grudgingly.

She glanced at Tish. Strands of her long hair whipped

out the half open passenger window, but Tish slept on, oblivious.

Kat smiled at her fondly.

Back at Superior Jewelers, Kat had never thought of Tish as other than her boss's wife. She'd been careful to keep her distance because Tish was also the woman she'd inadvertently wronged by sleeping with Fitz before she'd gone to work at Superior. When she'd met him, at a jewelry show, the bottom feeder had told her he was divorced.

Kat had never suspected that Tish would have the nerve to raid her husband's safe in the middle of the night. That she loved costumes and was a brilliant improv actress. That she could be fun, silly, and of all things, a turtle-napper.

On the road, Tish was relaxing into a true self she'd never shown anyone, at least anyone at the store. Or maybe she was relaxing because of the absence of Fitz.

Kat had never imagined she and Tish might become friends.

Can we be friends? thought Kat. After all, Tish didn't know who Kat truly was.

Do I even know any more?

Siobhan's friends and family had gotten her through the rough spots of her cancer surgery and treatment, she'd said. They'd sat with her, laughed and cried with her.

Who would Kat turn to when she needed friends?

She checked the guidebook, and hooked a left over the interstate, then right onto Highway Z running alongside it. Not long after, the Route bent away from the interstate, went in between two parallel strips of woods, then popped out onto four lanes of old concrete highway. Kat wondered if it was an original part of Route 66.

Not another car in sight. Four lanes all to herself.

She flexed her fingers in their leather driving gloves,

shoved her glasses up her nose, and relaxed, enjoying the power of the big car moving through the summer air, the tires humming on the concrete, bumping lightly over the expansion joints and the places where the surface had been repaired. The sound of freedom.

She almost missed the turn she wanted. The road immediately narrowed, and they were moving through countryside.

There was something in the road. Kat slowed.

Her shout of laughter woke Tish up.

"What?" said Tish. "What's so funny?"

"Turtle," gasped Kat. "Turtle in the road."

"Oh, stop," said Tish.

"Seriously." Kat wiped tears from her eyes. "He saw you coming, picked up his shell, and ran for the trees."

Tish glared at her.

"You're not going to let this go are you."

"Oh, I am *so* not letting this go." Kat glanced in the rearview mirror and started to laugh again. "I didn't know turtles could move that fast, except for your friend, Ruby. He's already in the weeds." She shot a sly look at Tish. "We should take him back to Cuba, enter him into the turtle races. We could clean up."

"Umm," said Tish thoughtfully. "You know what they say about payback."

Kat kept chuckling.

"You feeling better?" she finally asked.

Tish rolled her shoulders and stretched. "I am, a bit. Where are we?"

"Heading to a place called Devil's Elbow," said Kat. "I'm hoping we can find a spot by the river that's cool enough we can stop and eat something. Neither of us had breakfast."

"You're sure we're not heading to Montana?" asked Tish drily, referring to Kat's complete lack of a sense of direction.

"Oh! Oh!" Kat clutched her chest. "Stabbed in the heart." She grinned at her companion. "Is that the best you've got?"

Tish snorted. "I'm still hung over. Give me time."

Kat couldn't help it. "At the river, maybe we can find a turtle for you. Since you missed the last one." She started laughing again.

They came to a sharp bend where the road crossed a bridge over a river, running low between the banks.

Kat parked under the trees, and they found a shaded bit of coarse grass close to the water where they sat down. Tish sipped her warm Coke, gone flat in the heat. They split the toast and cinnamon rolls between them.

The nearness of the river created the illusion of coolness, but not a leaf twitched. The only sound was the distant, monotonous call of a lone tufted titmouse. Even the insects were too hot to fly.

Kat closed her eyes. Her skin prickled as perspiration popped out. Maybe if she didn't move...

"You know," Tish broke the silence, "despite the hangover, I had a really good time last night. Just being with friends."

Kat nodded. "It *was* fun."

Tish sighed. "It makes me wish we could just stop this."

"Stop this?" asked Kat, as if she didn't know what Tish meant.

"It's just that, being around the Geraghtys... They're such a nice family. And we keep lying to them."

"How did you lie?" asked Kat. "Nothing you told them wasn't the truth."

Tish looked at her. "I didn't know you could put that many negatives in a sentence."

"Doesn't make it not true."

"But..."

"You told them you left your husband."

"Yeees..."

"You told them you took the cash and jewelry you could and left."

"Yeees..."

"You told them about the Armentrouts following us."

"Okay..."

"You told them my dream was to drive Route 66."

"Fine..."

"Tish. You haven't lied."

"I told them we were cousins."

"Well, okay. That might have been a problem if they'd asked me about my Irishness or how we're related."

Tish looked guilty.

"What?"

"Something you should probably know..."

"Okay..." said Kat warily.

"I told Tim we'd owned a jewelry store."

Kat closed her eyes again. "And?" she asked.

"And that you worked for Fitz."

Kat sighed. She couldn't really get angry with Tish. She'd come very close to baring her soul to Siobhan the night before, too.

"Tish, this is why we can't collect people," she said, opening her eyes and turning a sapphire gaze on her friend. "Now we *do* have to figure out a lie. Two lies. How we're related, for one. Two, why and how I came to work for you. Three lies. Why I quit my job to run away with you."

"Maybe no one will ask."

"But we need a story in case they do."

"Sorry."

"Well, there's little chance we'll run into them again, so we probably won't need the story, and you won't have to lie."

"Oh."

A stricken look fell over Tish's face.

"There's something else, isn't there?" Kat asked.

"Deirdre invited us to stay with them in that house they've rented near Carthage."

Kat sighed again. "And you said yes."

"It sounded fun."

"Well, we can always change your mind."

Now Tish sighed, then nodded.

"Okay."

"Tish, I don't want to be the bad guy here."

"I'm just not cut out for this."

"Neither am I," said Kat.

Well, it wasn't *not* the truth. Exactly. She did, however, have more experience...editing...the truth than Tish had. Though she had to admit, Tish's ability to tell what wasn't *not* the truth was evolving rapidly.

"At least you watched all those heist movies," said Tish after a moment.

"Hardly practical experience." Kat leaned back and propped herself on her elbows. Was everyone's life this complicated?

"I wish we could just stop this," said Tish again.

This time Kat didn't pretend not to understand. "I do, too."

Tish looked at her. "Truly?"

"Of course. Tish, I don't like this any better than you do. The lying. The pretending." *Though I've been doing it all my life*, she thought. "But if we want to start new lives in California, we'll need money."

"We *have* money, though," said Tish, shifting to face Kat, her face bright with hope. "We have more than a million dollars! We can get jobs."

"Tish…" Kat trailed off. "I'm 45. You're 55. Are you prepared to work for minimum wage? I'm not."

Tish blinked, and her smile faded. Then brightened.

"We can open a store. I can do the designing, and you can manage it. We'd use my jewelry as starting inventory, along with the gemstones from Superior."

Kat felt sick. Tish had clearly been thinking about this.

"Look." Tish pointed at the river creeping past their lunch spot, her enthusiasm mounting. "We could dump Clapham's stones there. Like you dumped the gold in the Mississippi."

Kat levered herself from her elbows, folded her legs, and turned to face Tish.

"Tish," she said as gently as she could. "I don't want to spend the rest of my life working in a jewelry store. And as for the money…" she added, as she watched the happiness ebb from Tish's face, "…we're going to California. You can hardly get a fixer-upper house in California for a million dollars. Your house in Evanston was probably worth more than a million. You certainly can't open a business *and* get a home for that."

Tish's eyes grew large as the truth of that registered.

"And you won't have a million dollars," Kat went on relentlessly. "You'll have $650,000 and 65 percent of the stones. Remember what we agreed that night? Thirty-five percent of our inventory is mine. And Tish. I *need* that money. I need every dime we can get out of our inventory."

Her palms were sweating, and it wasn't due to the heat.

If Tish pulled out of their partnership, if she took all the stock from Superior—which she could do and there wasn't a thing Kat could do about it—and if she took the car—which she also had every right to do—Kat would have next to nothing.

"We've gotten ourselves into this, Tish. And I really don't know any way to get out of it other than to keep going forward. If you have any ideas, I'm open to them. I really am."

Tish turned and watched the river stumble over the rocks.

"No," she said finally. "I don't have any ideas. You're right."

Tish produced a large sigh and turned her dark brown eyes back to Kat. "If we each want our own fresh start, we have to get rid of the...the damned things. Stupid things," she corrected.

Kat hoped the relief didn't show on her face.

"So, we drive on?"

"We drive on," said Tish, pulling her feet under her and standing up.

They collected the paper trash and went back to the car. It wasn't any cooler inside the Buick.

"Are you feeling up for a sale?" asked Kat.

"Not really."

"I can try the next one alone, if you like." She really didn't want to. Tish always seemed to deflect suspicion. She wasn't sure she could do that by herself.

"No," said Tish, after thinking about it for a moment. "I think we work better as a team." She sighed. "And the sooner we get rid of the Clapham Collection, the happier I'll be."

"Maybe in Springfield?"

"Where's the guidebook?"

Kat handed it to her. Tish flipped through it, then got out her phone and searched.

"I think St. Robert would be better," she said.

"Why's that?"

"Fort Leonard Wood is right there," she said, "with all the Army personnel. They're always looking for jewelry for girlfriends and family. There's a small, family-owned chain of three stores nearby."

"You think it will be good for the Clapham diamonds?"

Tish nodded. "The Clapham stones aren't the basement of quality, and we can give them a good price, so it's probably a good fit. With the stores being owned by a family, they'll have the authority to buy, and hopefully the cash on hand, too."

Kat looked at Tish for a long beat.

"What?" asked Tish.

"We're getting frighteningly good at this," said Kat.

"I just want to get rid of all of this so we can be normal again."

That depends on us not getting caught, Kat almost said, but held her tongue.

"My only concern is that we're too close to the last place," said Tish.

"I really can't see a side-of-the-road pawnbroker who deals mostly in guns having much contact with a retail store like you describe," said Kat. "The two could probably even be in the same town and never even know the other one exists."

"Okay, then," said Tish. "The same story as at Jessup's?"

Kat nodded. "Let's find a place where we can change."

CHAPTER 28
HAYWIRE

"What do you mean you still can't find them?" asked Uly.

"Just what I said. They've dropped off the map," said Erma.

"You lost them yesterday."

"I know when I lost them," she snapped.

"So did the tracker fall off?"

"How the hell should I know? Maybe it's just a glitch."

Erma continued to fuss with the tablet. She checked it against her phone. She looked up troubleshooting advice for the tracker.

Uly kept his eyes on the road.

"You said the tracker was foolproof," he said.

"We're on Route 66, not in goddamn downtown Chicago. Signals are spotty."

"Then why are we depending on a tracker, if you're so smart?"

"I didn't know we'd get a flat tire, did I?"

"*Two* flat tires. I'll bet it was those bikers at the café let the air out of the tires. They looked the type."

"If you weren't such a chickenshit, we could have stolen the damned thing back in Illinois. But oh, no."

"I told you. There were too many damned people around."

"How many people were around that house? You could have broken into the garage."

"Oh, sure. Right. I didn't notice *you* volunteering to break in."

"You're the one with that kind of work experience," said Erma.

"That's right. And it's not an experience I want to have again. You want to steal a car, then you be the one goes to prison this time."

"Right, lover boy. You were so sure you could charm that red head. That worked out well, didn't it?"

"She's probably sleeping with that butch friend of hers."

"Oh, yeah. That must be it. That'd be the only reason she resisted your many charms."

"I don't know why we need *that* car anyway. There are plenty of places selling old cars along the Route. We should be able to find something to satisfy your buyer."

"We need *that* car because we have a buyer for *that* car. And now we don't have *that* car."

"Who cares?" asked Uly. "They're in Sweden. What do they know about cars? Send 'em something different. Tell 'em it's better."

Erma stared at him.

"I'd never make another sale if I don't deliver what people expect. I've spent years building this business."

"I'll bet they don't expect that half the cars you sell them are hot."

"They probably wouldn't care, even if they knew. And

they'll never know. Besides it keeps my costs down and increases my profit. Sometimes, baby brother, I wonder where you were when the brains were handed out."

"I noticed you didn't complain when I stole that last heap and went to prison fo..."

"Shut up! I've got them again. Jeee-zus! Where the *hell* have they been? And where are they going? They've gone off the Route."

"Why would they do that?"

"What am I? A psychic?" said Erma. "Get off at Rolla and follow my instructions. And be careful not to get too close."

"Yeah, yeah, yeah..."

JAMIE CAUGHT up with Connall at a park along the creek at Roubidoux Springs in Waynesville. His brother was sprawled on a bench, leaning against a picnic table under the trees, hands locked behind his head. He was watching the creek murmur by.

"You did it then?" asked Connall, seeing the look on his brother's face as Jamie walked up.

Jamie grinned. "Oh, sure," he said. "I found one of those big smiley gray delivery trucks. They'll maybe be halfway to New York by time they figure it out."

"You're a devil, you are," said Connall, getting up.

"I am that."

"I found a pub in town, or so it claims. Try it?"

"You're buying. I did the job."

Connall grinned. "Fair enough."

. . .

Late that afternoon, Uly and Erma found themselves on an empty country road, surrounded by fields. It was a long way north of Route 66. The only thing in sight was a giant, featureless warehouse surrounded by blacktop studded with grinning delivery trucks.

"The bitches," was all Erma had to say.

CHAPTER 29

BAD NEWS TRAVELS FAST

Johnny Beekman walked into his jewelry store showroom when the electronic buzzer on the door sounded. He took one look at the man closing the front door and started to sweat.

He'd had dealings with Clapham's errand boys before, but none like this. About six feet tall, he was dressed like a corner-office CEO just off the back nine. His ethnic mix was one Beekman couldn't identify, and he was damned if he'd ask about. The guy's face was like a road map of a bad detour. A twisted nose sat next to a glazed eye turned slightly outwards. The scar cutting through the eyebrow above and below it suggested the eye might be blind. The other eye was dark brown and as opaque as an alligator swamp.

"Beekman?"

"Yeah," croaked Johnny, then cleared his throat.

"Alf Clapham said you have something of his?"

Johnny wiped a damp hand on his pants as he reached into his pocket and laid a small plastic bag on the flimsy glass case between them while that dark eye stared at him.

The man's eyes flicked down and then back up.

"Who brought them in?"

"Runners for a pawnbroker out on the highway," said Johnny. "Harley Johnson. Said a couple sisters brought them in."

"Sisters? Like nuns?" said the stranger, irritation in his voice.

"No, no. Heh, heh. Nuns."

No amusement in that dark eye.

Johhny cleared his throat again. "No, like *sisters*. Mother died, left them the diamonds. Some kind of religious nut."

"These runners. They say what these sisters looked like?"

"Yes." Mr. Clapham's assistant had been—most—insistent about that: Find out what the women looked like.

Johnny repeated what Harley's boys had told him. They'd been very descriptive. Especially about the one with the hooters.

"Names?"

"Pauly Kelso and Marty Graves," said Johnny.

"The women were named Pauly and Marty?"

"Oh. Oh, the women's names. Heh. I thought you meant the runners..."

"I don't give a shit who the runners were, moron. The women. Their *names*."

"Yeah, yeah. Of course. Ummm..." Beekman dug around in his pocket and pulled out a crumpled piece of paper. "Kitty Carter and Terry Mason," he read, and before the scary stranger asked, he read off the address Kat had given the broker.

The scary stranger didn't even write it down.

"These guys see what the women were driving?"

Johnny's head bobbed up and down. Mr. Clapham's assistant had been most insistent about that, too.

"Some big old gas guzzler, like from the '50s."

"A Caddie?"

"Could be. Or maybe a Chevy. They didn't get a good look."

"Which way were they heading?"

"Harley's people said they went east, toward St. Louis. They tried to follow but lost them."

"They lost two old women in a gas guzzler." The stranger's lip curled in contempt.

Johnny nodded. There wasn't enough spit in his mouth to say anything.

The dark eye continued to stare while Johnny leaked sweat.

The lip curled again before the stranger scooped up the plastic bag and turned to the door.

The diamonds had cost Johnny more than two grand. His mouth opened to ask about payment, but his brain slammed it shut again. *Don't be that stupid*, said his brain.

When Johnny was sure the stranger was gone, he staggered to the door, flipped his sign to CLOSED, and returned to his office. Collapsing into his desk chair, he reached into a drawer and drew out a bottle. With a shaking hand, he poured himself a shot and thought about a vacation. In Alaska.

"THIS BETTER BE GOOD NEWS," said Alf Clapham.

"I got your stones."

"Fuck the stones. What did Beekman say about the women?"

"He didn't see 'em. Couple flunkies for some roadside

pawn shop brought the stones in. Said the women claimed to be sisters. In their 50s. Description was different from what you gave me, so they're using disguises."

"They know what they're doing, then."

The man in Springfield agreed.

"These flunkies know where the women went, after?"

"They thought St. Louis."

"They *thought*?"

"Assholes followed but lost them."

"*Lost* them?"

"That's the story."

The long silence from the office in Chicago was broken by the sound of a gold ingot tapping a wood desk.

"Smarter than I expected," muttered Clapham.

"So, I should head back to Houston?"

The man in Springfield certainly hoped so. He'd been halfway to that sprawling city and looking forward to his steak dinner, high-end hotel, and some accommodating female company, when Clapham had called. He'd had to drive all night just to get back to this ass-end of the world.

"No," said Clapham. "After they spooked in St. Louis, they'll stick to small towns where they think no one will find them. Why else stop at some nowhere hillbilly hock shop?"

Another pause, with the ingot tapping.

"You still in Springfield?" he finally asked.

"Yeah. I'm here."

"Check it out, then. What else is down there?"

"Hell, if I know."

"Well, find the fuck out! I want those bitches! Nobody takes what's mine."

Clapham couldn't slam the phone down, but then, he didn't have to.

Shit, thought the man in Springfield, thumbing the phone off and dropping it into the cup holder next to him.

Who'd've believed the goddamned bitches would turn up in Nowhere, Missouri? Smart money said he'd find them Houston where they could dump the stones and disappear.

He'd worked for Clapham for years. Things didn't always go smoothly, but nothing had ever been this fucked up from the beginning. The description he'd been given was wrong. These women weren't young, but they weren't a couple of fumbling gray-haired grandmas, either. Not amateurs but pros.

Again, his lip curled thinking of the time he'd wasted in St. Louis, hitting hotels and pawn shops.

If I'd been chasing the right goddamned car, I'd have found them in St. Louis. But I wasn't looking for a goddamned 1950s gas-guzzling Chevy, was I? I was told to look for a Caddie no more than ten years old.

Now I'm stuck here in Spring-fucking-field, Missouri, when I should have been done with this and sleeping in Houston.

Pros or not. He'd find these two bitches and finish the job. He'd never missed a hit for Clapham, and he wasn't going to start now.

CHAPTER 30
HAIR TODAY...

Kat was in the bathroom, water running. The Buick was stashed safely out of sight in the court at the center of the Rockwood Motor Court, another vintage Route 66 motel. The air conditioner had made short work of the heat and humidity, and Tish had a large cup of iced tea on the night table next to her.

Despite starting out with a hangover, the day had gone well, she thought. The owner of the stores in St. Robert had been happy to buy some of the Clapham Collection. Tish had judged the situation right. With the nearby military base, the market was hungry for reasonably priced stones.

Buying the diamonds for cash, and selling them the same way, was a good way for a small company to hide some of their transactions from the IRS, too.

Tish sighed as she settled back on one of the motel beds with her sketchbook and began drawing.

She'd sketched out a dozen pendant designs when there was an anguished cry from the bathroom.

"No! Oh, nonononono..."

Tish tossed her sketchbook aside and rushed to the bathroom door.

"Kat? Kat, are you okay?"

The answer was sobbing.

Kat? Crying?

"Kat, honey, what's wrong?" Tish asked urgently.

No answer.

She was about to violate Kat's right to be alone and open the door when Kat turned the knob and stepped out.

Tish gasped. Then choked and slapped her hand over her mouth to imprison the guffaw that she knew was the wrong response.

Kat's hair was bright orange. Flaming orange. Incandescent orange.

From the tears pouring down her partner's face, Tish was pretty sure this wasn't what Kat had wanted.

"What happened?" she croaked, as she fought to keep the grin off her face.

"Oh, God!" said Kat. She sank into a chair at the dining table in the center of the room and dropped her head on her folded arms.

Tish mastered her face, sat down next to her, and put her arm across Kat's shoulders.

"What were you trying to do?" she asked.

"I wanted to go blonde," Kat muttered to the table. "I did what it said. Why did this happen?"

"I don't know," said Tish. "Maybe the brand was different from what you've used before?"

"I've never done it before. I've always gone to the salon."

"Oooh..." said Tish. "So, you might have gotten the process wrong."

"How can I get it wrong?" wailed Kat. "Lots of women do it themselves. How hard could it be?"

Obviously harder than it looks, thought Tish, but she kept quiet and simply squeezed Kat's shoulders.

"Why did you want to go blonde all of a sudden?" asked Tish. "We have wigs. You could be any color you want."

Kat sat up. Tish quickly went to find some tissues and waited while Kat cleaned up.

"I used to be blonde, you know," said Kat.

"No, I didn't know," said Tish, surprised.

Kat swiped at her nose. "You're different, you know?"

"Different?" It wasn't what Tish had expected her to say.

Kat nodded.

"What do you mean?"

"You've changed since we started driving."

"How?"

"It's like you've gotten younger, I think," said Kat. "More...more real. More relaxed." She hesitated. "Prettier."

Tish was at a loss for words.

"You're happier, too. More like...more like a Tish Geraghty might have been before she married Fitz O'Donnell." Kat looked away, down at her hands. "I wanted some of that," she said quietly.

Tish stared. Kat wanted to be more like her? Self-assured, determined Kat?

She laid a hand on Kat's arm.

"It was the blonde wig," said Kat. "Wearing it... Wearing it, I remembered that I was someone else, once. But it's like the tits. When you're blonde, that's all anyone sees."

"So, you dyed your hair."

Kat nodded.

"I've had dark hair for so long. Since I left high school. I thought if I could go blonde again, maybe..."

Kat stopped. She wouldn't look at Tish.

"Maybe what?" Tish finally asked softly.

"Maybe I could be someone else. Be me again," she finished so quietly that Tish almost didn't hear her. "Maybe I could be normal, too."

Tish had never heard someone sound so lost. She waited a few moments, then patted Kat's arm gently.

"Tish, what am I going to do?" said Kat. "I can't live with this."

Good question, thought Tish.

"Well, at this point," she said, "I don't think you can go blonde without professional help. But maybe we could dye it back to dark?"

"Do you think that would work?"

Tish sighed. "Kat, I have absolutely no idea. I've never used hair color before. Isn't it just like painting a wall? Putting the dark color over the... the... this color? But we could certainly try. I don't think we could make it any worse."

"Anything would be better than this," said Kat.

"Unless we turn it green," said Tish, trying to lighten the moment. "Or it falls out altogether."

She was stunned by the look on Kat's face.

Tish stood up. "Dry your hair. Put a wig on," she said, "and we'll go back to that drugstore."

Kat refused to go into the CVS, choosing to wait in the Buick while Tish went in to find a hair color dark enough to cover Kat's colossal mistake. Even though she was wearing a dark wig, she felt like everyone could see through it to the almost fluorescent orange underneath.

To guarantee no one saw her, she'd parked at the back of the lot near the road, where there were few other cars.

Normal, she fumed. *Right. When did I ever have normal? What does that even mean? How ridiculous can I get?*

Pretty ridiculous, considering the state of her hair, she thought. *Stupid, stupid, stupid.*

It was that damned blonde wig, making her remember the girl she once was. She was lonely for that girl and all her dreams. She'd had possibilities. How did all that disappear?

It disappeared by trusting a friend. By her father trusting a friend.

She drummed her fingers on the steering wheel and watched the traffic on the road in front of her, while she called herself names.

And saw the Illinois plates flash as the SUV pulled into the hotel parking lot across the street.

CHAPTER 31
DETECTIVE CHUNG ON THE CASE

"What a family," muttered Detective Adam Chung. He rolled his shoulders, shrugged, and stretched his neck side to side.

Detective Lyons, who'd just passed the opening to Chung's cubicle, took two steps backward.

"The O'Donnells?" she asked, walking into Chung's tidy space.

"Can I get combat pay for this one?" asked Chung.

"Doubtful," said Lyons and sat down. "Tell me."

"I'm beginning to think the wife had the right idea, bailing out on this crew." He shook his head. "I need coffee," he said and got up. Lyons simply held out her empty cup to him. He took it, filled both mugs at the coffee station, and came back.

"You reached the son yet? The one in Oregon?" said Lyons, nodding her thanks as Chung sank into his chair. She took a hefty slug of coffee.

"You'd think it would be easy, right?" Chung shook his head again. "Hardly. O'Donnell didn't have his son's number. Said the mother was the one to stay in contact. The mother, as you know, is still not picking up. The brother didn't have a number. Said they really didn't speak. I'm not sure he speaks to anyone other than his broker.

"The sister wouldn't give it to me, saying it was our fault the store was robbed in the first place. The employees either didn't know there was another son, didn't know his name, or didn't know where he lived, so none of them had his number. I called the school where he used to work. The brother gave me that much. Administrative assistant there quoted privacy rules to me.

"Oh, you think this is funny," said Chung to Lyons's grin.

"There are perqs to being senior officer," she said.

Chung snorted.

"So, no luck?"

"No, I finally got it. I remembered Mrs. Fielding mentioned that she'd been to Luke O'Donnell's shows here in town. She gave me the number of the gallery. I called them, they had a contact number, and didn't have issues with privacy." Chung flipped a hand toward a notebook on his desk. "I'm about to call." He lifted his mug. "But I needed this first. If he's like the rest of them, I'm going to put in for a mental health day."

"You getting any more calls about customers' missing jewelry?"

Chung looked pained. "Oh, yes," he said. "But that's not all." He pulled a file up on his computer. "I've had a couple queries from suppliers in New York. They're not pressing charges yet, but I've got a feeling it won't be long."

"Locally, though?"

"Locally, I got four more calls from people in town who

had jewelry at the store. O'Donnell is still not being 'proactive,' as they say, about contacting people who'd left things with him. I expect we'll get more complaints as word spreads. But one of the calls was particularly interesting."

"Oh?"

"Yep. She was a former employee who bought her wedding set there. She left it for sizing. I'm not sure why, because she wasn't flattering about O'Donnell. Gave me an earful."

"I'm listening."

"The employees don't like him much. He's a phony, she said, claiming to be a designer when it's the wife who's the real artist, but she doesn't often work with customers."

"Why not?"

"The woman's opinion was that O'Donnell didn't want people to find out he really didn't know anything about designing. She said she went to the wife directly when she wanted her wedding set designed."

"What did Mrs. O'Donnell do at the store, then?"

"Worked the back office, mostly."

"Hmm. What else?"

"Employees really hated O'Donnell for cutting in to close their sales, especially the high-ticket ones. That way he didn't have to pay their commission."

"That would make him unpopular."

"It did. The word she used was 'scumbag.'"

Chung went on. "She complained that he schmoozed—her word—with the wealthy female customers in a smarmy way—also her word—and she was pretty sure he was sleeping with a few of them. He used to come on to all the female employees, too, she said, until the manager, Merevec, forced him to stop."

"How'd she manage that?" asked Lyons.

"She rewrote the employee manual to include a section that explained how to put in a sexual harassment complaint with the Illinois Department of Human Rights."

Lyons cocked her head and raised her eyebrows. "I'm impressed."

"Me, too. This woman said Merevec went to bat for them to get them raises. She suspected Merevec was the one to get them year-end bonuses as well, although the money didn't make up for the loss in the commissions when O'Donnell stole their sales."

"Sounds like she really liked Merevec."

"She did," said Chung. "A lot. She trusted her. Said she'd been about to quit when O'Donnell brought in Merevec six years ago. After that, it was Merevec who ran the day-to-day, with O'Donnell only crawling—again her word—out of his office to schmooze up the rich clients. Working at Superior became reasonably pleasant after that, she said. And after the raises, pretty well paid."

"Were they close? This woman and Merevec?"

Chung shook his head. "She said Merevec wasn't really close to anyone. Didn't talk about her private life or go out to lunch with the other employees. The woman I talked to couldn't tell me anything about her. But when it came to work, she said Merevec was very approachable. She worked hard and was good with customers, too. When she helped someone close a sale, she never took credit for it."

Lyons sipped her coffee, eyes half closed.

"Strange, then, that O'Donnell fired her, a hard worker like that, even if he did want to put his girlfriend in her place. But it's even stranger that she's disappeared. You'd think she'd be scrambling to find another job. We still have nothing on her?"

Chung shook his head. "Not her. Not her car. No one's

seen her at the condo complex. I checked again this morning. And I've been checking the jewelry stores in town and the surrounding area so see if she's been applying for jobs. Not a glimpse of her."

They were both quiet, thinking.

"You think maybe O'Donnell didn't fire her?" said Chung. "That he took the opportunity to get rid of her? Because she stopped the harassment and cost him money by getting the staff raises and bonuses."

"I can see him firing her because she was a thorn in his side, sure, dumb as it might be, but hardly a reason to make her disappear. Unless..."

Chung's eyes opened wide.

"You're thinking blackmail?"

Lyons looked down, absently swirling the coffee in her mug, as if she could see the truth there.

"If she caught him clearing out the store, and threatened him, or tried to blackmail him," she said finally, "that might make the thorn big enough to remove."

"You think he's got the stones for that?"

Lyons looked up. "What do you think?"

Chung scoffed. "Hardly."

"Hmm. I don't think so either," said Lyons. "But something has happened to her. I think it's worth asking him about, don't you?"

"Oh, yeah. He's easy to rattle."

Lyons stood and drank the rest of her coffee.

"Yeah. He is," she said.

She glanced at the digital clock on Chung's desk. "He's in Oregon, right? The son?"

Chung glanced at his notes. "Portland."

"Talk to him first. This afternoon, or over the weekend.

Maybe something will break with Merevec's disappearance. I'd like to have more information before we talk to O'Don-nell on Monday."

CHAPTER 32
KAT'S REVELATION

Kat's fingers froze in the air over the wheel. The Buick was a sitting duck here. Whoever was driving the SUV would surely see the car.

She was reaching for the ignition when the passenger door opened. Kat jumped a foot.

"Okay. I got something that's about the same color you had," said Tish, slamming the door. "Hey!" She yelped as Kat yanked the shift into REVERSE and gunned it out of the parking lot. "What's the hurry? Wait until I get buckled in at least."

Kat pulled onto the cross street, but instead of turning toward the motel again, she crossed at the light to drive alongside the hotel.

"Kat, you missed the turn."

"Sorry," she said, and turned into the hotel lot.

When she started cruising the lot, Tish protested.

"Where are you going?"

"Turning around," lied Kat.

"You could have done that two rows ago," said Tish. "What's going on?"

Kat hit the brakes. "That is," she said, pointing at the black Lincoln Navigator.

Tish's gaze followed Kat's pointing finger, then she turned back to Kat, clearly annoyed.

"I thought we'd settled this," she said. "It's a coincidence, seeing him here."

"Coincidences can get you killed," muttered Kat, staring at the SUV. Her voice was tight, her grip throttling the wheel.

"What?" said Tish. "What the hel... What on earth are you talking about?"

"Nothing," said Kat, shifting into gear and driving toward the exit.

"No. There's no 'nothing' now, Kat. I want to know what's going on, and no more cra...garbage about black SUVs with dark windows looking like they're up to no good. I want the truth." There was steel in Tish's voice. "I want to know why you freak out every time we see one."

"Maybe you'd freak out, too, if you'd been kidnapped in one of those things!" snapped Kat. She immediately regretted saying anything.

"*What?*" said Tish. "What the hell, Kat? What do you mean, 'kidnapped?' And don't you dare say 'nothing.'"

Kat turned onto the road and headed back toward their motel.

"I'm waiting," said Tish. But several blocks passed before Kat could bring herself to say anything. She wondered if she was making a mistake.

"I was six, I think," she said finally. "First grade. Miss Hennessey was my teacher. For some reason I remember that. One night—It was late. I was already in bed and asleep—my mom woke me. She was whispering. I had to get dressed. We had to go, she said.

"She was trying to make it seem like fun, like a game. But I kept complaining, I remember—I was sleepy. It was cold."

Kat no longer saw the Missouri summer evening. She saw only that starless winter night.

"Later, when I was older, I was sorry about that. About whining. I mean, I was just a kid. But even then I knew I was being difficult. And she was so frightened. I realized that later."

Kat blinked tears. Cleared her throat.

"I kept asking why. Where were we going? Even when she said we had to hurry, I dragged my feet. I wanted my dolls. I wanted to say good-bye to Winken."

"Winken?" asked Tish.

"The neighbor's cat." She'd loved that big blue-eyed Himalayan. Sometimes that loss still seared through her heart like a hot knife.

"She bundled me into warm clothes," Kat continued, "and gave me my favorite doll. My dad carried me out of the house. Snowflakes fell like stars from the darkness, but they touched my face like feathers. The snow squeaked as my dad went down the walk. I used to love that sound."

Not anymore, she thought.

"Then I saw the men." Kat's heart kicked and shook like a badly tuned engine whenever she remembered this part.

"I don't know how many there were. I was still complaining. It was dark. It was cold, and I was six. But the minute I saw them, I stopped." Her doll's arm had dug into her chest as she'd buried herself in her dad's wool jacket. "At the curb was a big black car. I knew something bad was happening."

"Oooh," breathed Tish.

"My mom got in and turned to reach for me. My dad

had to pry me off, I was holding on so tight. I started crying. I thought he was leaving us." Kat swallowed hard around the terror of that moment. "My mom pulled me into the backseat, and I wrapped myself around her. My dad climbed in next to me. Then he closed the door."

The thump of that door closing still woke Kat gasping from nightmares. Even in daylight, if it caught her unawares, the sound of a heavy car door slamming could turn her insides to slush.

Lost in the incomprehensible darkness of that night, Kat had forgotten Tish was there, listening, until Tish whispered, "Now I understand."

Kat shuddered and came back to the present.

"What was it all about?" asked Tish.

"I was never really sure," said Kat.

Well, it wasn't *not* the truth. She'd caught bits and pieces of her parents' conversations when she was small, and put more bits of information together after her dad had died. She had some pretty good guesses. But she didn't *know*. Not for *sure*.

."We ended up in Seattle. We stayed there a while. But none of us liked it. Gradually, we drifted back to the Midwest. Spent some time in Fargo. Ended up in Madison."

"You never asked questions?"

Kat shook her head. The fear that had lived in their family after that night always stopped her from asking questions. And honestly? She'd been a coward. She didn't want to learn something she could never unlearn.

"Anyway," she told Tish, clearing her throat again. "I grew up, and I got over being scared of big black cars." She made a wry face. "Otherwise, I'd have to stay home under the bed."

Tish didn't smile. "So why now?" she asked, quietly. "Why are they scaring you now?"

"I'm not sure," said Kat shrugging.

That wasn't the truth. Kat knew exactly why now. She had known from the moment she'd seen that convoy of black cars in Springfield, Illinois.

Her family had been running that starless winter night, running from something dark and terrifying.

Just like she and Tish were running now.

And big black cars seemed to be everywhere.

But Tish, who was so good at reading people, saw through her.

"You know they're not following us, Kat, the same men from that night. They're just black cars."

"Tell that to my six-year-old self."

"I understand that."

A half mile passed. A mile.

"I lost everything that night," said Kat, finally.

Winken. Her pretty bedroom. The giant tree her dad was teaching her to climb.

A few years later, she'd lose her mother.

After that, she'd been careful not to love anything again —not a tree, not a cat. It hurt too much to lose them.

But she'd ached all her life to belong. To have something that was hers. The vanilla bland condo and the cookie-cutter car that she'd walked away from—they weren't hers. They belonged to some caricature self she'd crafted a long time ago.

The only thing that was hers was her red shawl, the last thing her mother had wrapped around her before helping her into her puffer coat that frozen night.

She blinked to clear her eyes.

"I won't risk everything again." She didn't realize she'd said it aloud.

"Oh, Kat," breathed Tish, her own face wet with tears. "That's so lonely."

Kat shrugged as she turned into the driveway at the Rockwood Motor Court. "You get used to it."

Tish didn't say anything, but Kat knew she didn't believe her.

Kat didn't even believe it herself.

CHAPTER 33
...GONE TOMORROW

Kat stared in the mirror. Her eyes were edged with red and puddled with tears. She looked naked with her black-framed glasses lying on the small glass shelf above the sink.

"It didn't work," said Kat, stating the obvious. "It's just a different color of orange."

"We need professional help," said Tish. "Tomorrow we'll see if we can find a hairdresser..."

"No," said Kat. "Absolutely not."

"Why on earth not?" asked Tish.

"Because she'll remember us, Tish," said Kat fiercely. "That's why not."

"Maybe," said Tish. *Almost definitely*, she thought. "But surely any hairdresser has seen worse."

Kat was shaking her head. "No. We can't risk it."

Tish sighed.

"Then I don't know..." She paused. Kat wasn't going to like this.

"Yes, I do," she said, walking out of the bathroom.

"Wait. What?"

Tish plucked her phone off the table.

"Stop! What are you doing?" said Kat. "Who are you calling?"

"I'm calling Deirdre."

"What?" Kat grabbed Tish's wrist. "No, you can't."

"Kat," said Tish, trying to hold onto her temper. "You don't want to go to a hairdresser. Deirdre does hair and makeup for a living. She must know something about hair coloring."

Kat was shaking her head.

"No. They'll ask questions. I know you like them, but...no."

She dropped Tish's wrist and sat down at the table, her damp hair almost glowing in the dim light.

Angry with frustration, Tish was about to snap back at her, when Kat looked up, her eyes glazed with unshed tears.

"I can't do that, Tish. I just can't," she said.

Behind the tears, Tish saw raw fear and grief in Kat's eyes.

She understood why the sight of black SUVs shook Kat so badly, but something else was scaring Kat. Something Kat wasn't telling her. Tish had no idea what that might be, other than what they were both scared of: getting caught. Yet from the beginning, Kat had seemed up to that challenge.

Look at how she tricked those thugs from the pawn shop, thought Tish, though she was still annoyed at the way Kat had done that.

Whatever challenge *this* was, however, Kat did not feel up to it. Somehow, she'd lost her confidence.

So, thought Tish, *first we need to get her confidence back. To do that, she needs to get rid of that orange hair.*

Tish was coming to realize that, for Kat, her appearance was her armor.

She pulled up a chair next to Kat and took her hands.

"Kat. Back at the bridge, we decided to trust each other. Trust me now."

"I trust you. But I don't know *them*."

"Then trust my judgement. You said it was my super-power, my ability to read people. The Geraghtys are good people, Kat, and not because we joked about being family. I've watched them. Listened to them. Seen how they talk to and about each other. They want nothing from us. They've already helped us. More than once. I trust them, Kat. Trust *me*."

Kat looked away, across the room. Tish prepared to accept Kat's refusal, telling herself not to be angry when Kat said no.

She could almost see the forces inside Kat struggling against each other, one side wanting to run and hide, one side desperately wanting to fix this.

Kat bit her lip, closed her eyes for a moment, then turned back to Tish.

"Okay," she said. A deep breath. "Okay."

Tears stung Tish's own eyes.

"All right then."

She squeezed Kat's hands, took up her phone, and dialed.

"OH, DEAR," said Deirdre, the next morning, as Kat sheepishly pulled the blonde wig off exposing her hair.

Tish tried not to wince. Under the bright makeup lights in the master bath of the house the Geraghtys had rented, the orange was even more garish. Kat was looking hopefully at Deirdre's reflection in the large mirror, as the Irish woman felt her hair.

"Do I have this right?" asked Deirdre. "Your natural color was blonde. You had it colored sable brown and added purple...

"Burgundy."

"...burgundy...highlights. Now you've tried to bleach it back to blonde. When it went orange, you tried to go back to the sable brown again."

"You can't fix it?" asked Kat's dismayed reflection.

"Katherine, darlin'. I know something about coloring hair, but you need a lot more help here than I can give you with what's available at the chemist's."

Deirdre ran her fingers through Kat's hair again.

"The color is not the only problem," she said. "Whatever products you used were not very friendly to each other. There's a bit of damage here."

"You can't fix it." It wasn't a question this time.

Deirdre patted Kat's shoulder. "If I'm honest, girl, the best I can do for you is cut it right down. I can take it down to about a centimeter, and it will..."

"A centimeter?" asked Kat.

"About half an inch," said Deirdre, switching gears from metric for her American audience. "It'll only take a couple months to grow in..."

Deirdre stopped. Both she and Tish registered the horror on Kat's face.

"I can't," whispered Kat. "Not yet."

It was a strong reaction for a woman who'd had purple hair for the six years Tish had known her.

She put her hand on Kat's shoulder.

"You have the blonde wig, and..." Tish was about to admit to the dozen wigs they had in the Buick's trunk, and changed direction, "...it looks nice on you. You can use that if you don't want to have really short hair." *Really short, really* orange *hair*, she thought.

"About that," said Deirdre.

"What? What about it?" asked Kat.

"It's a bit dated, isn't it?" said Deirdre, picking the blonde wig up from the counter and fluffing it.

"It's natural hair," said Tish, before she remembered it was supposed to be Kat's wig.

"Which is good," said Deirdre. "But if you're going to wear it as your own," she addressed Kat's reflection, "once we've cut yours off, we'll pop this on, and I'll give it a bit of a trim. No one will guess it's not your own."

Kat put a hand up to her hair. Her face was covered in despair.

Tish squeezed Kat's shoulder. Then had an idea.

"Deirdre, after you cut Kat's, could you cut mine, too?" she asked.

Deirdre smiled. "I'd be happy to give you a trim," she said.

"No. Not a trim," said Tish, looking at herself in the mirror. "Short."

"How short?" asked Deirdre.

Tish put her hand at her jaw line. "This short."

Deirdre looked at Tish's thick auburn hair, tied back, but still lying between her shoulder blades.

"You're sure?" she asked.

"Yes," said Tish.

"You don't have to do that," said Kat.

"I know," said Tish. "But I've been thinking about it, and this seems to be a good time." She patted Kat again. "We'll both get a makeover."

"What do you say, Katherine?" asked Deirdre, wickedly. "Shall I practice on Mary Pat, first?"

"Oh, thanks," said Tish, rolling her eyes in mock annoyance. "I thought you were an expert."

Kat looked between the reflections of the two women standing behind her—and mustered a smile.

It's a weak smile, but at least it's a smile, thought Tish.

"Okay," said Kat, taking a deep breath. "Okay."

In the end, Kat went first. "If I don't, I'll lose my nerve," she said.

As Deirdre worked the scissors through Kat's orange disaster, Kat refused to watch.

"You look like you're Anne Boleyn waiting to have her head removed rather than just her hair," said Tish, standing just behind her friend. "If you'd open your eyes, you'd see Deirdre is really good at this."

Kat responded by squeezing her eyes even more tightly closed.

Deirdre raised an eyebrow at Tish's reflection in the mirror and smiled sympathetically. Tish watched as Kat's new cut slowly developed.

"You know, Kat," she said, "you look really good with your hair this short."

"Don't try to make me feel better," came the strangled response. "I'm bald. I can feel it."

"Well, it *is* very short," said Tish. "But you have a beautiful head and ears. I don't think many women could wear hair this short."

"Umm. I agree," said Deirdre. "When the blonde comes back, you might find yourself keeping it like this."

"Right," said Kat.

"No, seriously, Kat," insisted Tish. "Get some massive earrings, and you'll have women envying you. I'll even design them for you."

"I'll have to take your word for it," said Kat.

"Actually, it's very Fury Road," said Deirdre.

"I'm not sure that helps," said Kat.

"It's a compliment," said Deirdre. "Tough. Uncompromising. Warrior spirit."

Kat snorted but didn't open her eyes.

Deirdre caught Tish's eye in the mirror and winked.

Tish took a deep breath. The Kat she knew was coming back.

Even when Deirdre finished, Kat refused to look. So Deirdre fitted the blonde wig on her and began to look it over critically.

It took longer to evaluate and trim the wig because, unlike Kat's own hair, it would not grow back if Deirdre made a mistake. When she finally finished, Tish convinced Kat to look.

"Oh," she breathed, when she finally opened her eyes.

Deirdre had completely restyled the wig into a pixie cut with soft bangs and wisps in front of her ears. The back was slightly long, but not too much. It was similar to Kat's usual cut but suited her even more. It softened the harshness of the large-lensed black glasses.

"What do you think?" Tish asked nervously. This had been her idea, after all.

"I feel… I feel new," said Kat sounding as enchanted as Dorothy seeing the Land of Oz for the first time. "Like I haven't seen myself in years. In decades, maybe."

She tore her gaze from the mirror and looked up at Deirdre. "I didn't think anyone could fix that disaster," she said. "Thank you."

"My pleasure."

Deirdre turned to Tish, flourished a towel at the bench where Kat was sitting. "Next," she said.

"Are you sure?" asked Tish. "I didn't think about how long this would take when I asked before."

"It'll be my pleasure. Really," said Deirdre. "Hair styling was my first passion. I cut my little sister's hair when I was four, five." She laughed. "She still hasn't forgiven me. She swears she remembers, and I can't even deny it. Our mammy took a photo. This is a treat for me," she added as Tish sat down.

By the time Deirdre was finished, more than a foot of Tish's hair lay coiled in the waste basket, and her head was covered with a mass of auburn curls.

"I had no idea," said Tish, elated, as she admired the cloud of soft ringlets framing her face. "I've worn my hair long since... since forever."

"Deirdre," said Kat, after she'd examined Tish's new cut from all angles. "You're a magician."

"You like it then?" Deirdre asked Tish. "I was a bit worried, with you wanting so much taken off."

"I love it," said Tish. "I feel so...so...buoyant." It was as if Deirdre had severed away the dead weight of her past as well as her hair.

Deirdre smiled broadly.

"I can't thank you enough," said Tish. "I feel like a new person."

"Happy to do it," said Deirdre.

"I wish there was a way we could repay you," said Kat.

"You can," said Deirdre. "You can help me make lunch for this clan."

CHAPTER 34
FOOD FOR THOUGHT

Detective Sam Lyons wanted to call on Fitz O'Donnell first thing Monday morning, but Detective Adam Chung's phone started ringing almost as soon as he got in the door. Every time Lyons went by Chung's cubicle, he had his phone earbuds in and was typing rapidly, though as far as she heard, his part of the conversation consisted of, "Un-hunh. Un-hunh." The last time she'd passed by, she'd managed to catch his eye. He'd only shaken his head once, raised his index finger briefly, and gone back to typing.

She'd just refilled her coffee mug for the third time when Chung came into her office and dropped into the extra chair.

Lyons let him catch his breath. For about five seconds.

"So?"

"Oh, man," said Chung, and blew out a gust of breath. "Let's see..." He looked at his tablet. "First. I told you about the diamond and jewelry suppliers in New York, didn't I?"

Lyons nodded.

"I heard from their attorney. He's tracking down other

suppliers in New York who had merchandise in O'Donnell's store that hasn't been paid for. It's preparatory to suing if the his clients don't get some response from O'Donnell. But the lawyer really wanted to know if the rumors he'd heard were true, that O'Donnell might have been involved."

"To which you responded, 'no comment' because we're still investigating a variety of possibilities," said Lyons.

"I did," said Chung. "Then I got a call from Felicia Denham..."

"Oh, Lordy..."

Chung nodded. "Yep. She's been retained by Tish O'Donnell, who apparently is making good on her threat to divorce O'Donnell and sue him for everything but his socks. Ms. Denham's words. She said we should stop harassing her client, who is the wronged party here. When Ms. O'Donnell is settled, she'll be happy to make an official statement about what she knows—which is nothing, says Denham—about the store robbery."

"Settled where?"

"Ms. Denham declined to share."

"Until now O'Donnell probably thought *we* were his big problem."

"Yeah. Is he in for a surprise."

"Would be interesting to know where Ms. O'Donnell is getting the money to pay such a pricey attorney," said Lyons.

"Ms. Denham, when carefully pushed on that point by a well-trained detective," said Chung, "noted that, when the divorce is final, Ms. O'Donnell will have more than enough to pay Ms. Denham's fee."

"I'll bet. Is that all?"

"Not yet. I got another call, this one from Henry Fox." Chung paused, looking at Lyons expectantly.

She frowned. "Fox? Henry Fo..." Lyons stopped. "You're kidding. About this case?"

"Cross my heart," said Chung. "O'Donnell hired him to find Ms. O'Donnell. He had questions about some of the information he'd been given. And he wondered if I had Ms. O'Donnell's phone number."

"Why does O'Donnell want to find his wife?"

"The divorce. O'Donnell wants his wife to sign papers. I think he's hoping for a quiet settlement so he can slip out of town with the barista. Ahead of all the lawsuits."

Lyons laughed. "Not with Denham in her corner. Ms. O'Donnell won't be signing anything until he's wrung dry."

"So true," said Chung.

"No doubt Denham will force Fox to stop 'harassing' her client, too."

"Highly likely," said Chung. "I did reach the younger son, Luke, by the way, the one in Oregon. He goes by his married name, Fonseca. Luke O'Donnell Fonseca."

Lyons perked up. "Does he know where his mom is?"

Chung's face was a picture in skepticism. "He says not, but he's not a good liar. I suspect he knows. He's adamant that his mother would not have been involved in the burglary. When I asked if he thought his father might have planned it, he laughed, and said he'd have nothing to gain. When I asked about the insurance, he said this."

Chung turned on his phone's record function.

"The store doesn't own most of the jewelry and gemstones in it," said an unknown voice, presumably Luke's. "Suppliers give jewelers their stock 'on memo.'"

Lyons frowned in puzzlement, but Luke was explaining to Chung.

"It's kind of like consignment, Detective," said Luke. "Suppliers provide a jeweler with inventory. The jeweler pays for it when it's sold. If it isn't sold, the jeweler sends it back to the supplier. If my dad had robbed the store, he'd have to use the insurance money to pay back his suppliers. He'd have nothing to gain."

"Doesn't he own any of the jewelry and gemstones in the store?" asked Chung's recorded voice.

"Sure. But only a small part of the product is his. If he tried to cash it out, he'd only get a fraction of the value," said Luke, "even if he knew who to sell it to. Which I doubt. No, Detective. Fitz O'Donnell would not risk going to jail for that small a reward."

"Not even for a younger girlfriend?"

Luke laughed. "My father's an idiot. But no matter how much of his brain is functioning below the belt right now, even for Hilary, he wouldn't risk self-destruction."

"Is there anyone you can think of among your family, their friends, store staff, disgruntled employees who might take that risk?"

"Of course not."

"The store manager?"

"Kat? Good Lord, no. Kat's cool. I'd trust her more than my dad. Kat's straight. The staff love her."

"What about your sister? She seemed pretty desperate for money."

"Madison? She used to take jewelry from the cases to show off at school dance when she was a teenager. Then my mom caught her and barred her from the store. After that, she just got Pop to give her whatever she needed. No. She wouldn't try anything like this. She wouldn't have any idea of where to start."

"Your brother, Carlisle?"

There was a long, long pause.

"Mr. Fonseca?" Chung's voice prodded.

Luke's long, indrawn breath was audible even on the recording, and Lyons realized that Luke was struggling with his conscience.

"I shouldn't say this," said Luke, sounding reluctant, "because he *is* my brother, after all. But...if there's anyone in my family who'd be willing or able to plan something like that—and I'm not saying he actually would or that he did —but it would be Carlisle."

CHAPTER 35

ANOTHER UNWANTED VISIT

As they pulled out of the police parking lot, Lyons got a call from the Wisconsin State Patrol. She and Chung listened on her phone's speaker as they drove to O'Donnell's house. It was grim news.

Lyons disconnected and dropped her phone in her pocket as Chung parked in front of the residence.

"Finding Merevec's car changes things," said Chung.

"Hmm," said Lyons thoughtfully. "It does. But what?"

"It's clear something happened there."

"But what?" said Lyons again. "There wasn't enough blood in the car to indicate she'd been killed, at least not in the car. There was none found in the area around the car."

"Probably not carjackers, or she would have reported it."

"If she could," said Lyons.

"Hmm. Could have been joyriders who dumped it in those woods. Could be their blood."

"True. That makes the most sense, because someone did empty her purse, and there was no phone found.

Joyriders don't normally bleed on the cars they steal, though," said Lyons.

"Could still happen, though."

"It could."

Lyons pursed her lips and sat thoughtfully for a moment. "The missing purse's the one thing that could support O'Donnell's story," she said finally, almost to herself.

Chung frowned. "The story that he didn't break into his own store? How does finding Merevec's purse support that?"

"She still had the store keys with her, Adam. Or so O'Donnell said."

"Oh, right. She did."

"So, there's an outside chance that someone waylaid Merevec, forced her to open the store, turn off the alarm, then took her with them after they were done. She may have been hurt in a struggle. We'll have to wait and see if the blood samples Wisconsin took are a match for Merevec."

"If there was someone else involved, they had plenty of time over the Memorial Day weekend to break into the store, but how could they circumvent the time lock on the vault?" asked Chung. "They'd have to wait until 8 a.m. on Tuesday and risk someone seeing the break in."

Lyons rubbed her eyes. "I know. Too many holes in that theory."

"I still think O'Donnell knows something about all this," said Chung.

"So, do I. But what?"

"What do we tell him now, then?"

"I think," said Lyons, reaching for the door release, "we throw around the scary words, like blood, kidnapping, and murder, but we keep the piece about the keys to ourselves. I don't want to give him any ideas. But it might be worthwhile to see how he reacts to the rest of it."

"Let's go rattle his cage, then," said Chung.

"Now what?" said Fitz, trying for bravado and failing, when he opened the front door to find Detectives Lyons and Chung on the doorstep. "I hope you've caught the people who robbed my store."

"We're still working on that," said Lyons. "But we have some other news. May we come in?"

Fitz shifted and looked over his shoulder. "Yeah, okay. Fine," he said, opening the door. "We'll have to sit in the kitchen, though."

The reason became clear as Lyons stepped into the foyer. The living room was empty except for the coffee table. The dining room held only dents in the carpet where the table and chairs had sat.

"Redecorating?" she asked.

"That's not a crime," said Fitz.

"It's not, Mr. O'Donnell. A strange time for it, though. As there are so many people about to sue you."

Fitz waved a hand. "That's just a misunderstanding. The insurance company will take care of all that."

"Oh," said Chung. "They've changed their mind about it being fraud, then?"

Fitz staggered a bit. "There was no fraud," he blustered.

"The kitchen?" said Lyons, before he could go on. She lifted her hand in that direction.

Fitz snapped his mouth shut and showed them to high stools at the kitchen bar.

"So, what's your news?" he asked, putting the granite

bar between the detectives and him. He picked up a fork lying on the counter and began waggling it between his index and middle finger.

"You said you fired Ms. Merevec, the weekend of the robbery," said Lyons.

"Yeah, what of it?"

There were footsteps on the stairs.

"Was that the last…"

"Fitzy!" said Hilary calling from the front hall. "Is that ugly wooden cabinet up there worth anything?"

She braked to a halt inside the kitchen door.

"In a minute, sweetness. The police are here." Fitz waved a hand toward the two detectives.

"Was that the last time you saw her?" continued Lyons.

"Saw who?" said Hilary.

"Yeah, sure."

"Saw *who*?" repeated Hilary.

"What's this about? Is she complaining, too?" asked Fitz.

"It's not my Fitzy's fault!" said Hilary, coming to stand by O'Donnell. "Saw who?"

"What isn't his fault, Ms. Schoenmeyer?" asked Lyons.

"Well…well… Whatever it is people are blaming him for!" she said.

Lyons glanced at Chung who opened his tablet and held his stylus poised.

"As far as blame goes," said Lyons, "we have ten customers who want answers about their stolen jewelry…" She looked at Chung for confirmation, and he nodded. "And four—with likely more to follow—New York suppliers who want answers about their missing merchandise."

"They can't hold me responsible for that," said Fitz, fumbling the fork, which rang like a closing cell door as it hit the tile floor. "It's the insurance company that won't pay."

"Actually, they *can* hold you responsible, Mr. O'Donnell. But that's the least of our concerns right now," said Lyons. "Because we have something of greater concern. A missing woman."

"Tish isn't missing," said Fitz, thumping his fist on the counter. "You," he pointed at Chung. "You talked to her that day. Right here in our living room."

"No, Mr. O'Donnell, I didn't speak to her that day," said Chung. "I left her a message."

He paused as the color slowly drained from Fitz's face.

"I did, however, speak to her subsequently," added Chung.

Lyons noted that Chung was enjoying his role as "bad cop" a little too much, but she couldn't deny that his significant pause had given O'Donnell an effective jolt of adrenaline.

"That's not the woman we're concerned about," said Lyons.

"What?" Fitz snapped his attention back to Lyons. "Who then? Who's missing?"

"Yes, Fitzy. What woman are they talking about? What woman have you been seeing?" Icicles hung on every one of Hilary's words.

"Sweetness, whatever you're thinki…"

"Kat Merevec," said Lyons. "Kat Merevec is missing."

"Oh. Her," said Hilary, dismissing Kat's disappearance with a wave of her hand. "Fitzy fired her. Tell them, Fitzy."

"She's not missing," said Fitz. "I fired her. You know that."

"We know that's what you *said*," said Chung.

"Are you calling me a liar?" said Fitz.

"Are you calling my Fitzy a liar?" Hilary's show of indignation was marred by the side-eye she gave O'Donnell.

"Kat Merevec's car's been found. In Wisconsin," said Lyons.

"So? What does that..."

"Her blood was found on the seats and wheel," said Lyons.

Fitz froze, though his jaw continued to move up and down soundlessly.

"You mean...like *blood*?" said Hilary, sounding more titillated than horrified.

"Blood?" Fitz croaked. "You think..." He licked his lips. "You think... I.... I... I..."

"Did you?" asked Lyons. "Did you kill Kat Merevec?"

"Fitzy? Fitzy, you didn't. Did you?"

Now Hilary sounded shocked, but Lyons also registered the look of speculation the young woman was giving her lover.

"Of course not," Fitz whispered.

As denials went, thought Lyons, it was as flimsy as soggy bread.

"What about you, Ms. Schoenmeyer?" asked Chung. "Did you have any reason to harm Ms. Merevec?"

"Me?" squealed Hilary. "What?"

"Perhaps you discovered Ms. Merevec was having an affair with Mr. O'Donnell here, who was *not* going to fire her, as he'd promised you. So, you..."

"Her?" said Hilary. "*Her?* She's *old*. My Fitzy wouldn't be interested in *her*." There was a small hesitation. "Would you, Fitzy?"

"Or perhaps she discovered you and Mr. O'Donnell emptying the safe at the store," said Lyons watching her closely.

"Of course not," said Hilary, hands on her hips. "She wasn't..."

Fitz's right hand shot out like a striking rattler and yanked Hilary into his side. He wrapped his other arm around her, trapping her face against his chest.

"How can you suggest such a thing!" he said, dramatically. Hilary struggled to breathe, but O'Donnell had her head clamped tightly to his shirt front with his left arm. "My Hilary wouldn't harm a fly. I can't believe you'd suggest she killed someone."

Then he said the magic words.

"I'm going to talk to my lawyer. I won't have you saying such terrible things about my Hilary."

Hilary was mumbling something into O'Donnell's buttons. Lyons was frankly surprised O'Donnell had enough strength to hold her.

She'd heard enough for now. Since O'Donnell had invoked his lawyer, it would be better to wait and see what story they came up with.

But the girlfriend... Pushing her again just might be worthwhile, at least before she invoked a lawyer, too.

Lyons rose.

"We may have more information or more questions later," she said, as Chung, too, stood up. "But Mr. O'Donnell," she added. "Please let us know if you plan to leave Evanston. You, too, Ms. Shoenmeyer. Because honestly, the only reason we're not arresting either of you right now is because your fingerprints are not in Ms. Merevec's car."

"My fing..." Fitz's eyes were almost spinning.

Outraged mumbling from Hilary.

"Though the FBI will probably be going over the car for DNA evidence."

"The FBI?" squeaked Fitz.

"Of course, Mr. O'Donnell," said Lyons. "We call them in whenever we believe there's been a kidnapping."

"Kidnap...?"

"Especially if there might be murder involved."

"*Murder?*

"Thank you for your time, Mr. O'Donnell. Ms. Shoenmeyer," said Lyons, and she and Chung showed themselves out.

When they reached the bottom of the driveway, Chung spoke up. "Definitely does not have the stones to kill her," he said.

"I agree," said Lyons, opening the car door. "But always instructive to ask. And raises the question: Who *might* killer her? And why?"

"The girlfriend might do it, if she were jealous enough. She knows more than she's saying," said Chung, getting in and starting the car.

"I agree with you there, too," said Lyons. Then she gave him a look. "But, Adam, can you see her keeping it a secret?"

"Not without O'Donnell to stuff a shirt in her mouth," said Chung, and started to laugh.

CHAPTER 36

GONE IN SIXTY SECONDS

"This *is* luxury," said Siobhan from the depths of the Buick's leather backseat, as Kat pulled the big car into a diagonal parking spot on the old courthouse square in Carthage. Three big motorcycles pulled in next to them.

"Luxury is not having to cook again tonight," said Maureen, unbuckling her seat belt. "I'm glad you suggested this, Mary Pat."

"Thank Jamie," said Tish. "I didn't think he was joking about finding a McDonald's for his night of 'cooking.'"

"He wasn't," said Maureen, and they all laughed.

"Besides," said Tish, as they all got out of the big car, "we owe you something for putting us up and feeding us for the last three days."

After Deirdre had fixed Kat's hair disaster on Saturday, the Geraghtys had offered Kat and Tish the guest cottage on the property they'd rented.

"It's empty," Deirdre had told them. "You can put that big car in the barn with the motorcycles and rest for a few days. Honestly, the two of you look like you could use the break."

"We'll be out most days tracking down family history," said Maureen.

Jamie groaned from across the room.

His mother grinned. "Though I suspect the boys will be off trying to find roads to challenge their bikes."

"Too right," said Jamie.

Tish put her hand on Kat's arm before her friend could decline again.

"We could use a rest," she said, and Kat had caved in.

The Geraghtys had refused all payment, so Kat and Tish were taking the family to dinner.

"How did you get lucky enough to park almost in front of this place?" Tish asked Kat, as they pulled into a restaurant on Fourth Street, right across from the Jasper County Courthouse.

"I have excellent parking karma," said Kat, smiling.

It was good to see her smile, thought Tish. She'd wondered if Kat would ever smile again after the hair fiasco. But she was like a new woman after Deirdre had restyled the wig. She'd even abandoned her usual all-black attire for the evening, wearing a sapphire blue top over her black jeans. She did, however, open the trunk and grab her black jean jacket.

Tish was beginning to recognize the signs of Kat camouflaging herself. Though willing to use her amazing figure to distract buyers from asking too many questions about their "inventory," at other times, Kat disguised it as much as possible.

"So, this place is good, is it?" asked Connall, dismounting from his motorcycle and stepping up on the curb.

"So says Tripadvisor," said Tish, as he held the door. "We'll blame them if it goes bad."

The eight of them were spread out over two tables, and, as always, the waitress was quickly besotted with the Irish accents—and Jamie's shameless flirting.

There were a lot of tempting choices on the menu, and a lot of banter between the tables about who was getting what and why and how much and explanations of American oddities like chicken-fried steak and grits. But they finally placed their orders, Jamie once again lamenting his age and the drinking age in the US, Maureen again reminding him that she'd truss him up before she allowed him to drink and get on his motorcycle.

Tish rubbed her arms.

"It *is* a bit cool in here," said Siobhan, noticing.

"I didn't think I'd need my sweater," said Tish, "but I've changed my mind. Kat, would you hand me the...oh. Thanks," she finished as Kat reached across the table and handed her the car keys. "Back in a sec."

The heat coming off the sidewalk hit her like a wet cloth as Tish pushed out of the restaurant door. As she glanced toward the car, the lowering sun blinded her for a moment, so she didn't react as quickly as perhaps she should have.

The big Buick was pulling away from the curb.

"Hey! Stop!" she shouted.

A young male face threw her a startled glance, and said something she didn't hear. The driver hit the gas.

"Shit!" cried Tish. She whipped around and caught the restaurant door just before it closed.

"Kat!" she screamed into the room. "Kat! The car! Someone's stealing the car!"

Kat bolted out of her seat as if catapulted. The pack of Geraghtys was right behind her.

"There!" Tish hollered, pointing down the street. The Buick was turning onto Grant, at the corner of the court-house square. "Quick! Call the police!"

"No time." Connall grabbed her arm, pulling her toward his bike. "Get on!"

"What?"

"Get on! We can catch them," he said, giving her his helmet.

Tish mounted the big bike like a pro, pulled on the helmet, and grabbed Connall around the waist.

"You, too, Katherine!" Jamie shouted, as Connall backed the bike.

Tish caught a brief glimpse of Tim running to his machine. Then Connall gunned it.

Tish clutched Connall as he leaned the bike into the turn onto Grant. The Buick passed the courthouse and kept going, picking up speed. It was already two blocks down.

"They're heading for Route 66!" Tish shouted.

Connall nodded.

Tish felt the deep-throated rumble of Jamie's Ducati as he pulled the bike alongside. He was grinning like mad, but Kat's face promised retribution when they caught up to the car thieves.

But even the big bikes weren't a match for the blue Nissan Cube that shot out of the side street ahead of them to race alongside the Buick, its horn peeping like an enraged chickadee.

The Cube darted in front of the convertible, and Tish gasped. The Buick swerved and bounced over the curb in front of a storefront church. The driver slammed on the brakes, hurling the massive car to a stop, its big chrome-plated bumper less than 18 inches from the side of the Cube.

Tish, peering around Connall, saw Uly and Erma Armentrout explode from the Cube. They lunged toward the Buick tearing open the doors. Uly wrapped a hand in the driver's gray T-shirt, dragged the skinny boy over to the Cube, and shoved him against the side. The small car rocked on its wheels.

"You asshole!" Uly screamed.

"Lemme go, you shithead!" the kid yelled back, aimed a booted foot, and kicked Uly hard on the shins. Uly yelped.

On the passenger side of the Buick, Erma wrestled the other teen out of the car. He spun and started to run, but she grabbed his ponytail, hauling him to a stop. He spun, hit at her, and she punched him in the face, knocking him to the ground.

"You fucking bottom feeder!" she yelled, slapping at him as he desperately tried to cover his head with his arms. "That's my fucking car! You freaking moron!"

"Bloody hell," muttered Connall, as he stopped.

"Better than telly," said Jamie, still grinning as he pulled alongside.

Tim rolled up on his bike, a look of disbelief on his face.

Bent on vengeance, the Armentrouts didn't notice they were the center of attention. Customers were starting to come out of the restaurant across the street.

"You won't have a better chance to get the car back," said Connall calmly.

Kat was already sliding off Jamie's bike.

"Tish! Come on!" she shouted. "Let's get the car."

"Go on, girl," said Connall.

Tish tore off the helmet and shoved it at Connall as she jumped off and hurried to the Buick.

"Meet us back at the house," called Tim, and steered around the melee.

Kat was already behind the wheel when Tish slipped by Erma and her victim and jumped into the passenger seat. As she slammed the door, Kat jerked the gear shift into REVERSE, revved the car backward, threw it back into DRIVE, and shot forward around the Cube and down the street. The Irish riders were ahead of them, already turning east onto 66, heading back to the house on the river.

"Hey! *Hey!*" Tish heard Uly yell. In the side mirror, she saw the strobing lights of a police car a block or so behind them. A moment later she heard the siren.

"Go, go, go," she muttered to Kat.

But Kat was already going.

"No! Wait!" she cried.

"What? Are you crazy? That's the police! You think our IDs will stand up to police scrutiny? The faster we get out of here the better." Kat stopped decorously at the Route 66 junction.

"We can't! We left the women at the restaurant!"

"Shit," said Kat,

"Go left. Go left!"

Kat spun the wheel, turning onto 66 heading west.

"Next left, here," said Tish, pointing, and Kat turned onto Main.

"You know where we're going?"

"Of course, I do," said Tish. "Slow down! Stop sign!"

"No one will notice..." Kat started to say.

"Sheriff's office!" Tish stabbed a finger at the cars parked in the lot across the street.

She was tossed forward against the seat belt when Kat hit the brakes.

"That's all we'd need right now," said Kat. Then she took a breath and drove carefully through the cross street.

"Where are we?" she asked.

"Courthouse is just up ahead. There's another stop sign."

"Why the hell do they have stop signs every freaking block?" muttered Kat, slowing.

She hit the brakes hard.

"Shit."

"Well, you don't have to be..."

Then Tish saw what Kat did.

A black Navigator with smoked glass windows slid out from Third and turned right onto Main. Right in front of them.

The driver didn't seem to notice the Buick, as he moved forward. Toward the courthouse.

"It's him," said Kat.

CHAPTER 37

THE SUV AGAIN

"It can't be him," said Tish.

Kat spat out a license plate number.

"What's that?"

"The plate number of the car in Springfield," said Kat.

It matched the car in front of them.

"Besides. There's the ding we made in his windshield. He's following us," said Kat.

"He can't be, Kat."

"Tish! How can you be so...so...thick about this?"

"How often do we have to go over this? Those men are probably long dead. They can't be following you."

"I know that! I'm not stupid. But *somebody's* following us. You'd see that if you'd just open your eyes."

"Kat..."

"Get us back to the house," said Kat. "I don't know where we are."

"We're not going anywhere until..."

"We can hash this out at the house," said Kat. "I don't want to do it while I'm driving."

Tish took a couple deep breaths, but her voice was tight

when she told Kat, "We are not going anywhere. We still have to get Siobhan, Deirdre, and Maureen from the restaurant. They came with us. Remember?"

"Shit. Shit shit shit," Kat muttered. "I don't want to get that close to him."

Tish turned at the terror in Kat's voice. Her face was bloodless, her body rigid. Kat was always relaxed when she drove, like she was part of the car. For the first time since Kat had told her about being kidnapped as a child, Tish truly understood how much these black cars frightened her friend.

"Then let's just wait a minute and see where he goes," she said gently.

As she spoke, a truck pulled out of Third and turned up Main, putting itself between the SUV and the Buick.

"Kat, we only have another block to go," said Tish, quietly. "If we take it slowly, he'll have time to get a long way from us."

She crossed her fingers on the seat next to her. If he stopped in the courthouse square, she'd never get Kat to pick up the Irish women.

"Okay," said Kat. "Okay." She flexed her fingers from the steering wheel, then slowly drove forward.

Tish felt a wave of panic from Kat as the truck turned left onto Fourth, leaving space between the Buick and the SUV, but they both relaxed when they saw the black car was continuing straight down Main. Moving away from them.

When they got back to the restaurant on Fourth, though, no women.

"They grabbed your food to go," said the waitress.

"Oh. Of course, they did," said Tish who'd gone into the restaurant to get Maureen, Deirdre, and Siobhan.

"Did you get your car back?" asked the waitress as Tish turned to leave.

"What? Oh, yes." She pointed out the front window. "Yes. The thieves were...were very cooperative when we confronted them."

"I'm not surprised," laughed the waitress. "You looked like something out of Fury Road when you pulled out of here!"

Tish managed to smile as she left.

WHEN KAT and Tish got back, Maureen, Deirdre, and Siobhan were setting up the table on the wide porch that wrapped two sides of the rented house. Maureen spotted the Buick as it came down the driveway, pointed, and grinned.

"We thought we might have to walk back here, when you ran off like that," she said, as Kat and Tish came up the steps after parking the Buick in the barn. "Then Tim called to say we were going to eat at home instead. The restaurant was good enough to pack up our dinners as takeaway. They were very understanding."

"Sorry," said Tish. "We seem to have ruined the evening."

"Don't be," said Deirdre, as Kat picked up the silverware to help lay places. "Jamie has decided you and Katherine are more fun than cemeteries. He said it was like a real-life American police drama."

"I only wish I'd been there," said Siobhan. "Something to write about."

"Perhaps Jamie got a video," said Deirdre, and the women laughed.

Tish felt her face freeze, and she saw Kat startle.

Video?

Siobhan's smile faded as she registered Tish's look. "Did I say something wrong?" she asked.

"No," said Tish. "We're just a bit...shaken by this whole thing." She tried to brush it off. "Nothing that dinner won't cure, I'm sure. I hope that's as good as it smells."

Video. What if someone in Evanston saw it? she thought. *The police... Fitz...*

"Oh, love. I'm sorry," said Siobhan. She came over and put her hand on Tish's arm. "Here we are joking, like this is something that happens on the telly. That was cruel, that was."

"No," said Tish. "It's okay. It's just... You mentioned video..."

"Oh, of course," said Maureen. "Cruel and thoughtless. Is it your husband you're worried about? Give me a moment."

Without waiting for an answer, she slipped into the house. Through the large windows, Tish saw her talking to Jamie.

"No worries," said Maureen, sliding the door closed behind her as she came back to the porch a minute later. "Jamie's disappointed he didn't get any video, so nothing's gone online."

"So, if you don't mind," said Siobhan, "what happened? How did you get the car back? Did you just pull alongside and shout 'Stop, thief?'"

Tish glanced at Kat.

"We didn't stop them," said Tish. "It was the Armentrouts."

"Those awful people tracking your car?" said Siobhan.

"Yep," said Tish. "Them."

"How on earth did they find the car?" asked Deirdre.

"Jamie is very good at that. If he said the car was clean, it should have been clean."

"Dumb luck?" said Tish.

"The dumb part is right anyway," said Kat, taking the first deep breath Tish had seen her take in almost an hour. "Did you see the way they went after those kids?"

"What kids?" asked Siobhan.

"Two kids hotwired the car," said Kat. "Idiots," she muttered under her breath as she turned back to the table.

"So, the old couple didn't steal it?" asked Siobhan.

"No. A couple teenagers," said Tish. "The Armentrouts came out of nowhere. Forced the kids to stop, dragged them out of the car, and jumped them."

"One kid got in a couple good licks, though," said Kat. She glanced at Siobhan. "Kicked Uly right in the shins."

"His partner was getting it worse from Erma," said Tish. "I imagine they had some explaining to do to the sheriffs."

"The police came?" said Maureen.

Too late, Tish heard the unasked part of that question—why didn't you stay to talk to them?—and realized that guiltless people would have done just that.

But they were not guiltless, and they had fake IDs in their wallets.

She could tell that Kat, too, had heard the unasked question in Maureen's tone.

"We'd already retrieved the car," she explained quickly and smoothly. "So, we left the kids and the Armentrouts to explain," said Kat.

"I wonder if they'll get arrested for helping us," said Tish.

"They weren't helping us," said Kat. "They were helping themselves. Did you hear Erma say it was 'her' car?"

"Do you think they might have hired those kids to steal the car?" asked Tish.

"Not the way they were whaling on them," said Kat.

"Do you think Tim was right, then?" asked Maureen. "They want the car to sell in Europe?"

Kat shook her head. "I can't believe they're that sophisticated, but they certainly want it for some reason. They're willing to steal it, too. I doubt they would have brought it back to us."

"Jamie's right," said Siobhan. "You are more fun—more interesting anyway—than cemeteries."

"I agree," said Deirdre. "Sorry, Maureen."

"Who knew the living could be so entertaining?" said Maureen.

"Well, that takes care of the Armentrouts, anyway," said Tish.

"To be sure, though, you might ask Connall and Jamie to look over the car once again, after we eat," said Maureen. "Shall we bring the food out?"

CHAPTER 38
REPRIEVED

Uly touched his nose gingerly. There were streaks of blood on his T-shirt, and his cap had disappeared.

"It's broken," he said.

"It's not broken," said Erma, tossing the hotel room key card onto the bureau. "Stop whining."

Erma looked in the mirror. She looked a little ragged herself. She had a long scratch down one cheek where that little bastard's swing had caught her before he went down. And her hair...

Uly was poking at his nose again.

"Stop jabbing at it," she said. "It's not bleeding. Cops did that much for you anyway."

"So grateful for your concern." Uly's voice dripped sarcasm.

Erma held her hands out to her sides, palms up. "I'd have thought you learned something in prison. Christ, Uly. That kid was half your weight and half your age, and look at you."

"Little shit sucker-punched me!"

"Yeah. Right." She dropped onto one of the beds and put an arm over her eyes. "We're lucky those cops didn't check your background. You'd have been back in the can."

"You would have been right there with me this time, sis," said Uly, nastily. "That kid you beat up was only 15. His mother really wanted to press charges against you."

"Yeah? If she's doing such a great job, what's her kid doing stealing cars?" Erma dropped her arm back by her side. "I can't believe we lost that fucking Buick again!" Her fist thumped the mattress. "Where the hell did those bitches even come from?" She gave Uly a suspicious look. "You sure it was them?"

"It was them," said Uly, turning his head from side to side and examining his nose in the mirror. "I think we should give up on that..."

Erma glared. "We are *not* giving up on the Buick."

Uly glared back. "We got lucky this time, spotting them in Carthage. How do you expect to find them without the tracker?"

"We keep looking, that's how. Check out more hotels here and in Joplin, first thing tomorrow. See if we can catch them. If not, we stay with the Route. They're heading west."

"For now," said Uly, dropping onto the other bed in the room. "They could decide to go back to Illinois, for all you know."

"Then we'd better find them soon. In the meantime, we need another vehicle. There's that show..."

Erma paused.

"Well, shit," she said. "That show in Oklahoma. I'll bet that's where they're heading. That dark-haired bitch didn't buy the car. They're going to sell it in Oklahoma." She smiled evilly. "We'll get them there, for sure, if we don't get them before."

"What if we miss them again?"

"We won't. They can't hide that car forever."

She glanced at her brother. He was prodding his nose again. She sighed.

"Food, Uly. Call."

CHAPTER 39
REVEALED

Kat and Tish were in the barn, after dinner, washing and cleaning the Buick. Kat was determined to remove any and all traces of the teenagers and the Armentrouts from Beauty's exterior and interior. They'd nixed the idea of taking it to a car wash in Carthage, especially after the brawl.

She was absolutely furious about the theft of the Buick. Someone could have walked into her condo in Evanston and taken everything, and Kat would have shrugged. But this car... She was special. No one should touch Beauty, but her.

Well, and Tish...

Though right now she was angry at Tish, too.

"I don't know how else they could have stolen it," she said. She was lying across the bench seat, head dangling under the steering column. "You *must* have forgotten to lock the door. If those little bastards have damaged anything," she muttered to herself as she checked the wiring, "I'll go back and kill them myself."

"I did *not* forget to lock the door," said Tish, for the third time, as she spritzed the driver's window with cleaner. "Why are you blaming me? Maybe *you* forgot."

"I distinctly remember locking it."

"And your memory is so much better than mine?" Tish slapped the paper towel back against the windshield and rubbed furiously.

Kat slid back up onto the seat and sat up.

"We should get back on the road," she said, almost to herself. "We're sitting ducks here. If that guy spotted us... First the damned Armentrouts. Now...*him*."

"We are not being followed, Kat. I'm sympathetic to your feelings but this has got to stop."

"We *are* being followed," said Kat, her voice climbing. "It's the same damned car we've seen for the last three hundred miles! What do I need to do to convince you? I saw him turn a block past the courthouse. He was quartering the area. He was looking for us!"

"Well, he couldn't have missed us, Kat. We were sitting right there. You can hardly hide this thing." Tish flicked the damp paper towel toward the Buick. "How many other times could he have seen us?"

Kat held onto her temper. She needed Tish on her side. "I know you think I'm crazy," she said. "But it's not my past haunting me. We're being followed, Tish. It's the same car. I'm sure of it."

"It's not just that ugly blue thing after you, then?"

Kat and Tish jumped at the voice. Tim and Jamie had come into the barn unseen.

Speechlessly, they stared at the Geraghtys, father and son.

"You know that's sure to bring rain, don't you?" said Jamie, gesturing at the wash bucket still standing next to the Buick's front wheel. "Washing the car? At least that's the case in Ireland."

"Here, too," managed Tish.

"Yes," said Kat. "I don't know why any of us bother." She tried to smile. It probably looked as forced as it felt.

"Katherine—or Kat and Tish, if I may?" said Tim. "After the events of this evening, I think we all should talk."

Kat shot Tish a look. Her dinner, what she'd eaten of it, was threatening to come up. Tish, it was clear, felt the same.

Tim's eyes softened. "You're not that good at pretending," he said. "Besides. It's what we do. We work with frightened people." He gestured at Jamie. "All of us. We've seen how scared you are and have been since we met you. We may be able to help you. But we need the truth. I need to know that you've not involved my family in anything illegal."

Kat gulped.

"Illegal?"

"You didn't talk to the police about the theft of your car."

Silence hung in the barn while Kat's mind spun close to panic. She frantically tried to remember what they'd told the Geraghtys. How had they slipped up? What had given them away?

"You're right, Tim. We are scared," said Tish. She came around the open car door and put her hand out to her partner. "We *do* need help, Kat," she said quietly.

The blood slipped from Kat's face as she took Tish's hand and slid out of the Buick. She looked into Tish's eyes... and saw "trust me" written in them as surely as if they were a flashing, ten-foot neon sign.

Tish, the great improviser, had a plan.

"Okay," she said to Tish's eyes. "Okay."

"We keep seeing an SUV, a black Lincoln Navigator," Tish told the two men. "Katherine—Kat's—sure it's the same car, and that it may be following us."

"It is," said Kat.

"Have you seen the registration?" asked Jamie.

"Yes," said Kat.

"Easy enough to find out who it is," said Jamie. "We'll give the number to Connall. He'll soon tell you who owns it."

"He can do that?" asked Tish. "I thought only police could do that?"

Jamie laughed. "For Con, a car tag is like a red flag to a bull. He can't wait to charge. If you're done with the Beauty, then, go talk to him."

He waved an electronic gizmo at them. "In the meantime, I'll go over this car again. I doubt I missed something, but we'll make sure this time, yes?"

Kat looked at Tish. They both nodded.

"Come on then," said Tim. "I came out to get you for tea and cake anyway. We'll make Connall earn his. And you'll tell us who and what you're running from."

Kat hoped Tish's story would hold up to Tim's shrewd gaze.

"I DESPISE STALKERS," said Connall. "Give me his registration number, and we'll have him."

Kat wrote it down, and Connall turned to his laptop, set up in a corner of the dining room, overlooking the river.

He looked up at Kat standing behind him, shifting from one foot to the other. "It'll take a bit of time, Katherine. Go get your cake."

"It's just..." She looked out the window at the river rippling by, flashing in the evening light.

"It's just what?"

"Mary Pat...Tish thinks I'm imagining things. I don't want her to be right. And... I'm afraid she might be."

"Better to know one way or the other, don't you think?" said Connall kindly.

Kat stared into his unblinking gaze, and finally sighed.

"Yes," she said. "I suppose it is."

Connall's smile was understanding.

"Go have a cuppa. It'll set you right. Not like that watery stuff you Americans go for. No offense intended, but I speak as I find." Now he produced a grin that was the twin of Jamie's.

I will not cry. I will not cry, thought Kat, so unused to kindness.

First Tish, and now these people.

"That does sound good," she said, and went to join the others outside.

"THAT IS WITCHCRAFT, THAT IS," said Deirdre. "It can't be natural."

They were gathered on the large porch as the evening darkened. Citronella candles glowed softly in hurricane lamps, discouraging—mostly—the mosquitoes. Fireflies flashed messages to potential lovers in the darkness of the unmown grass at the river's edge. The Geraghtys were charmed by the mysterious lights winking on and off in the growing dark.

"It's worth coming all these thousands of miles," said Deirdre, "just to see that. Can we import them, do you think?"

"They'd fit right in with all of Ireland's mythical creatures," said Siobhan.

"Will you write about them?" Deirdre asked her.

"I'm not sure I can," said Siobhan. "How do you describe magic?"

Connall pushed open the sliding doors. A burst of air-conditioned air flowed out for a brief moment before he closed it again.

He had his laptop with him.

"That took longer than I expected," said Tim. "You've lost your touch?"

Connall grinned in the darkness. "It was a welcome challenge," he said. "It's usually pretty easy."

"I'm almost afraid to ask," said Kat. "Who is it?"

"It's not a who, it's a what," said Connall.

"A what?" said Tish. "What do you mean?"

"It's registered to a company called Lakeside Acquisitions, Inc.," said Connall.

"Are you sure?" said Kat, grateful for the darkness that covered her blush of embarrassment.

"Yes. Your motor vehicles department does not have a sense of humor," said Connall.

"So, you've been right all along," said Kat to Tish. "Nothing more than a salesman on his route. How stupid could I have been?"

"You weren't stupid," said Tish.

"However," Connall continued, "being that you two seem to have more than your share of admirers, I thought a deeper look might be called for. So, I dug for the owner of the company. That was what took me the time. It was a bit of a puzzle, and that made me curious. But I finally found the man at the top." Connall popped his laptop up. "It's some fellow in Chicago named Alfred Clapham. He..."

Connall stopped. Kat and Tish had gasped so hard the candles around them flickered with their indrawn breaths.

"Holy Jesus, Mary, and Joseph," whispered Tish. "Mother of God. It *is* him."

CHAPTER 40

CONFESSIONS, OF A SORT

"Holy shit," was Kat's more profane response. She had *not* expected Clapham. Despite what she'd told Tish, she truly *had* thought the darkness of the past was coming to swallow her. "How? How did he find us?"

"You know this guy?" asked Connall. "It says he's a dealer in antiques."

"He's a dealer in stolen property," said Kat. "He's a fence."

"That's not all he is," said Tish. "He's a killer."

"Tish."

"That's why we had to leave," Tish said into the shocked silence. "We discovered my husband was working with him."

Well, thought Kat. *It wasn't not the truth.*

Kat wanted to believe Tish had a plan, and she knew Tish was very good at telling almost the truth. But she also knew her partner had wanted to confess ever since they'd left Evanston. Kat was afraid that it was all about to bubble out, plan or no plan.

"We should go," said Kat, leaning forward to get up. "We've put you all at risk. Tish…"

Maureen, sitting next to her, put her hand on Kat's arm.

"You're forgetting, Katherine. Security is our business. I don't think we're at risk," she glanced at Tim, who gave her a slight shake of the head, "but if this man is what you say, you and Mary Pat *are*. Let us help."

"Kat. Kat," said Tish, reaching for her other hand. "Please. We need help. If Clapham is looking for us…"

Kat looked around the ring of faces, all of them concerned. Saw the tears standing in Tish's eyes.

She was right. They needed help. For better or worse, the Geraghtys were offering it.

It made her uneasy but also almost fatalistically relieved. "Maybe you're right," she said, sitting back. "But promise us, please, that you won't put yourselves in his way."

Jamie chortled. There was no other word for it.

"Oh, darlin'," he said, rubbing his hands together. "This is meat and drink."

"I can see we're going to need more tea," said Siobhan. She stood up and tapped Deirdre on the shoulder. "As non-security experts, we're of more use in there," she tipped her head toward the house and the kitchen, "than out here."

"I agree with you there," said Deirdre, getting up and gathering loose plates and glasses. "If only to get away from these mosquitoes. They seem to be getting hungrier."

"Okay," said Tim, as he sat down on the raised hearth in front of the cold fireplace. They'd all moved inside to evade blood-hungry insects. "Tell us."

Kat lifted a hand toward Tish, giving her the floor.

They'd had a hurried conversation in the guest house where they'd gone to get Tish's sweater and Kat's mother's shawl, which she now had wrapped around her, giving her comfort. They'd agreed to let Tish do the talking, sticking as close to the truth as she could, but not giving the Geraghtys all of it.

"They're in security, Tish. Remember. They said they do a lot of contract work in the US. They probably have good noses for anything even passingly illegal. If they get a whiff of what we've done, they'll have to report us, even if they're sympathetic. So, be careful. And if you have to lie to them, lie."

"I don't think I can," said Tish.

"Then when you can't tell the truth about something, let me talk."

"What will you say?"

Kat shook her head. "I have no idea. None whatsoever. I'll just try not to make it worse."

Tish took a breath to begin, but Maureen interrupted her.

"First," she said, "do you want to tell us your real names? I assume Geraghty it is not."

Tish and Kat exchanged glances. They'd discussed this, too. Even Kat agreed they owed the Geraghtys this much.

"My name really *is* Mary Patrice Geraghty," said Tish. "When I'm finally divorced, that's the name I will use. But my family name was Ryan. Everyone has always called me Tish."

Kat waited a beat. But when Tish turned to her, she knew that she wasn't going to lay claim to O'Donnell.

She had a split second to decide on Miller or Merevec.

"My family name is Merevec," she said, having realized in that brief flash that Connall, with his ability to search dark corners of the internet, would find her out in no time. "I truly am Kat."

"And you're not cousins," said Maureen. "Your knowledge of each other has some gaping holes. Like you, Katherine…Kat, not knowing Mary Pat played pinball."

"Or that she's a shark at it," said Jamie, making Tish smile.

"No," said Tish. "We're not related. I think I mentioned…my family owns a jewelry store. Kat was our manager."

Tish turned back to Tim.

"Fitz, my husband, told me he was leaving me for a woman half his age. That's also true," she said. "It was the last straw after years of his cheating. I knew I'd get nothing in a divorce. So, I gathered up my jewelry and all the cash I could and was packing when Kat called.

"Fitz had fired her with no warning, no cause, and no severance. She was very upset because she'd worked for my husband for six years and had done a wonderful job with the store. But Fitz wanted to install his…new girlfriend in that job."

Kat could heard all of Tish's contempt and pent up fury at being supplanted in that small pause.

"So, I met her at the store," Tish continued, "to pay her what I knew she was owed from cash we kept on hand in the office safe. It was the least I could do for her. But when I opened the safe, we discovered a bag of money and some gemstones in there that didn't belong to the store."

Tish sipped tea that had to be only lukewarm.

"It didn't take a lot of thinking to realize that Fitz was laundering money. We quickly figured out he was working with Alfred Clapham because of an appointment I'd seen in his calendar."

"The man who owns the car following you."

"Yes."

"So why didn't you go to the police?" asked Tim.

"Frankly, I panicked. The store is in Fitz's name, not mine, Tim, but he's still my husband. I was afraid the police would think I was involved in the laundering, too. And Clapham..."

Tish stopped. Kat laid a hand on her arm and Tish covered it with her own. Took a deep breath.

"Clapham," continued Tish, her voice shaking a bit, "well, people who know too much tend to disappear. And we were afraid we knew too much. So. The long and the short of it is, we simply ran away. Kat said she'd always wanted to drive Route 66 to California, so we took the Buick, and we just...left."

Kat kept her face neutral. For someone who couldn't lie, Tish was doing a fine job of using the truth to hide...well, the truth.

"Even then, though," said Connall, "you could have contacted the police."

"Maybe we should have," said Tish. "But then my daughter called. She told me the store had been robbed, and everything had been taken. Kat and I are sure Fitz did it, meaning to run away with his girlfriend. But if he took what belonged to Clapham, and he thought I was involved in the robbery, too..."

"Then you might not live to tell your side of the story," said Jamie, when Tish hesitated.

"Exactly," said Kat.

"The police could protect you," said Connall.

Kat shook her head. "Lately, all the witnesses against Alfred Clapham either 'die in suspicious circumstances,' as they say in the movies, or they disappear. Even those in police protection," she said. "We were too afraid to take that risk."

"We thought if we just kept going, sticking to small towns and backroads, no one would be able to find us," said Tish. "That's why we didn't stay to talk to the police when the car was stolen this afternoon."

Kat started to relax. Tish was rewriting their story quite well, without telling the Geraghtys anything illegal that they'd have to report.

"I wonder, then, why this Clapham is following you, Mary Pat, if your husband took everything and did a runner," said Connall

"We think that was the most likely plan," said Kat. "But Fitz and his girlfriend haven't left town."

"How do you know they haven't?"

"Fitz keeps leaving me messages. He says I need to come back and sign papers for the divorce," said Tish.

Maureen frowned. "It seems strange that he'd worry about a divorce, if he's taken valuables that belong to this criminal."

"We've wondered about that, too," said Kat glancing at Tish. "We thought that Fitz might really want Tish to come back so he can, as you said, Connall, do a runner and leave her holding the bag. But now that we know that SUV belongs to Clapham...well, maybe Fitz has told Clapham that *Tish* has what belongs to him, to keep Clapham from going after *him*."

"One way or another, he's trying to shift the blame," said Tim thoughtfully.

"I think so, yes," said Kat.

"I'm surprised the police haven't asked you to come back to answer questions," said Maureen to Tish.

"They've called a couple times," said Tish. "But they've never asked me to come back to Evanston."

Damn, thought Kat. *She is getting good at this*. The police *had* called several times. But Tish had only answered their calls once.

"They didn't ask about the robbery?" said Connall.

Tish shook her head. "No. Well, yes. They *did* ask what I knew about the robbery, and I told them what my daughter had told me. But mostly they wanted to be sure I was all right."

"Why did they think you might not be?" Maureen asked, surprised.

"Oh. Well," said Tish, her rosy complexion getting rosier. "I was a bit...upset...when Fitz told me about...about *her*. I threw a few things."

Kat put her hand to her mouth, pretending to smother a cough. Tish had thrown a *lot* of things. Breakable things. Kat had seen the destruction first-hand.

Siobhan cocked a curious eyebrow. "Did you hit him?"

Tish shook her head, sheepishly. "I'm afraid not."

"Too bad," said Siobhan, shaking her head.

"But what about you?" Tim asked, turning to Kat. "Couldn't Mary Pat's husband or this Clapham be looking for you, too?"

Kat shook her head. "I wouldn't think so. Clapham has no reason to even know I'm alive," she said. "And Fitz fired me before all this happened. I'm sure he's forgotten all about me."

"But surely if you both disappeared at the same time...?" Maureen left the question hanging.

"We were co-workers," Kat said, "but we weren't friends. As far as we know, there's no reason for anyone to suspect we're together."

"That's changing though," said Tish, looking at Kat fondly.

The chilly hole in Kat's heart got a bit smaller.

"Still," said Tim. "A disgruntled employee should also be a prime suspect. The police haven't called you?"

"They may have," said Kat. "But my phone is missing. I think I left it on the kitchen counter when we left that night."

Very much *not* the truth, thought Kat.

Tim seemed to accept it, however.

"Add in a generous dollop of sex, Gran, and you'll have a best seller," said Jamie.

Even Kat and Tish laughed.

"It does sound like a made-for-television movie, doesn't it?" said Tish.

"It may be a dangerous situation for real, though," said Connall, as his smile faded. "This Clapham fella sounds like no one you want to cross."

Too late, thought Kat, a wave of guilt flowing over her.

Tish had been right that night. Once they'd discovered Clapham was involved, they should have taken the diamonds, the cash, and the gold back to the store and put it back in the safe. Fitz would be gone, and Clapham would be chasing him.

Kat was still pretty sure, though, that Clapham would have come after Tish, an easy target sitting in an empty store.

Kat suppressed a shudder.

Either way, once they knew Clapham was involved, there was no way out.

"I just don't know how he found us," said Tish.

"Your phone," said Jamie. "Almost certainly."

And he grinned like a demon.

CHAPTER 41
OUR PLUCKY HEROINES

Tish stood on the guest house porch in the dark. Across the lawn, in the main house, the bedroom windows upstairs glowed. Downstairs, in the brightly lit dining room, Tim and Maureen sat next to each other talking, a pot and cups on the table between them.

She watched as Tim raised Maureen's hand to his lips and kissed it. Maureen laughed and tipped her head toward him. He responded, resting his forehead against hers. Tish saw him say something, and Maureen smiled. They rose and walked toward the back of the house. The lights went out.

Tish's face was soft, and a gentle smile filled the corners of her mouth as she watched the fireflies' flash dance in the dark above the grass.

How long had it been since she'd sat out on a warm evening and watched fireflies?

Not since Luke was a boy, she thought. She remembered him chasing the luminescent beetles through the night, reaching for the flashing lights as they blinked out, and laughing as he missed catching them...again.

Before that...

She thought.

It had been years. Not since that perfect summer on the lake.

Tishie.

"Tish?" said Kat behind her.

"Umm?"

"Tish. Are you okay?"

"Umm," said Tish and turned, still smiling. "Just thinking."

"You miss Luke, don't you?"

"Like an arm cut off."

Kat stepped up next to her. Tish watched the struggle on her face.

"We could...you know... Maybe instead of going to California, we could go to Oregon. You could see your son."

Tish stared at her.

"But your dream," she said. "Your dream of driving Route 66. All the way to the end."

"Oh. Well," said Kat in a small voice. "Maybe that's all it will ever be."

Tish waited, but Kat wouldn't look at her.

"Well," said Tish finally, turning back to the lightning bug display, "I can't say it's not tempting. Especially since it seems that Alf Clapham knows—or guesses—where we are. But as you've said before, Portland isn't that far from Southern California. It's only a short plane trip to go to see him."

"You could always drive, too," said Kat.

"I think, after this, I'll have had all I want of road trips for a while."

"Maybe you're right."

Tish glanced sideways at Kat.

"Besides, Kat. I think you deserve this. You deserve to have your dream."

They stood quietly for a while watching the fireflies turn on and off in the dark.

"Do you have a dream, Tish? Something you've always wanted to do?"

A simple question. But it ripped open the dark around her.

Her throat closed, blocking the words she could have said.

Kat waited.

"I did, once," said Tish finally.

"Not now?"

"No. Not anymore."

Kat sighed. "I'm sorry."

"Yeah. Me, too," said Tish.

"So," she added, in a stronger voice. "That's why we're going to finish this drive for you. Alf Clapham be damned."

"Damned?" asked Kat, and Tish could almost hear the raised eyebrow.

"Yep. Damned. Shot. Hanged, drawn, and quartered. Run out of town on a rail."

Kat tsked. "Lots of penance there."

"You're right," said Tish. "I should probably start now. Hail Mary..."

Kat laughed.

"Maybe start tomorrow," she said. "I'd like to get some sleep tonight. We're heading out early."

Tish's smile faded.

"You think it's safe? We could wait a few days. Maureen and Tim did ask us to stay longer. Maybe Clapham's guy will have gone on. Or back."

She turned to Kat.

"What would your favorite caper movies advise?" she added, trying to lighten the dread that suddenly hung in the air.

Kat thought a moment.

"Having scraped through their last close call with the villain," she said, "our plucky heroines would decide to trust to fate and plunge courageously onward."

Tish produced a crooked smile.

"Somehow," she said, "I was afraid you were going to say that."

"Besides," said Kat, serious now, "despite what Tim says, I'm really a bit concerned that the longer we stay with the Geraghtys, the greater the danger we put them in. Especially if Jamie is right and, somehow, they've been tracking your phone."

"But he said he's fixed that now. Turned it off. Taken the whatsis out of it. Blinded its all-seeing eye. Whatever he did. And they gave us those burner phones."

"Along with that long list of do's and don'ts," said Kat.

"Makes me wonder about using them at all."

Kat sighed. "I do think they're right about using the internet at public libraries to look for hotels and rentals, though. It's the internet use that will target us with the phones."

Tish closed her eyes, felt the tension tightening her forehead again.

"I guess you're right," she said. "We'd better move on. From one plucky heroine to another."

Kat put her hand on Tish's arm. Tish opened her eyes and looked at her friend.

"We'll be okay, Tish. Plucky heroines always are."

"I hope you're right," said Tish, as they turned to go into the guest house.

But she found the words flowing through her mind: *Hail Mary, full of grace...*

ACKNOWLEDGMENTS

Books are never a solo effort, and *The Missouri Run,* the second book in *The Route 66 Steal* series, is no different. I am sincerely grateful to my beta readers, Helen Lewis, Merle White, and Lauri Martin, who read the first draft with care and enthusiasm. Their suggestions were invaluable.

As I have before and no doubt will again, I depended on Devon Monk, author of more than twenty urban fantasy novels, for her ability to see deep inside the structure of a story to what is missing. She is almost always right. With gratitude, my dear friend.

The Route 66 Steal series would not have been possible if I had not actually made the drive along Route 66. Anyone with the desire and the chance to follow the Route should do so. You'll never look at the US in the same way again. While there are many ways to drive Route 66, the turn-by-turn directions in Jerry McClanahan's irreplaceable *EZ66 Guide for Travelers* made it possible for us to enjoy the drive without the frustration of getting lost. I highly recommend it.

Thank you to Kim Killion at Killion Publishing for the delightful cover and for always getting it right.

Many gracious women of PEO greeted us, fed us, and

made us feel welcome across the country: Carol in Spokane, WA (my first port of call on the way to Chicago); Sally and Nan in St. Louis, MO; Vicki, Carol, Sheryl, Sherry, Bobbie, and Susan in Claremore, OK; Sabrina, Deanah, Lauren, Sammie Jo, Sarah, Judy, Ann, and Karla in Amarillo, TX; Mayor Ruth Ann in Tucumcari, NM; and Kathy, Ann, Margaret, Lynn, Laura, Bernadette and Lynda (with a number of spouses) in Santa Fe, NM. It was a pleasure.

Last, but not in any way least, the drive would not have been possible without my friend, intrepid traveler, and navigator extraordinaire, Gayna Morris, without whom I might still be circling St. Louis. Gayna deftly shifted between phone(s), iPad, itineraries, and our *EZ 66 Guide*. Without her, the drive would have been a heck of a lot less fun. Who else could I laugh with at the mere mention of the word "turtle"? Just remember, Gayna, what happened in Gallup, stays in Gallup.

Thank you all.

Liz

About the Author

Liz Hartley is the author of *The Route 66 Steal* series, *The Eden Beach Main Street Novels*, and *The Eden Beach Crime Novels*.

She has worn jewelry and picked up rocks since she was old enough to stand, so Liz was probably fated to spend more than twenty-five years writing about jewelry and gemstones. It's why, in all her novels, crime and passion swirl around gemstones and jewelry.

An enthusiastic traveler, Liz has lived and studied in Japan, traveled with gem and mineral enthusiasts to Brazil, journeyed to southern Africa, made two "grand tours" in Europe, and driven Route 66 from downtown Chicago to the Santa Monica boardwalk.

She does not own a television but loves movies and will read just about anything that doesn't get out of her way.

9 781955 720021